Albergo Empedocle and other writings

Albergo Empedocle and other writings

BY

E. M. FORSTER

EDITED, WITH INTRODUCTION
AND NOTES BY
George H. Thomson

LIVERIGHT   NEW YORK

International Standard Book Number: 0-87140-540-7
Library of Congress Catalog Card Number: 79-162435

DESIGNED BY BETTY BINNS
MANUFACTURED IN THE UNITED STATES OF AMERICA

Contents

Introduction, ix

An Early Short Story, 1

Albergo Empedocle   5

Cambridge Humor, 37

ON GRINDS   45
A BRISK WALK   48
ON BICYCLING   51
A LONG DAY   53
THE PACK OF ANCHISES   55
THE CAMBRIDGE THEOPHRASTUS,
    Being a guide for the inexperienced to characters that may be
    met with in the University World: The Stall-Holder   57
THE CAMBRIDGE THEOPHRASTUS:
    The Early Father   59
A TRAGIC INTERIOR
    Being an attempt to interpret the inner meaning of the Aga-
    memnon of Aeschylus   61
A TRAGIC INTERIOR, 2
    Being a further attempt to assist the earnest student of Aeschy-
    lus, by means of an interpretation of the Choephori   68
STRIVINGS AFTER HISTORICAL STYLE
    With apologies to a certain series of Oxford Textbooks   77
A DAY OFF   80
AN ALLEGORY   86

v

Contents

Bourgeois Values versus Inspiration, 91

ROSTOCK AND WISMAR	97
LITERARY ECCENTRICS: A REVIEW	102
MR. WALSH'S SECRET HISTORY OF THE VICTORIAN MOVEMENT	109
INSPIRATION	117

For the Working Men's College, 122

PESSIMISM IN LITERATURE	129
DANTE	146
THE BEAUTY OF LIFE	169
THE FUNCTIONS OF LITERATURE IN WAR-TIME	176

India, 185

IRON HORSES IN INDIA	193
THE AGE OF MISERY	198
THE INDIAN BOOM	203
THE INDIAN MIND	207
A GREAT ANGLO-INDIAN	211
THE ELDER TAGORE	216
THE GODS OF INDIA	220
THE MISSION OF HINDUISM	224

The Arts and War, 229

THE WEDDING	235
THE ROSE SHOW	239
TO SIMPLY FEEL	242
A NEW NOVELIST	248
SHORT STORIES FROM RUSSIA	253

Contents

TATE VERSUS CHANTREY   259

RECONSTRUCTION IN THE MARNE AND THE MEUSE   263

Forster's Publications 1900-1915: A Chronology, 269

Introduction

Forster thought well of his writing. That is the judgment of P. N. Furbank, his friend and official biographer. It is a judgment confirmed by Forster's statement at the beginning of B. J. Kirk-patrick's *Bibliography:* "The longer one lives the less one feels to have done, and I am both surprised and glad to discover from this bibliography that I have written so much." The sur-prise is occasioned by the cumulation of material quietly lost in the obscurity of forgotten periodicals and long defunct news-papers. Miss Kirkpatrick's work of identification, carried out with Forster's full cooperation, is the first step in making avail-able the uncollected writings. The next step is the reprinting of them. That is the purpose of this volume which includes, as far as possible, everything published between 1900 and 1915 which has not previously appeared in book form.

A brief review of Forster's literary career during these years will help to place the uncollected writings in perspective. In

1900 and 1901, while in his third and fourth years at Cambridge University, he contributed ten sketches, parodies, and satirical essays to a student magazine. After Cambridge he traveled and began writing fiction. Between 1903 and 1910 he published four novels, nine short stories, and nine occasional pieces. With the single exception of "Albergo Empedocle," all the stories have been reissued. Of the nine nonfictional items, four have been collected.

The two years following the publication of *Howards End* on 18 October 1910 were not productive: in 1911, two stories and two essays, as well as the first collection of short stories; in 1912, one story and two essays. However, in the fall of 1912 Forster traveled to India, where he stayed until at least March 1913; and in the fall of 1915 he went to Egypt to work with the International Red Cross. It now appears that between his return from India and his departure for Alexandria, he was exceptionally active.

As a result of his experiences in the East he began work on *A Passage to India*. He wrote almost half before difficulties with the episode in the Marabar caves stopped his progress. Meanwhile, in the spring of 1914 he wrote "Arctic Summer (Fragment of an Unfinished Novel)," included in *Tribute to Benjamin Britten on His Fiftieth Birthday,* edited by Anthony Gishford (London, 1963). Martin Whitby is on his way through Switzerland when he accidentally falls under a train. He is rescued by a young man named March. The part of the story that has been printed—it is not all that Forster wrote—shows the beginning of the friendship between Martin, the civilized man of thirty, and March, who is the "hero" type. The commentary which follows describes the difficulties of portraying a hero in the modern world, but it does not tell us at

precisely what point these difficulties got the better of the author or how extended the manuscript fragment may be.

Finally, between 1913 and 1915, Forster completed *Maurice*, a novel with a homosexual theme. Because he did not wish
to endure the fuss its publication would arouse, he suppressed
it during his lifetime. According to Anthony Lewis in a *New
York Times* article of 11 November 1970, he wrote across the
top of the manuscript "Publishable but is it worth it?" Whatever its merits, it will be of great interest to see how it relates
to his other work. Will it enhance our appreciation of the relations of Rickie, Ansell, and Stephen in *The Longest Journey?*
Will it give us new insight into the characters of Tommy and
Harold in "Albergo Empedocle," the early story which Forster
did not exactly suppress but which he left to languish in the obscurity of the periodical *Temple Bar?* And at the same time,
will the uncollected writings throw light on *Maurice* or themselves take on fresh significance from its publication?

After this burst of activity there is a lull, nothing apparently
in 1916, and a series of essays relating to Egypt in 1917 and
1918. So 1915 is a natural breaking point for a volume of Forster's uncollected early writings. By that date, in addition to
the eleven short stories which he reprinted, he had published
forty-five pieces in newspapers and periodicals. Of these, nine
have since been included in *Abinger Harvest:* four works of
historical reconstruction and five short essays and reviews on
India. The remaining thirty-six pieces, representing four-fifths
of the total, have not been collected. They comprise the present
volume.

My aim has been to reproduce these early writings faithfully
but without fuss. They are arranged in groups, for the most
part chronologically, but with changes in order where logic or

the convenience of the reader dictated. In each case the date has been inserted at the end. Spelling, especially in the matter of hyphenation, has been somewhat modernized, obvious misprints and misspellings have been silently corrected, but technical errors in grammar, such as oddities in the agreement of subject and verb, have been retained where there is a reasonable possibility that Forster himself is responsible. Quotations from other writers are reproduced as Forster transcribed them, with a variety of minor inaccuracies. In only one instance has the text been significantly changed. In "To Simply Feel," I have substituted *learn* for *leave* (the reverse process would be easy in setting print from a handwritten manuscript) in the account of the lessons little Lesbia mastered (p. 246), though not without falling into the Irrawaddy (mistakenly spelled with a single "d" by Forster).

Not everything in this collection is of equal interest, not everything is in itself worthwhile. But it is the mark of the good writer that the lesser may add to our understanding of the greater. It is easy to condescend to Forster. A number of critics have done so. They usually praise one novel, maybe two, and find all manner of fault with the rest. They follow the same procedure with the essays, picking to tatters the author's lifetime stance as a liberal and intellectual. Forster's lively balance of sensitivity and judgment, and his refusal to be pompous, is sufficient answer to such criticism.

George H. Thomson

AN EARLY
SHORT STORY

After Forster left Cambridge in 1901, he visited Italy for a year. In the Introduction to *The Collected Tales* (1947), he says that in May 1902 as he was walking near Ravello, Chapter I of "The Story of a Panic" rushed into his mind. He wrote it down as soon as he got back to his hotel and added the other parts a few days later. This was the first story he wrote. It was published in August 1904. We do not know precisely when he wrote "Albergo Empedocle," but it must have been very early, possibly his second story, for it was published in December 1903.

Albergo Empedocle

The last letter I had from Harold was from Naples.

"We've just come back from Pompeii," he wrote. "On the
whole it's decidedly no go and very tiring. What with the
smells and the beggars and the mosquitoes we're rather off Naples altogether, and we've changed our plans and are going to
Sicily. The guide books say you can run through it in no time;
only four places you have to go to, and very little in them. That
suits us to a T. Pompeii and the awful Museum here have fairly
killed us—except of course Mildred, and perhaps Sir Edwin.

"Now why don't you come too? I know you're keen on Sicily,
and we all would like it. You would be able to spread yourself
no end with your archaeology. For once in my life I should have
to listen while you jaw. You'd enjoy discussing temples, gods,
etc., with Mildred. She's taught me a lot, but of course it's no
fun for her, talking to us. Send a wire; I'll stand the cost. Start
at once and we'll wait for you. The Peaslakes say the same, especially Mildred.

"My not sleeping at night, and my headaches are all right
now, thanks very much. As for the blues, I haven't had any

since I've been engaged, and don't intend to. So don't worry any more. Yours,

"Harold.

"Dear Tommy, if you aren't an utter fool you'll let me pay your ticket out."

I did not go. I could just have managed it, but Sicily was then a very sacred name to me, and the thought of running through it in no time, even with Harold, deterred me. I went afterwards, and as I am well acquainted with all who went then, and have had circumstantial information of all that happened, I think that my account of the affair will be as intelligible as anyone's.

I am conceited enough to think that if I had gone, the man I love most in the world would not now be in an asylum.

Chapter I

The Peaslake party was most harmonious in its composition. Four out of the five were Peaslakes, which partly accounted for the success, but the fifth, Harold, seemed to have been created to go with them. They had started from England soon after his engagement to Mildred Peaslake, and had been flying over Europe for two months. At first they were a little ashamed of their rapidity, but the delight of continual custom-house examinations soon seized them, and they had hardly learnt what "Come in," and "Hot water, please," were in one language, before they crossed the frontier and had to learn them in another.

But, as Harold truly said, "People say we don't see things properly, and are globe-trotters, and all that, but after all one travels to enjoy oneself, and no one can say that we aren't having a ripping time."

Every party, to be really harmonious, must have a physical and an intellectual center. Harold provided one, Mildred the other. He settled whether a mountain had to be climbed or a walk taken, and it was his fists that were clenched when a porter was insolent, or a cabman tried to overcharge. Mildred, on the other hand, was the fount of information. It was she who generally held the "Baedeker" and explained it. She had been expecting her Continental scramble for several years, and had read a fair amount of books for it, which a good memory often enabled her to reproduce.

But they all agreed that she was no dry encyclopedia. Her appetite for facts was balanced by her reverence for imagination.

"It is imagination," she would say, "that makes the past live again. It sets the centuries at naught."

"Rather!" was the invariable reply of Harold, who was notoriously deficient in it. Recreating the past was apt to give him a headache, and his thoughts obstinately returned to the unromantic present, which he found quite satisfactory. He was fairly rich, fairly healthy, very much in love, very fond of life, and he was content to worship in Mildred those higher qualities which he did not possess himself.

These two between them practically ran the party, and both Sir Edwin and Lady Peaslake were glad that the weight of settling or explaining anything should be lifted off their shoulders. Sir Edwin sometimes held the "Baedeker," but his real function was the keeping of a diary in which he put down the places they went to, the people they met, and the times of the trains. Lady Peaslake's department was packing, hotels, and the purchasing of presents for a large circle of acquaintance. As for Lilian, Mildred's sister, whatever pleased other people pleased her. Altogether it was a most delightful party.

They were however just a little subdued and quiet during that journey from Palermo to Girgenti. They had done Palermo in even less time than Baedeker had allowed for it, and such audacity must tell on the most robust of tourists. Furthermore they had made an early start, as they had to get to Girgenti for lunch, do the temples in the afternoon, and go on the next morning to Syracuse.

It was no wonder that Lady Peaslake was too weary to look out of the window, and that Harold yawned when Mildred explained at some length how it was that a Greek temple came to be built out of Greece.

"Poor boy! you're tired," she said, without bitterness, and without surprise.

Harold blushed at his impoliteness.

"We really do too much," said Lady Peaslake. "I never bought that Sicilian cart for Mrs. Popham. It would have been the very thing. She will have something out of the way. If a thing's at all ordinary she will hardly say thank you. Harold, would you try at Girgenti? Mind you beat them down. Four francs is the outside."

"Certainly, Lady Peaslake." His method of purchasing for her, was to pay whatever was asked, and to make good the difference out of his own pocket.

"Girgenti will produce more than Sicilian carts," said Mildred, smoothing down the pages of the guide book. "In Greek times it was the second city of the island, wasn't it? It was famous for the ability, wealth, and luxury of its inhabitants. You remember, Harold, it was called Acragas."

"Acragas, Acragas," chanted Harold, striving to rescue one word from the chaos. The effect was too much for him, and he gave another yawn.

"Really, Harold!" said Mildred, laughing. "You're very much exhausted."

"I've scarcely slept for three nights," he replied in rather an aggrieved voice.

"Oh, my dear boy! I'm very sorry. I had no idea."

"Why did not you tell me?" said Sir Edwin. "We would have started later. Yes, I see you do look tired."

"It's so queer. It's ever since I've been in Sicily. Perhaps Girgenti will be better."

"Have you never slept since Naples?"

"Oh, I did sleep for an hour or so last night. But that was because I used my dodge."

"Dodge!" said Sir Edwin, "whatever do you mean!"

"You know it, don't you? You pretend you're someone else, and then you go asleep in no time."

"Indeed I do not know it," said Sir Edwin emphatically.

Mildred's curiosity was aroused. She had never heard Harold say anything unexpected before, and she was deter-mined to question him.

"How extremely interesting! How very interesting! I don't know it either. Who do you imagine yourself to be?"

"Oh, no one—anyone. I just say to myself, 'That's someone lying awake. Why doesn't he go to sleep if he's tired?' Then he—I mean I—do, and it's all right."

"But that is a very wonderful thing. Why didn't you do it all three nights?"

"Well, to tell the truth," said Harold, rather confused, "I promised Tommy I'd never do it again. You see, I used to do

9

it, not only when I couldn't sleep, but also when I was in the blues about something—or nothing—as one is, I don't know why. It doesn't get rid of them, but it kind of makes me so strong that I don't care for them—I can't explain. One morning Tommy came to see me, and I never knew him till he shook me. Naturally he was horribly sick, and made me promise never to do it again."

"And why have you done it again?" said Sir Edwin.

"Well, I did hold out two nights. But last night I was so dead tired, I couldn't think what I wanted to—of course you understand that: it's rather beastly. All the night I had to keep saying 'I'm lying awake, I'm lying awake, I'm lying awake,' and it got more and more difficult. And when it was almost time to get up, I made a slip and said, 'He's lying awake'—and then off I went."

"How very, very interesting," said Mildred, and Lilian cried that it was a simply splendid idea, and that she should try it next time she had the toothache.

"Indeed, Lilian," said her mother, "I beg you'll do no such thing."

"No, indeed," said Sir Edwin, who was looking grave. "Harold, your friend was quite right. It is never safe to play tricks with the brain. I must say I'm astonished: you of all people!"

"Yes," said Harold, looking at a very substantial hand. "I'm such a stodgy person. It is odd. It isn't brain or imagination or anything like that. I simply pretend."

"It is imagination," said Mildred in a low determined voice.

"Whatever it is, it must stop," said Sir Edwin. "It's a dangerous habit. You must break yourself of it before it is fully formed."

"Yes. I promised Tommy. I shall try again tonight," said Harold, with a pitiful little sigh of fatigue.

"I'll arrange to have a room communicating with yours. If you can't sleep tonight, call me."

"Thanks very much, I'm sure not to do it if you're near. It only works when one's alone. Tommy stopped it by taking rooms in the same house, which was decent of him."

The conversation had woke them up. The girls were quiet, Lilian being awed, and Mildred being rather annoyed with her parents for their want of sympathy with imagination. She felt that Harold had so little, that unless it was nourished it would disappear. She crossed over to him, and managed to say in a low voice, "You please me very much. I had no idea you were like this before. We live in a world of mystery."

Harold smiled complacently at the praise, and being sure that he could not say anything sensible, held his tongue. Mildred at once began to turn his newly-found powers to the appreciation of Girgenti.

"Think," she said, "of the famous men who visited her in her prime. Pindar, Aeschylus, Plato—and as for Empedocles, of course he was born there."

"Oh!"

"The disciple, you know, of Pythagoras, who believed in the transmigration of souls."

"Oh!"

"It's a beautiful idea, isn't it, that the soul should have several lives."

"But, Mildred darling," said the gentle voice of Lady Peaslake, "we know that it is not so."

"Oh, I didn't mean that, mamma. I only said it was a beautiful idea."

"But not a true one, darling."

"No."

Their voices had sunk into that respectful monotone which is always considered suitable when the soul is under discussion. They all looked awkward and ill at ease. Sir Edwin played tunes on his waistcoat buttons, and Harold blew into the bowl of his pipe. Mildred, a little confused at her temerity, passed on to the terrible sack of Acragas by the Romans. Whereat their faces relaxed, and they regained their accustomed spirits.

"But what are dates?" said Mildred. "What are facts, or even names of persons? They carry one a very little way. In a place like this one must simply feel."

"Rather," said Harold, trying to fix his attention.

"You must throw yourself into a past age if you want to appreciate it thoroughly. Today you must imagine you are a Greek."

"Really, Mildred," said Sir Edwin, "you're almost too fanci-ful."

"No, father, I'm not. Harold understands. He must forget all these modern horrors of railways and Cook's tours, and think that he's living over two thousand years ago, among palaces and temples. He must think and feel and act like a Greek. It's the only way. He must—well, he must *be* a Greek."

"The sea! the sea!" interrupted Harold. "How absolutely ripping! I swear I'll put in a bathe!"

"Oh, you incorrigible boy!" said Mildred, joining in the laugh at the failure of her own scheme. "Show me the sea, then."

They were still far away from it, for they had hardly crossed the watershed of the island. It was the country of the mines,

barren and immense, absolutely destitute of grass or trees, producing nothing but cakes of sallow sulphur, which were stacked
on the platform of every wayside station. Human beings were
scanty, and they were stunted and dry, mere withered vestiges
of men. And far below at the bottom of the yellow waste was
the moving living sea, which embraced Sicily when she was
green and delicate and young, and embraces her now, when she
is brown and withered and dying.

"I see something more interesting than the sea," said Mildred. "I see Girgenti."

She pointed to a little ridge of brown hill far beneath them,
on the summit of which a few grey buildings were huddled together.

"Oh, what a dreadful place!" cried poor Lady Peaslake.
"How uncomfortable we are going to be."

"Oh dearest mother, it's only for one night. What are a few
drawbacks, when we are going to see temples! Temples, Greek
temples! Doesn't the word make you thrill?"

"Well, no, dear, it doesn't. I should have thought the Pesto
ones would have been enough. These can't be very different."

"I consider you are a recreant party," said Mildred in a
sprightly voice. "First it's Harold, now it's you. I'm the only
worthy one among you. Today I mean to be a Greek. What
hotel do we go to?"

Lady Peaslake produced her notebook and said "Grand
Hôtel des Temples. Recommended by Mr. Dimbleby. Ask for
a back room, as those have the view."

But at the Girgenti railway station, the man from the Temples told them that his hotel was full, and Mildred, catching
sight of the modest omnibus of the "Albergo Empedocle," sug-

13

gested that they should go there, because it sounded so typical.

"You remember what the doctrine of Empedocles was, Harold?"

The wretched Harold had forgotten.

Sir Edwin was meanwhile being gently urged into the omnibus by the man from the "Empedocle."

"We know nothing about it, absolutely nothing. Are you— have you clean beds?"

The man from the "Empedocle" raised his eyes and hands to Heaven, so ecstatic was his remembrance of the purity of the blankets, the spotlessness of the sheets. At last words came, and he said, "The beds of the Empedocle! They are celestial. One spends one night there, and one remembers it for ever!"

Chapter II

Sir Edwin and Lady Peaslake were sitting in the temple of Juno Lacinia and leaning back on a Doric column—which is a form of architecture neither comfortable as a cushion nor adequate as a parasol. They were as cross as it was possible for good-tempered people to be. Their lunch at the dirty hotel had disagreed with them, and the wine that was included with it had made them heavy. The drive to the temples had joggled them up and one of the horses had fallen down. They had been worried to buy flowers, figs, shells, sulphur crystals, and new-laid antiquities, they had been pestered by the beggars and bitten by the fleas. Had they been Sicilian born they would have known what was the matter, and lying down on the grass, on the flowers, on the road, on the temple steps—on anything, would have sunk at once into that marvellous midday sleep which is fed by light and warmth and air. But being northern born they did not know—nor could they have slept if they had.

"Where on earth are Harold and Mildred?" asked Lady Peaslake. She did not want to know, but she was restless with fatigue.

"I can't think why we couldn't all keep together," said Sir Edwin.

"You see, papa," said Lilian, "Mildred wants to see the temples that have tumbled down as well as these, and Harold is taking her."

"He's a poor guide," said Sir Edwin. "Really, Lilian, I begin to think that Harold is rather stupid. Of course I'm very fond of him, he's a thoroughly nice fellow, honest as the day, and he's good-looking and well made—I value all that extremely—but after all brains are something. He is so slow—so lamentably slow—at catching one's meaning."

"But, father dear," replied Lilian, who was devoted to Harold, "he's tired."

"I am tired, too, but I can keep my wits about me. He seems in a dream; when the horse fell he never attempted to get down and sit on its head. It might have kicked us to pieces. He's as helpless as a baby with beggars. He's too idle to walk properly; three times he trod on my toes, and he fell up the temple steps and broke your camera. He's blind, he's deaf—I may say he's dumb, too. Now this is pure stupidity, and I believe that stupidity can be cured just like anything else, if you make the effort."

Lilian continued the defence, and repeated that he had hardly slept for three nights.

"Ridiculous. Why can't he sleep? It's stupidity again. An effort is needed—that is all. He can cure it if he chooses."

"He does know how to cure it," said Lilian, "but you thought—and so did he—that——"

She produced an explosion of ill-temper in her father, which was quite unprecedented.

"I'm very much annoyed with him. He has no right to play tricks with his brain. And what's more I am annoyed with Mildred, too."

"Oh, father!"

"She encourages him in his silliness—makes him think he's clever. I'm extremely annoyed, and I shall speak to them both, as soon as I get the opportunity."

Lilian was surprised and pained. Her father had never blamed anyone so strongly before. She did not know—indeed, he did not know himself—that neither the indigestion nor the heat, nor the beggars, nor the fleas were the real cause of his irritation. He was annoyed because he failed to understand.

Mildred he could pardon; she had merely been indiscreet, and as she had gone in for being clever when quite a child, such things were to be expected from her. Besides, he shrewdly guessed that, although she might sometimes indulge in fancies, yet when it came to action she could be trusted to behave in a thoroughly conventional manner. Thank heaven! she was seldom guilty of confusing books with life.

But Harold did not escape so easily, for Sir Edwin absolutely failed to understand him, for the first time. Hitherto he had believed that he understood him perfectly. Harold's character was so simple; it consisted of little more than two things, the power to love and the desire for truth, and Sir Edwin, like many a wiser thinker, concluded that what was not complicated could not be mysterious. Similarly, because Harold's intellect did not devote itself to the acquisition of facts or to the elaboration of emotions, he had concluded that he was stupid. But now, just because he could send himself to sleep by an unexplained device, he spied a mystery in him, and was aggrieved.

He was right. There was a mystery, and a great one. Yet it was trivial and unimportant in comparison with the power to love and the desire for truth—things which he saw daily, and, because he had seen daily, ignored.

His meditations took shape, and he flung this challenge at the unknown: "I'll have no queerness in a son-in-law!" He was sitting in a Doric temple with a sea of gold and purple flowers tossing over its ruins, and his eyes looked out to the moving, living sea of blue. But his ears caught neither the echo of the past nor the cry of the present, for he was suddenly paralyzed with the fear that after all he had not done so well for his daughter as he hoped.

Meanwhile, Mildred, at the other end of the line of temples, was concentrated on the echoes of the past. Harold was even more inattentive to them than usual. He was very sleepy, and would only say that the flowers were rather jolly and that the sea looked in prime condition if only one could try it. To the magnificence and pathos of the ruined temple of Zeus he was quite dead. He only valued it as a chair.

"Suppose you go back and rest in the carriage?" said Mildred, with a shade of irritation in her voice.

He shook his head and sat yawning at the sea, thinking how wonderfully the water would fizz up over his body and how marvellously cold would be the pale blue pools among the rocks. Mildred endeavored to recall him to higher pleasures by reading out of her "Baedeker."

She turned round to explain something and he was gone.

At first she thought it was a mild practical joke, such as they did not disdain to play on each other; then that he had changed his mind and gone back to the carriage. But the custodian at the gate said that no one had gone out, and she returned to search the ruins.

The temple of Zeus—the third greatest temple of the Greek world—had been overthrown by an earthquake, and now re-sembles a ruined mountain rather than a ruined building. There is a well-made path, which makes a circuit over the mass, and is amply sufficient for all rational tourists. Those who wish to see more have to go mountaineering over gigantic columns and pilasters, and squeeze their way through passes of cut stone.

Harold was not on the path, and Mildred was naturally an-noyed. Few things are more vexatious for a young lady than to go out with an escort and return without. It argues remissness on her own part quite as much as on that of her swain.

Having told the custodian to stop Harold if he tried to come out, she began a systematic hunt. She saw an enormous block of stone from which she would get a good view of the chaos, and wading through the gold and purple flowers that separated her from it, scrambled up.

On its further side were two fallen columns, lying close to-gether, and the space that separated them had been silted up and was covered with flowers. On it, as on a bed, lay Harold, fast asleep, his cheek pressed against the hot stone of one of the columns, and his breath swaying a little blue iris that had rooted in one of its cracks.

The indignant Mildred was about to wake him, but seeing the dark line that still showed beneath his eyes, stayed her voice. Besides, he looked so picturesque, and she herself, sitting on the stone watching him, must look picturesque, too. She knew that there was no one to look at her, but from her mind the idea of a spectator was never absent for a moment. It was the price she had paid for becoming cultivated.

Sleep has little in common with death, to which men have compared it. Harold's limbs lay in utter relaxation, but he was tingling with life, glorying in the bounty of the earth and the warmth of the sun, and the little blue flower bent and fluttered like a tree in a gale. The light beat upon his eyelids and the grass leaves tickled his hair, but he slept on, and the lines faded out of his face as he grasped the greatest gift that the animal life can offer. And Mildred watched him, thinking what a picture might be made of the scene.

Then her meditation changed. "What a wonderful thing is sleep! How I would like to know what is passing through his brain as he lies there. He looks so peaceful and happy. Poor boy! When he is awake he often looks worried. I think it is because he can't follow the conversation, though I try to make it simple, don't I? Yet some things he sees quite quickly. And I'm sure he has lots of imagination, if only he would let it come out. At all events I love him very much, and I believe I shall love him more, for it seems to me that there will be more in him than I expected."

She suddenly remembered his "dodge" for going to sleep, and her interest and her agitation increased.

"Perhaps, even now, he imagines himself to be someone else. What a marvellous idea! What will he say if he wakes? How mysterious everything is if only one could realize it. Harold, of all people, who seemed so ordinary—though, of course, I love him. But I am going to love him more."

She longed to reach him in his sleep, to guide the course of his dreams, to tell him that she approved of him and loved him. She had read of such a thing. In accordance with the advice of the modern spiritualistic novel she pressed her hands on her temples and made a mental effort. At the end of five minutes she had a slight headache and had effected nothing. He had not moved, he had not even sighed in his sleep, and the little blue flower still bent and fluttered, bent and fluttered in the regular onslaught of his breath.

The awakening, when it did come, found her thoughts un- prepared. They had wandered to earthly things, as thoughts will do at times. At the supreme moment, she was wondering whether her stockings would last till she got back to England. And Harold, all unobserved, had woken up, and the little blue flower had quivered and was still. He had woken up because he was no longer tired, woken up to find himself in the midst of beautiful flowers, beautiful columns, beautiful sunshine, with Mildred, whom he loved, sitting by him. Life at that moment was too delicious for him to speak.

Mildred saw all the romance melting away: he looked so natural and so happy: there was nothing mysterious about him after all. She waited for him to speak.

Ten minutes passed, and still he had not spoken. His eyes were fixed steadily upon her, and she became nervous and un- comfortable. Why would he not speak? She determined to break the silence herself, and at last, in a tremulous voice, called him by his name.

The result was overwhelming, for his answer surpassed all that her wildest flights of fancy had imagined, and fulfilled be- yond all dreaming her cravings for the unimagined and the un- seen.

He said, "I've lived here before."

Mildred was choking. She could not reply.

He was quite calm. "I always knew it," he said, "but it was too far down in me. Now that I've slept here it is at the top. I've lived here before."

"Oh, Harold!" she gasped.

"Mildred!" he cried, in sudden agitation, "are you going to believe it—that I have lived before—lived such a wonderful life—I can't remember it yet—lived it here? It's no good answering to please me."

Mildred did not hesitate a moment. She was carried away by the magnificence of the idea, the glory of the scene and the earnest beauty of his eyes, and in an ecstasy of rapture she cried, "I do believe."

"Yes," said Harold, "you do. If you hadn't believed now you never would have. I wonder what would have happened to me."

"More, more!" cried Mildred, who was beginning to find her words. "How could you smile! How could you be so calm! O marvellous idea! that your soul has lived before! I should run about, shriek, sing. Marvellous! overwhelming! How can you be so calm! The mystery! and the poetry, oh, the poetry! How can you support it? Oh, speak again!"

"I don't see any poetry," said Harold. "It just has happened, that's all. I lived here before."

"You are a Greek! You have been a Greek! Oh, why do you not die when you remember it."

"Why should I? I might have died if you hadn't believed me. It's nothing to remember."

"Aren't you shattered, exhausted?"

"No: I'm awfully fit. I know that you must have believed me now or never. Remembering has made me so strong. I see myself to the bottom now."

"Marvellous! marvellous!" she repeated.

He leapt up on to the stone beside her. "You've believed me. That's the only thing that's marvellous. The rest's nothing." He flung his arms round her, and embraced her—an embrace very different from the decorous peck by which he had marked the commencement of their engagement. Mildred, clinging to him, murmured "I do believe you," and they gazed without flinching into each other's eyes.

Harold broke the silence, saying, "How very happy life is going to be."

But Mildred was still wrapped in the glamor of the past. "More! more!" she cried, "tell me more! What was the city like—and the people in it? Who were you?"

"I don't remember yet—and it doesn't matter."

"Harold, keep nothing from me! I will not breathe a word. I will be silent as the grave."

"I shall keep nothing. As soon as I remember things, I will tell them. And why should you tell no one? There's nothing wrong."

"They would not believe."

"I shouldn't mind. I only minded about you."

"Still—I think it is best a secret. Will you agree?"

"Yes—for you may be right. It's nothing to do with the others. And it wouldn't interest them."

"And think—think hard who you were."

"I do just remember this—that I was a lot greater then than I am now. I'm greater now than I was this morning, I think—but then!"

"I knew it! I knew it from the first! I have known it always. You have been a king—a king! You ruled here when Greece was free!"

"Oh! I don't mean that—at least I don't remember it. And was I a Greek?"

"A Greek!" she stammered indignantly. "Of course you were a Greek, a Greek of Acragas."

"Oh, I daresay I was. Anyhow it doesn't matter. To be believed! Just fancy! You've believed me. You needn't have, but you did. How happy life is!"

He was in an ecstasy of happiness in which all time except the present had passed away. But Mildred had a tiny thrill of disappointment. She reverenced the past as well.

"What do you mean then, Harold, when you say you were greater?"

"I mean I was better, I saw better, heard better, thought better."

"Oh, I see," said Mildred fingering her watch. Harold, in his most prosaic manner, said they must not keep the carriage waiting, and they regained the path.

The tide of rapture had begun to ebb away from Mildred. His generalities bored her. She longed for detail, vivid detail, that should make the dead past live. It was of no interest to her that he had once been greater.

"Don't you remember the temples?"

"No."

"Nor the people?"

"Not yet."

"Don't you at all recollect what century you lived in?"

"How on earth am I to know!" he laughed.

Mildred was silent. She had hoped he would have said the

fifth B.C.—the period in which she was given to understand that the Greek race was at its prime. He could tell her nothing; he did not even seem interested, but began talking about Mrs. Popham's present.

At last she thought of a question he might be able to answer. "Did you also love better?" she asked in a low voice.

"I loved very differently." He was holding back the brambles to prevent them from tearing her dress as he spoke. One of the thorns scratched him on the hand. "Yes, I loved better too," he continued, watching the little drops of blood swell out.

"What do you mean? Tell me more."

"I keep saying I don't know any more. It is fine to remember that you've been better than you are. You know, Mildred, I'm much more worth you than I've ever been before. I do believe I am fairly great."

"Oh!" said Mildred, who was getting bored.

They had reached the temple of Concord, and he retrieved his tactlessness by saying, "After all I'm too happy to go back yet. I love you too much. Let's rest again."

They sat down on the temple steps, and at the end of ten minutes Mildred had forgotten all her little disappointments, and only remembered this mysterious sleep, and his marvellous awakening. Then, at the very height of her content, she felt, deep down within her, the growth of a new wonder.

"Harold, how is it you can remember?"

"The lid can't have been put on tight last time I was sent out."

"And that," she murmured, "might happen to anyone."

"I should think it has—to lots. They only want reminding."

"It might happen to me."

"Yes."

"I too," she said slowly, "have often not been able to sleep. Oh, Harold, is it possible?"

"What?"

"That I have lived before."

"Of course it is."

"Oh, Harold, I too may remember."

"I hope you will. It's wonderful to remember a life better than this one. I can't explain how happy it makes you: there's no need to try or to worry. It'll come if it is coming."

"Oh, Harold! I am remembering!"

He grasped her hands crying, "Remember only what is good. Remember that you were greater than you are now! I would give my life to help you."

"You have helped me," she cried, quivering with excitement. "All fits together. I remember all. It is not the first time I have known you. We have met before. Oh, how often have I dimly felt it. I felt it when I watched you sleeping—but then I didn't understand. Our love is not new. Here in this very place when there was a great city full of gorgeous palaces and snow-white marble temples, full of poets and music, full of marvellous pictures, full of sculptures of which we can hardly dream, full of noble men and noble thoughts, bounded by the sapphire sea, covered by the azure sky, here in the wonderful youth of Greece did I speak to you and know you and love you. We walked through the marble streets, we led solemn sacrifices, I armed you for the battle, I welcomed you from the victory. The centuries have parted us, but not for ever. Harold, I too have lived at Acragas!"

Round the corner swept the Peaslakes' carriage, full of excited occupants. He had only time to whisper in her ear, "No Mildred darling, you have not."

Chapter III

There was a dirty little sitting room in the Albergo Empedocle, and Mildred was sitting there after dinner waiting for her
father. He had met some friends at the temples, and he and she
had agreed to pay them a visit. It was a cold night, and the
room smelt of mustiness and lamp oil. The only other occu-
pant was a stiff-backed lady who had found a three-year-old
number of *Home Chat*. Lady Peaslake, Lilian, and Harold were
all with Sir Edwin, hunting for the key of his Gladstone bag.
Till it was found he could not go out with her, for all his clean
collars were inside.

Mildred was thoroughly miserable. After long torture she
had confessed to herself that she was self-deceived. She had
never lived in Acragas. She remembered nothing. All her glow-
ing description was pure imagination, the result of sentimental
excitement. For instance she had spoken of "snow-white marble temples." That was nonsense, sheer nonsense. She had seen
the remains of those temples, and they were built of porous
stone, not marble. And she remembered now that the Sicilian
Greeks always covered their temples with colored stucco. At
first she had tried to thrust such objections away and to believe
that she had found a truth to which archaeology must yield.
But what pictures or music did she remember? When had she
buckled on Harold's armor, and what was it like? Was it
probable that they had led a sacrifice together? The visions, always misty, faded away. She had never lived in Acragas.

But that was only the beginning of her mortification. Harold
had proved her wrong. He had seen that she was a shifty, shallow hypocrite. She had not dared to be alone with him since her

exposure. She had never looked at him and had hardly spoken. He seemed cheerful, but what was he thinking? He would never forgive her.

Had she only realized that it is only hypocrites who cannot forgive hypocrisy, whereas those who search for truth are too conscious of the maze to be hard on others—then the bitter flow of her thoughts might have been stopped and the catas-trophe averted. But it was not conceivable to her that she should forgive—or that she should accept forgiveness, for to her forgiveness meant a triumph of one person over another.

So she went still further towards sorrow. She felt that Har-old had scored off her, and she determined to make the score as little as she could. Was he really as sincere as he had seemed? Sincere he might be, but he might be self-deceived even as she was. That would explain all. He too had been moved by the beauty of the scene, by its wonderful associations. Worn out he had fallen asleep, and, conscious perhaps that she was in a fool-ish sympathetic state, had indulged in a fit of imagination on awaking. She had fallen in with it, and they had encouraged each other to fresh deeds of folly. All was clear. And how was she to hide it from her father?

Each time she restated the question it took a more odious form. Even though she believed Harold had been as foolish as herself, she was still humiliated before him, for her folly had been revealed, and his had not. The last and worst thought pressed itself upon her. Was he really as simple as he seemed? Had he not been trying to deceive her? He had been so careful in speaking of his old life: would only say that he had been "greater," "better"—never gave one single detail by which archaeology might prove him wrong. It was very clever of him. He had never lost his head once. Jealous of her superior acquirements, he had determined to put her to ridicule. He had laid a cunning bait and she had swallowed it. How cleverly he had lured her on to make the effort of recollection! How patiently he had heard her rapturous speech, in order that he might prove her silly to the core! How diabolically worded was his retort—"No, Mildred darling, you have not lived at Acragas." It implied, "I will be kind to you and treat you well when you are my wife, but recollect that you are silly, emotional, hypocritical: that your pretensions to superiority are gone for ever; that I have proved you inferior to me, even as all women are inferior to all men. Dear Mildred, you are a fool!"

"Intolerable! intolerable!" she gasped to herself, "if only I could expose him! I never dreamt it of him! I was never on my guard!"

Harold came quickly into the room, and she was at once upon the defensive. He told her that her father was ready and she got up to go, her ears aching in expectation of some taunt. It came—a very subtle one. She heard him say, "Kiss me before you go," and felt his hands grasp her elbows.

"No!" she said, shrinking from his touch, and frowning towards the stiff-backed lady, who sat a little stiffer.

"You'll have to," was his reply, and catching hold of her—he was very strong—he lifted her right above his head, and broke the feathers in her hat against the ceiling. He never completed his embrace, for she shrieked aloud, inarticulate with passion, and the voice of Sir Edwin was heard saying "Come, come, Harold, my boy—come, come!"

He set her down, and white with rage she hissed at him, "I never thought I should live to find you both charlatan and cad," and left the room.

Had she stayed, she would have been gratified at the prompt

effect of her rebuke. Harold stood where she left him, dumb
with misery, and then, without further warning, began to cry.
He cried without shame or restraint, not even turning his head
or covering his face with his hands, but letting the tears run
down his cheeks till they caught in his moustache, or dropped
on to the floor. Sir Edwin, not unmoved, stood before him for a
moment, stammering as he tried to think of something that
should both rebuke and console.

But the world has forgotten what to say to men of twenty-
four who cry. Sir Edwin followed his daughter, giving a de-
spairing look at Lady Peaslake and Lilian as he departed.

Lady Peaslake took up the line of behaving as if nothing
had happened, and began talking in a high voice about the
events of the day. Harold did not attempt to leave the room,
but still stood near the table, sobbing and gulping for breath.

Lilian, moved by a more human impulse, tremulously asked
him why he cried, and at this point the stiff-backed lady, who
had sat through everything, gathered up her skirts as if she had
seen a beetle, and slipped from the room.

"I cry because I'm unhappy: because Mildred's angry with
me."

"Er—er," said Lady Peaslake, "I'm sure that it would be
Mildred's wish that you should stop."

"I thought at dinner," he gasped, "that she was not pleased.
Why? Why? Nothing had happened. Nothing but happiness,
I mean. The best way, I thought, of showing I love her is to
kiss her, and that will make her understand again. You know,
she understood everything."

"Oh yes," said Lady Peaslake. "Look," she added to divert
him, "how do you like my new embroidery?"

"It's hideous—perfectly hideous!" was his vigorous reply.

"Well, here is a particular gentleman!" said good-natured Lady Peaslake. "Why, it's Liberty!"

"Frightful," said Harold. He had stopped crying. His face was all twisted with pain, but such a form of expressing emotion is fairly suitable for men, and Lady Peaslake felt easier.

But he returned to Mildred. "She called me a cad and a charlatan."

"Oh, never mind!" said Lilian.

"I may be a cad. I never did quite see what a cad is, and no one ever quite explained to me. But a charlatan! Why did she call me a charlatan? I can't quite see what I've done."

He began to walk up and down the little room. Lady Peaslake gently suggested a stroll, but he took no notice and kept murmuring "Charlatan."

"Why are pictures like this allowed!" he suddenly cried. He had stopped in front of a colored print in which the martyrdom of St. Agatha was depicted with all the fervor that incompetence could command.

"It's only a saint," said Lady Peaslake, placidly raising her head.

"How disgusting—and how ugly!"

"Yes, very. It's Roman Catholic."

He turned away shuddering, and began his everlasting question—"Why did she call me a charlatan?"

Lady Peaslake felt compelled to say—"You see, Harold, you annoyed her, and when people are annoyed they will say anything. I know it by myself."

"But a charlatan! I know for certain that she understands me. Only this afternoon I told her——"

"Oh, yes," said Lady Peaslake.

"Told her that I had lived before—lived here over two thousand years ago, she thinks."

"Harold! my dear Harold! what nonsense are you talking?" Lady Peaslake had risen from her chair.

"Over two thousand years ago, when the place had another name."

"Good heavens; he is mad!"

"Mildred didn't think so. It's she who matters. Lilian, do you believe me?"

"No," faltered Lilian, edging towards the door.

He smiled, rather contemptuously.

"Now, Harold," said Lady Peaslake, "go and lie down, there's a good boy. You want rest. Mildred will call you charlatan with reason if you say such silly, such wicked things—good gracious me! He's fainting! Lilian! Water from the dining room! Oh, what has happened? We were all so happy this morning."

The stiff-backed lady re-entered the room, accompanied by a thin little man with a black beard.

"Are you a doctor?" cried Lady Peaslake.

He was not, but he helped them to lay Harold on the sofa. He had not really fainted, for he was talking continually.

"You might have killed me," he said to Lady Peaslake, "you have said such an awful thing. You mean she thinks I never lived before. I know you're wrong, but it nearly kills me if you even say it. I have lived before—such a wonderful life. You will hear—Mildred will say it again. She won't like talking about it, but she'll say it if I want her to. That will save me from—from—from being a charlatan. Where is Mildred?"

"Hush!" said the little man.

"I have lived before—I have lived before, haven't I? Do you believe me?"

"Yes," said the little man.

"You lie," said Harold. "Now I've only to see people and I can tell. Where is Mildred?"

"You must come to bed."

"I don't speak or move till she comes."

So he lay silent and motionless on the sofa, while they stood around him whispering.

Mildred returned in a very different mood. A few questions from her father, followed by a few grave words of rebuke, had brought her to a sober mind. She was terribly in fault; she had nourished Harold's insanity first by encouraging it, then by rebuffing it. Sir Edwin severely blamed her disordered imagina-tion, and bade her curb it; its effects might be disastrous, and he told her plainly that unless Harold entirely regained his normal condition he would not permit the marriage to take place. She acknowledged her fault, and returned determined to repair it; she was full of pity and contrition, but at the same time she was very matter-of-fact.

He heard them return and rushed to meet her, and she rushed to meet him. They met in the long passage, where it was too dark to see each other's faces.

"Harold," she said hurriedly, "I said two dreadful words to you. Will you forgive me?"

She tried to touch him, but he pushed her off with his arm, and said—"Come to the light."

The landlord appeared with a lamp. Harold took it and held it up to Mildred's face.

"Don't!" she said feebly.

"Harold!" called Lady Peaslake. "Come back!"

"Look at me!" said Harold.

"Don't!" said Mildred and shut her eyes.

"Open your eyes!"

She opened them, and saw his. Then she screamed and called out to her father—"Take him away! I'm frightened. He's mad! He's mad!"

Harold said quite calmly, "This is the end."

"Yes," said Sir Edwin, nervously taking the lamp, "now it's bedtime."

"If you think I'm mad," said Harold, "I am mad. That's all it means."

"Go to bed, Harold, to please me."

"Six people say I'm mad. Is there no one, no one, no one who understands?" He stumbled up the passage as if he were blind, and they heard him calling "Tommy."

In the sitting room he caught his foot in the carpet and fell. When they picked him up, he was murmuring—"Harold can't stand up against six. What is Harold? Harold. Harold. Harold. Who is Harold?"

"Stop him!" cried the little man. "That's bad! He mustn't do that."

They shook him and tried to overtalk him, but he still went on. "What is Harold? Six letters. H.A.R.O.L.D. Harold. Harold. Harold."

"He's fainted again!" cried Lady Peaslake. "Oh, what has happened?"

"It's a sunstroke," said Sir Edwin. "He caught it through sleeping in the sun this afternoon. Mildred has told me all about it."

They took him up and carried him to his room.

As they were undressing him, he revived, and began to talk in a curious, thick voice.

"I was the last to go off the sofa, wasn't I? I counted five go—the wisest first—and I counted ten kinds of wine for certain before I slipped. Your conjurers are poor—but I liked the looks of the flute-girl."

"Go away, dears," said Lady Peaslake. "It's no good our stopping."

"Yes, I liked the flute-girl; is the porter I gave you last week a success?"

"Yes," said the little man, whose cue it was always to agree.

"Well, he'd better help carry me home. I don't want to walk. Nothing elaborate, you know. Just four porters for the litter, and half a dozen to carry the lights. That won't put you out."

"I'm afraid you must stop here for the night."

"Very well, if you can't send me back. Oh, the wine! the wine! I have got a head."

"What is he saying?" asked Mildred through the door.

"Is that the flute-girl?" said Harold raising an interested eye.

Sir Edwin laid hold of him, but he was quite passive, and did not attempt to move. He allowed himself to be undressed, but did not assist them, and when his pyjamas were handed to him, he laughed feebly and asked what they were for.

"I want to look out of the window." They took him to it, hoping that the fresh air would recall his wits, and held him tight in case he tried to leap out. There was no moon, and the expanse of trees and fields was dark and indistinguishable.

"There are no lights moving in the streets," said Harold.

"It must be very late. I forgot the windows were so high. How odd that there are no lights in the streets!"

"Yes, you're too late," said the little man. "You won't mind sleeping here. It's too far to go back."

"Too far—too far to go back," he murmured. "I am so sleepy, in this room I could sleep for ever. Too far—too far—oh, the wine!"

They put him into the bed, and he went off at once, and his breathing was calm and very regular.

"A sunstroke," whispered Sir Edwin. "Perhaps a good night's rest—I shall sit up."

But next morning Harold had forgotten how to put on his clothes, and when he tried to speak he could not pronounce his words.

Chapter IV

They had a terrible scene with him at the Girgenti railway station next morning when the train came in. However they got him on to it at last, and by the evening he was back at Palermo and had seen the English doctor. He was sent back to England with a keeper, by sea, while the Peaslakes returned by Naples, as soon as Mildred's health permitted.

Long before Harold reached the asylum his speech had become absolutely unintelligible: indeed by the time he arrived at it, he hardly ever uttered a sound of any kind. His case attracted some attention, and some experiments were made, which proved that he was not unfamiliar with Greek dress, and had some knowledge of the alphabet.

But he was quite blank when spoken to, either in ancient

or modern Greek, and when he was given a Greek book, he did not know what to do with it, and began tearing out the pages.

On these grounds the doctors have concluded that Harold merely thinks he is a Greek, and that it is his mania to behave as he supposes that a Greek behaved, relying on such elementary knowledge as he acquired at school.

But I firmly believe that he has been a Greek—nay, that he is a Greek, drawn by recollection back into his previous life. He cannot understand our speech because we have lost his pronunciation. And if I could look at the matter dispassionately —which I cannot—I should only rejoice at what has happened. For the greater has replaced the less, and he is living the life he knew to be greater than the life he lived with us. And I also believe, that if things had happened otherwise, he might be living that greater life among us, instead of among friends of two thousand years ago, whose names we have never heard. That is why I shall never forgive Mildred Peaslake as long as I live.

Most certainly he is not unhappy. His own thoughts are sweet to him, and he looks out of the window hour after hour and sees things in the sky and sea that we have forgotten. But of his fellow men he seems utterly unconscious. He never speaks to us, nor hears us when we speak. He does not know that we exist.

So at least I thought till my last visit. I am the only one who still goes to see him: the others have given it up. Last time, when I entered the room, he got up and kissed me on the cheek. I think he knows that I understand him and love him: at all events it comforts me to think so.

1903

CAMBRIDGE HUMOR

Forster was born on New Year's day 1879 and went up to Cambridge in the autumn of 1897. In 1900, when he was twenty-one years old, he started publishing a variety of items in the student magazine *Basileona*. They are the work of a young man with a good eye for detail and a liking for the countryside around Cambridge. Since the educated Englishman at the turn of the century had a notorious predilection for walking, Forster is in the best company with his very first contribution "On Grinds," or what used to be called constitutionals.

"On Grinds" suggests that walking is a way of life. "A Brisk Walk" shows the unfortunate side of such a philosophy and Forster's unqualified rejection of it. In his paper on "The Beauty of Life" (1911) he firmly tells his readers never to study a subject that bores them, however important others say it is. "A Brisk Walk" expresses the same outlook in 1901.

The next best thing to getting about on your own two feet on a decent day is careening through the countryside on a bicycle. But it is a precarious situation as Forster pictures it, especially since the Cyclists' Touring Club has not posted signs in the Cambridge area warning of the precipitousness of the hills. The reason is that the warnings are scarcely needed. Cambridge is situated, as Baedeker puts it, "in a somewhat flat but not unpleasing district." It is against this plain fact that Forster builds his account of the perils and humiliations of the bicyclist.

In these three short essays Forster devises a pleasant mixture of land-scape and human foibles. In "A Long Day" his interest is more psy-chological as he describes how a few hours may stretch themselves out interminably when one has visitors on one's hands. One looks at every landmark, church, library, chapel, the Fitzwilliam Museum (outstand-ing library, good collection of art), the Union (reading, writing, and smoking rooms, fine debating hall, library of 20,000 volumes); one re-peats the jokes about the Pitt Press (the large and ecclesiastical-looking University Printing Office was nicknamed the Freshmen's Church); and at last one is reduced to debating: is Cambridge better than Oxford?

What happens to the weight of tradition during the three long years of an undergraduate's life? "The Pack of Anchises" tries, with little success, to explore the question. As Aeneas flees Troy, he carries with him his old father Anchises who, in his turn, carries the household gods. Such a burden of the past is a continuing hindrance to Aeneas and what does he gain for his trouble? Though his piety and patience are re-warded by the natural death of his father and though he founds a great nation, yet he is not a happy man. And how does a young man in 1900 handle the traditions which he carries into manhood with him? Forster sets up the allegory but does nothing with it. He is interested in the psy-chology of the problem but he is not prepared to say where he stands in relation to tradition.

"The Stall-Holder" and "The Early Father" are illustrated char-acter types after the manner of the Greek, Theophrastus. Again the in-terest is primarily psychological, but the stress here is on realistic sur-face as Forster displays his novelistic eye for detail. Anyone who has read *The Longest Journey* will immediately recognize the girl in "The Stall-Holder" as the prototype of Agnes Pembroke. She has the same straightforward aggressive charm, the same self-deception and dishon-esty. Brief though it is, this sketch has bite.

A rather similar character, still aggressive, but weaker, older, and more ridden by foibles, is the center of "The Early Father" which is in fact about the early mother who comes up with her son to college and, instead of entrusting him to the good offices of his tutors and to the mercies of the Maker of Beds (if he lives within a college) or of the Landlady (if he takes rooms in town), intervenes on his behalf.

"A Tragic Interior" and its sequel are schoolboy spoofs of the Orestes trilogy by Aeschylus. The first is most notable for the authoritative character of Clytemnestra who entirely dominates the ineffectual Agamemnon. The choice of subject tells us something about Forster's interests at this time. Even in 1900 he is attracted by the figure of the dominant woman who is to play so large a part in his fiction. She may be threatening like Agnes Pembroke or sterile and deadly like Aunt Emily in *The Longest Journey;* she may be a life-sustaining priestess like Mrs. Wilcox or a source of cultural and genetic continuation like Margaret and Helen Schlegel in *Howards End;* but in either case, Forster's fascination can be related to his own childhood experience, to the early death of his father and his upbringing by his mother in a family dominated by women. "The Stall-Holder" and "A Tragic Interior" are the first literary consequences of that upbringing.

"A Tragic Interior, 2" is based on the second play of the trilogy in which Orestes returns to avenge the death of his father. It is not as effective as Forster's first parody because it lacks a dominant character to focus the action. It continues, however, to play on the absurd machinery of Greek tragedy with its eccyclema whereby the interior scene, bath and all, is wheeled outdoors to stage front; and it ends on a note of bathos with a reference to Dr. A. W. Verrall (1851–1912), the indefatigable editor of school texts of the Latin and Greek classics.

More generally, these parodies suggest that extreme notions of fate are ridiculous and tiresome. Forster, in 1900, did not appreciate that life closes in on one, that choices continually narrow. In fact he never appreciated this truth, which may be a way of saying that he always remained young in spirit. He refused to see life as either dull routine or grandiose fate. The refusal had nothing to do with metaphysical freedom. Forster was profoundly uninterested in metaphysics. Life is life; it is made up of expectations and surprises, of blessings and misfortunes. It may be a dull routine for characters like Cecil Vyse in *A Room with a View* and Adela Quested in *A Passage to India.* But Cecil meets Lucy and Adela enters her cave. If they had the spirit to under-stand what life was offering, they would cease to be the victims of dull-ness and fate.

Aeschylus's third play, in which Orestes is pursued by the avenging deities, escapes parody. The reason may be Forster's profound sym-pathy for this part of the story in which the Furies, representing re-morse and punishment, are brought within the framework of civilized rational control. Near the beginning of Chapter XLI of *Howards End* we read: "Remorse is not among the eternal verities. The Greeks were right to dethrone her. Her action is too capricious, as though the Erin-yes selected for punishment only certain men and certain sins." The Furies or Erinyes appear for just a moment at the end of "A Tragic Interior, 2" and leave behind one detached blue snake. This image also reappears in *Howards End,* late in the same chapter. The guilt-ridden Leonard Bast sees blue snakes of moonlight running up his blanket; then one part of his mind tells him that Time, Death, Judgment, and "the smaller snakes" of remorse are alive in the moon whose tenta-cles of blue light are reaching out to him. Forster understands Leo-nard's feelings of regret and sin, but he does not approve them. Re-morse is a wasteful form of regeneration. It may cleanse but it inevitably narrows. It is, I would suggest, a kind of self-imposed fate. And fate of any kind is for Forster the enemy of life and spontaneity.

"Strivings after Historical Style" is a crude take-off of four textbook modes of historical writing. Forster shows an eye for cliché, tired idiom, and mixed metaphor. But behind the verbal panache, the real butt of the satire is not the style at all but the assumption of historical neces-sity; running through all four parodies is the idea that someone "was to" do something and that "it was none the less inevitable." Or to put it more graphically—it hardly matters that the reference is to France—"her enemies were but hatching the eggs that she herself had laid forty years before." Here again, Fate displeases Forster.

On the other side from fate is spontaneity which defies the force of destiny and escapes the rule of cause and effect. In "The Beauty of Life" Forster says that holidays give spontaneity a chance because they make us more open to unexpected and lively happenings. "A Day Off" (1904) is a record of such happenings. It is not, of course, a

Cambridge essay, but the humor is strictly of the student variety. In addition to its praise of spontaneity, the essay is most notable for its tribute to Italy, a subject Forster rarely touches upon except in the fiction.

In 1912 Forster published a final Cambridge essay, or dialogue to be more precise, which the editors claim to have named "An Allegory" and which another Cambridge journal, *Granta,* when it reprinted the work in 1956, entitled "Back to the Backs." In bringing together boats on the Cam and a large steam engine which travels ponderously by road and is capable of pulling heavy loads, Forster develops a miniature confrontation between ancient Cambridge and modern industrial England. The boats are frolicsome, the river is silent, and the engine says: "I am the squalor of experience. I shall come." It is the situation in *Howards End* again. The red rust of roofs and the grey amorphousness of the megalopolis seem to be spreading, spreading, over all of England, all of the world. But the novel does not end on this note. Out in the country there is yet some hope. An island of happiness remains, or possibly a hundred islands, or a thousand. Likewise here, the river continues mysteriously silent, the traction engine huffs and puffs and passes on, and the flexible little canoe turns over happily.

On Grinds

Every afternoon the academic population falls into two classes —those who go for grinds and those who do not. Endless sub-divisions of the latter are realized, and the performance of some is watched by vast crowds. But no one cares to look at the grinders, or notes that they grind not all alike, but according to their natures. Look at the parent of grinds, the Grantchester, the great artery through which the intellect of the place daily circulates. Here, rather than to the Senate House or the University Church, do we bring visitors who wish to see Cambridge as a home of learning. But let no one confound those who walk by Trumpington to Grantchester with those who walk by Grantchester to Trumpington. All are great, but the former are the more solid thinkers, who are perfectly indifferent which way they go, and start by the Trumpington Road because it is easier to find; the latter are more esthetic, they hide the horrid main road from their thoughts and plunge into the green meadows of the golf links and the lane through Grantchester to the Mill, oblivious of the dull return. Of course, it is possible to come back the same way, but no proper person would ever think of doing that.

The best spot for studying the two classes is on the mill bridge. Those who approach from the right wear the strongest spectacles; those from the left have smarter ties and are attended by more dogs. At the bridge a small percentage will hang over the rail, and of these a few—who have come from the extreme left—will affirm that they are laughing with Chaucer in the hawthorn shade. But esthetics are here tempered with erudition; the real person of soul is to be found on the Madingley Road. This indeed is a particularly interesting highway. Those who tread it are either obviously unenterprising and fat, turning back at the base of the hill, or else in search of the beautiful. Of these a part ascend the hill and quote Ruskin, or if they have got past him, write an account of the view themselves, beginning "With what varied emotions did I behold this striking scene," and introducing Ely Cathedral, and Girton, which lies like a pink slug on the left. Here, too, Wordsworth's three sonnets on King's may be quoted, especially the one beginning "What awful perspective." The other part pursue the lower road to thrid the sombre boskage of Madingley, and a happy few find the little chalk pit this side of the village where they may wander among the firs and undergrowth, folded off from the outer world.

Other grinds there are, but less famous and less attractive. Members of the Fabian Society find the walk through Barnwell to Cherry Hinton stimulating, and there is a blind alley by the Trumpington Road known as the Senior Wrangler's walk, down which candidates for the Mathematical Tripos go to school themselves to disappointment and the blows of fate. These do but turn because they must, but abhorred be they who go to the second milestone on the Barton or Huntingdon road, and having reached it revolve with expressionless features and retrace their path. Unloved, unlovely, may they return through rain and mist and settle down unrefreshed to their irksome and unnecessary tasks.

1900

A Brisk Walk

It is after luncheon and a fog. The unnecessary friend comes in and suggests a brisk walk. You say you think no. He replies that it will do you good. You are morally certain that it will not, but in things athletic he who affirms is stronger than he who denies, and you put on your boots.

"Which (uter) way shall we go? The Madingley or the Grantchester?" You decide on the Madingley, and start off in the embarrassed silence peculiar to people taking exercise in bad weather. After a time you observe—

"What a perfectly foul day."

"It all depends how you look at it," the unnecessary friend replies in an offended voice. He is a bit of a philosopher, and if the weather were decent you would like to hear him talk and might even understand him. But the fog immures you both in one chamber; you cannot even look away or touch your prison walls; the moving pavilion must encircle you until you return. You are two amoebas in one cell, and if one amoeba is intellectual the other dies. So it is best to be silent. All along the road, in front and behind, could you but see them, are other moving cells filled with other amoebas, some single, most in pairs, all depressed. You hear a wild ring close behind you, and a cell collides with yours. It holds an amoeba on a bicycle, who with an inadequate apology gathers himself together and speeds on.

"Isn't it strange," remarks the unnecessary friend, after a long silence, "to think of the limited area of a fog. It never rises far above the ground, and I dare say that in many parts of England they are having glorious weather."

You make no reply.

"It reminds me of Matthew Arnold," he continues, cheer- fully:

> *"Smoky dwarf houses*
> *Hem me in everywhere,*
> *A vague dejection*
> *Weighs down my soul.*
> *Yet on the convent roof*
> *Of Holy Lassa*
> *Bright shines the—*

but I dare say people quoting may get on your nerves."

It does, and so does the knowledge that they are enjoying excellent weather in Tibet. And to think that not a thousand feet above is bright sunshine and blue sky, and the blessed gods reclining.

But even the blessed gods notice something is wrong.

"I cannot see the Eastern counties today," Jupiter remarks. "They are veiled in mist. Just go, Mercury, and see that man- kind are all right and safe there."

Mercury obediently plunges into the pea soup and emerges with the news that mankind are taking brisk walks. Then is the pity of the blessed gods turned to laughter, and they deplore the cost of thunderbolts and the decreased cultivation of hellebore.

Meanwhile you are saying "Here is the Observatory pillar-box; shan't we turn now?" and the unnecessary friend replies, "Why, you'll get no good from this; we must go up the hill. On a fine day you get a beautiful breeze and a really fine view."

You sullenly comply, and he says you do not seem to like walking as you did. Your head aches violently, your feet are tender, you have a pain in the stomach. All this he attributes to the liver, a circular organ in the small of the back, the one part of you which seems unaffected. At the hill top he has a brilliant idea. "Let us go over the fields to Coton and so home." Mercury is sent to see if you will actually comply. You do. The unnecessary friend, now most necessary, misses the path, and you get into a ploughed field. Your feet grow larger at every stride, and a great flower of mud caresses your trousers. You stop to pluck it off, and when you look up the cell is divided and your fellow is no more. You call and hear him answer, and go the wrong way. Mercury returns to the blessed gods. You stumble through mud, ditch, hedge, fence, and finally regain a road and, oh, joy! a carriage-amoeba comes along it and takes you back to Cambridge. After all you are an hour before the unnecessary friend, who was some time in the field looking for you, yet he still sings the praises of the brisk walk and will take you for many another ere winter ends.

1901

On Bicycling

Bicycling is separated from all other employments by the new position in which it places the outside world. The world of the athlete consists of opponents and spectators: the pedestrian, sane and unpretentious, has neither, but contents himself with looking on: the bicyclist endeavors to be both actor and spectator and fails in both. He is too insignificant to be admired, too much imperilled to have time to admire. His world consists of things that have got out of his way, things that cannot, and things that will not. The first class is very small: the second comprises stones, overturned carts, and drunken men: the third the greater part of the animal kingdom. Children, hitherto harmless and even attractive, become noxious beings of enormous power, bent on breaking their victim's limbs and then claiming compensation. Their tactics differ according to the locality. In Hertfordshire they simulate insanity, in Kent they make patterns with tin tacks, in Lancashire they throw bricks. Here in

Cambridge they flee at the first note of the bell: the bicyclist speeds happily on, and when he is close at hand they rush back into the road and form a dense phalanx, the weakest in the van.

Besides children, the Cambridge bicyclist must beware of steep hills. They can indeed be descried at a considerable distance, but are none the less insidious. The C.T.C. have missed this part of England in their paternal survey: as far as I know only one hill near has their sign-board—the Haslingfield. It is short and steep, ending in a low wall, which not unsuitably forms the boundary of a grave yard. The Gog Magogs are unmarked. The precipitous Madingley, however, has gained notoriety. Many years ago, the then Vice-Chancellor used to descend it at a terrific rate, carried by his impetus past the sunny pleasure domes of the observatory right into the scene of his labors. One day the hill rebelled at the insult and threw him off. An enterprising tire company profited by this to erect a circular caution on the top, but democratic England has not brooked classification with a Vice-Chancellor and the caution has been stoned till it is illegible.

Beset by such perils how can the bicyclist admire his surroundings? and who will admire the bicyclist? Too incompetent to play games, too proud to go for grinds, he is the type of man who aims at two things and misses both, skidding between two stools and breaking his machine into the bargain.

1900

A Long Day

Of all days a long day is the longest, a day that is when friends or relatives arrive by the first train in the morning and stop till the last train at night. If they stop the night, the spell is broken and time runs out his envious course at a reasonable rate. But a long day does not bow to the rules of nature. The sun stays in his path, neither does the evening come. Long distances are traversed even by elderly visitors with marvellous celerity. Meals are scarcely served before they are finished. There is time, and ample time, to see the whole of the colleges, the University Church and Library, the Fitzwilliam, and the Union, to go to service in the chapel, and in a boat on the backs, for in a long day there are many days. Whether the visitors are enthusiastic or apathetic, whether they require detailed information about obscure buildings, taxing truth and chronology beyond all limits, or whether they greet everything with civil assent varied by "how beautiful," or "how pretty,"

or "how you must enjoy yourselves to be sure," the result is still the same. Early in the visit it is found necessary to relate the humorous stories about the Pitt Press and the balls on Clare bridge, and to engage in discussion on one of the usual topics—"Is Cambridge better than Oxford," or "Do the men at different colleges know each other," or "What a pity it is so flat?" On no account omit to point out the stone rose inside the chapel "in which appears a female form, due probably to a fancy of the workman." It is an excellent subject for conversation and has been known to occupy more time than all the windows put together.

As the shadows lengthen so do the hours, and "seeing off" seems a process that can have no end. The train will not go, nor will you, although they implore you earnestly and have nothing more to say to you, nor you to them. At last they start, and then comes that supremely important communication that you just fail to catch as the train glides away. They are gone and have had a happy day, and so have you; but it has been long.

1900

The Pack of Anchises

Looking back may be profitable, but it is hardly an exhilarating performance. Nevertheless there is a certain fascination on nearing the end of our three years' life here to consider the time when we entered on it and suddenly became "men." Between it and now stretches a road glittering with smashed penates that have one by one slipped from the pack. Those that still remain we finger critically, marvelling at their un' couth workmanship and insipid smiles, and submit them to the weighing machine to see whether it is not better to replace them with lighter and more commodious articles. The worst of it is that though a portable god is very brittle he is not easy to replace, and we may find it better to have none.

But besides the penates we also carry Anchises—who shall signify enthusiasm, so far as the contradictions of allegory will allow. When we loaded up before the walls of Troy he made an extensive selection of gods, declaring that he should not find them a bit too much to carry. You gently suggested that since he rode on your shoulders you would ultimately bear the weight of the gods, but Anchises was never remarkable for his brain power, nor for his powers of selection, choosing both well and ill made penates, but showing a decided prefer- ence for those that were heavy. The result was that your pantheon was both too extensive and incomplete, and that Anchises let a good many drop on the way. And what with the loss of dilatory Creusa and the bother of seeing to Iulus and the misfortunes at Crete, owing to Anchises hailing it as the promised land when it wasn't, you have at times an unholy longing to be rid of the silly old man and carry your penates for yourself. Then you could choose rationally, no longer hampered by his silly impulses, and keep in your pack either perfect gods or else none at all. And how you would economize your strength and swiftly reach the end of your journey with such gods as pleased you!

But when the piety of Aeneas was rewarded by his father's natural death, he took the penates and sailed to Carthage, and got no good therefrom, and though he returned to Sicily and mourned long over the grave his life was but toil and battle till the end, and success itself brought him no happiness. Virgil gives us no account of the housewarming after his marriage with Lavinia, but it must have been a dismal function, for few of either her relatives or his friends were left alive to grace the proceedings. And the penates drop out of the story en- tirely.

It is worth while looking back to see how our belongings have stood the great move. Has Anchises dropped the gods, or have we dropped Anchises and gods together?

1900

The Cambridge Theophrastus

BEING A GUIDE FOR THE INEXPERIENCED TO CHARACTERS
THAT MAY BE MET IN THE UNIVERSITY WORLD

The Stall-Holder

A stall may be defined as a place in which dumb animals are penned, and a stall-holder is one who pens them.

She is one who, being at other times generous, straight-forward and magnanimous, is able, at the call of Charity, to put all these things away from her and devote herself solely to the acquisition of wealth. She addresses herself chiefly to those who are young and in possession of money that is not their own but entrusted to them by their absent parents, using such expressions as "Now you must buy something from *me*," and "Let me pin this flower in your coat," and "If you will take both these egg cosies I will reduce them to four-and-sixpence." Or she will offer a pincushion fashioned like a star-fish, of great price and inconvenient shape, and if he affirms he has no use for it, will reply "It will do to throw at a burglar," under cover of the witticism completing the bargain. And if he demand change she will reply that "she is just out of it," though audibly jingling with many small coins, and thus ends by acquiring in its entirety a sovereign, from which she ought to have yielded back twelve shillings and ninepence, being the acknowledged excess of the article purchased. And she practises these and many other tricks which, were she not in a bazaar, would assuredly bring her beneath the jurisdiction of the magistrates, as, for example, fortunetelling and raffles, and falsifying the price when the purchaser seems eager and inducing people to dip in a lucky bag whence they only draw wood and bits of coal, justifying herself on the score of humor. This, however, is particularly to be observed about her, that she persuades people to buy not by affirming the justice of her cause or the indigence of those whom her gains are intended to assist, but by representing the matter as a personal favor, and that she will be treated very ill if they do not comply. So that they, being overcome by shame, are compelled to make many and useless purchases. And as she returns home she might be overheard saying that "she has made twenty-eight pounds nine shillings and twopence though the articles on her stall were only valued at twenty pounds," and that "she, for one, will never hesitate to labor personally in a Good Cause."

1900

The Cambridge
Theophrastus

The Early Father

The Early Father is one who, having determined to send his
son to acquire learning, deems it fitting to accompany him in
order that he may start with greater ease and comfort on his
career. And though he always intends kindly he does not
always act with wisdom, as, for instance, when he asks the
tutor questions to which he, though learned and affable, is at
sore straights to make reply, such as "how is the drainage
planned?" and "must he come to his lessons when it rains?"
and "will they see that he changes his socks?" To which the
tutor, answering at random, is apt to give an impression of
negligence and incompetency, even though none such exists.

And with the Early Father must be classed the Early
Mother, who is determined to protect her son from extortion,
saying to him "dear, you shall not be put upon." So, for instance, having gone out with him to make purchases, she will
say in loud tones to those who are proferring goods "How

now! do you ask two drachmae for these dish-clouts when in my own city I get them not worse for half that price?" And they being covered with confusion and fearing that the by-standers will overhear and so desist from buying, allege I know not what excuse, such as the war with the Medes or the superior quality or that different cities excel in different goods. To which she in a high voice replies "by your rapacity you have overreached yourselves, for my son here, though not being extravagant, no indeed, would nevertheless have made many profitable purchases at your booth! but now being forewarned he will go elsewhere." And if the youth himself says that after all the price is small and the dish-clouts very requisite, she only replies "No, dear, you shall not be put upon," and leads him from the shop to the mirth of the bystanders and the no little mortification of himself.

And also she is likely to alienate the landlady or the Maker of Beds—whichever fate has allotted—by asking what becomes of such bread and butter as the youth shall have not consumed when even falls, or why so vast a quantity of knife-powder and hearth-brushes is necessary—unseemly questions which no wise woman and no man would ask. Moreover, she states that her son is a delicate eater and of frail health, wishing to enlist sympathy but omitting the means by which sympathy is best attained. And having done many other similar things and given much advice concerning the necessity of warm clothing and the perpetual use of rain-averters when the heavens threaten, she departs to her own city, having so far erred in her purpose that if one were to say that she of all women has most tried to do one thing and succeeded in effecting another, he would not be far wrong.

1900

A Tragic Interior

BEING AN ATTEMPT TO INTERPRET THE INNER
MEANING OF THE AGAMEMNON OF AESCHYLUS

SCENE: *Interior of the palace of Agamemnon at Mycenae. Big outer door in front. To right and left are doors leading to inner chambers. The room is simply furnished with jars of oil, wine, etc., and a hip-bath. An axe hangs on the wall. In the corner of the room stands an expensive roll of carpet. In the middle is the eccyclema—a small truck on a line of rails which run through the big front doorway.* CLYTEMNESTRA *is discovered with a recipe book, making a libation. On the roof the watchman is delivering his opening speech. He cannot of course be seen, but when he performs his dance the palace rocks violently. Enter* WATCHMAN.

WATCHMAN: O, Queen! Troy is taken and Agamemnon returns.

CLYTEMNESTRA: Very well. Go to the inner store cupboard and bring back a clot of the best oil. Don't lose the key.

(Exit watchman. Chorus outside are heard singing their opening ode. CLYTEMNESTRA, *who has listened to their senti-*

ments for ten years, yawns wearily, and completes her libation with the best oil. The watchman tidies the room on his return.)

WATCHMAN: Hadn't I better take the bath away?

CLYTEMNESTRA (*severely*): Leave the bath where it is. And go.

(*Exit watchman.* CLYTEMNESTRA *goes out by the big front door, and amid great applause delivers her speech about the bonfires. She returns and rings the bell. Enter maid servants.*)

CLYTEMNESTRA: Your master is coming home this afternoon.

SERVANT: Yes'm. From Troy m'm?

CLYTEMNESTRA: Yes. He will want a bath. Get it ready here. (*Indicates eccyclema.*)

SERVANT: Zeus Ma'am! Master always had his bath in the dressing-room. And how is one to hoist it up?

CLYTEMNESTRA: Shall I have to speak twice?

(*After frantic efforts the bath is hoisted up.*)

SERVANT: What will he like for his supper, ma'am?

CLYTEMNESTRA: He will not want any. When was the eccyclema used last?

SERVANT: Thyestes ma'am—that is I mean Atreus, the time he murdered the two young gentlemen. They do say as how they can be seen walking with their insides——

CLYTEMNESTRA: That will do. Listen to me. Take that carpet and undo it. I shall be making a speech outside and when I get to "the hum of the buzzing gnat" push it up to the front door. Then when I say "servants, why tarry ye?" open the doors and let the carpet unroll itself down the steps. Be careful to stand on the end, or the whole thing will slip down and make the horses shy.

SERVANT: Master won't half like the best carpet undone.

(*The sounds of a somewhat lugubrious triumph song are*

heard from outside. Enter, running, CHRYSOTHEMIS *with a wax doll and* ELECTRA *with a wooden one.)*

CHRYSOTHEMIS: Oh, mummy dear, we can count thirteen bonfires from the nursery window——

ELECTRA: And a lot of people all shouting——

CHRYSOTHEMIS: And papa in a carriage——

ELECTRA: With a strange lady——

CHRYSOTHEMIS: And do let us go out and meet them! Oh, do!

CLYTEMNESTRA: No, dear.

ELECTRA: But why, mamma?

CLYTEMNESTRA: Because, dear, I say not.

ELECTRA: But we want to, and why . . .

CLYTEMNESTRA (*to* SERVANT): Take the young ladies back to the nursery.

SERVANT (*nervously*): Come, Miss Electra; do as your mamma tells you.

ELECTRA: I won't, I shan't go. I want to see papa and I——

(*Enter* AEGISTHUS.)

CLYTEMNESTRA: Aegisthus!

ELECTRA: I hate you, mamma, and I believe you hate me and hate papa, and——

CLYTEMNESTRA: Aegisthus, take the children away—at once —and put them in the back attic.

(*Exit* AEGISTHUS, *leading* CHRYSOTHEMIS *weeping and* ELEC- TRA *kicking his shins. Sound of wheels outside. Exit* CLYTEM- NESTRA *to meet her husband. The servants execute her orders about the carpet. Finally enter* CLYTEMNESTRA *and* AGAMEM- NON.)

AGAMEMNON: It's not the impiety I object to, but the extrav- agance. Think of the carpet! It'll never be the same again, even though I did take off my shoes. The bloom's off it for ever. Of course, dear, you meant it kindly, but you might have known me better. And—Apollo save us!—why have you put the bath on the eccyclema?

CLYTEMNESTRA: Surely after your journey, a bath——

AGAMEMNON: My dear, my dear, you must be mad. If I did have a bath, should I have it in the front sitting-room? Highly indecent—to say nothing of splashing the furniture. Dear, dear!

CLYTEMNESTRA: Oh—by the by, while I remember—who was that in the carriage with you?

AGAMEMNON: Who?—oh yes, that is Cassandra, daughter of Priam and Hecuba. Pleasant, very pleasant, but just a little fanciful at times. Of course, as you know, she had fifty brothers, not to mention her parents, and after losing them all one would be naturally a little—overwrought shall we say? But I am sure you will like her.

CLYTEMNESTRA: I suppose then I should ask her in?

AGAMEMNON: Who? Oh—yes—do you see the maids have trodden the soap into the carpet. Most provoking. And why on earth did you put the bath . . .

(*Exit* CLYTEMNESTRA. AGAMEMNON *wanders disconsolately round, reviewing the breakages that have occurred in his absence. Re-enter* CLYTEMNESTRA.)

CLYTEMNESTRA: I can do nothing with her; she seems a perfect fool—won't speak a word.

AGAMEMNON: Quite a fool? Yes, perhaps that is so. Eh? What? Oh, you were speaking of Cassandra. I was wondering what on earth induced you to put . . .

CASSANDRA (*outside*): Otototoi popoi da!

AGAMEMNON: Bless us and save us!

CASSANDRA: Otototoi popoi da.

CLYTEMNESTRA: I told you she was a fool.

AGAMEMNON: She is only relieving her feelings. I was about to say, why is the eccyclema——

CASSANDRA: Apollo, oh, Apolio!

CLYTEMNESTRA: You will have no supper till you have taken the bath, and if that noise does not stop we shall have——

CASSANDRA: Apollo, oh, Apollo! (*Her interruptions continue all through the dialogue.*)

AGAMEMNON: Now, Clytemnestra, I have given in to you about the carpet and the result is it's spoilt. I will not give in about the bath.

CLYTEMNESTRA: Servants! retire. (*The servants retire.*)

AGAMEMNON: What are you going to do, pray?

CLYTEMNESTRA: Kill you. In the bath. With the axe.

AGAMEMNONS Wh-wh wh-at!

CLYTEMNESTRA: The chorus have been foretelling it for years. There will be a revolution if it does not happen. You know that.

AGAMEMNON: I refuse, object, protest. I don't care if there is.

CLYTEMNESTRA: I do. Why Cassandra outside—she's prophesying it now.

CASSANDRA: Wow! wow! keep the bull from the cow!

AGAMEMNON: Yes, dear, she certainly does refer to you there. Apt, very apt. She always had a way of putting things.

CLYTEMNESTRA: Listen, she's prophesying her own death now. Well, when I begin I don't object to go on.

AGAMEMNON: I forbid you to murder me!

(*A long and unprofitable argument ensues. Finally enter CAS-*

SANDRA *tragically reeling with excitement and fatigue but conscious of having acquitted herself creditably. Her face falls on seeing them.*)

CASSANDRA: You aren't ready! There's not a minute! Quick.

CLYTEMNESTRA: Quick indeed! When I can't catch him, and if I did he's sixteen stone to hoist up into the bath!

CASSANDRA (*to* AGAMEMNON): Look here, don't be a fool.

CLYTEMNESTRA: I think, madam, you forget you are addressing my husband.

CASSANDRA: Don't talk. You must pretend you are dead—or else there will be a revolution. Ah! they've stopped! Quick now, say your death-line. Anything; but groan.

AGAMEMNON: I don't know—(*she pricks him with a hairpin.*) Oh my! I'm struck a bloody blow inside!

CLYTEMNESTRA: The young hussy! (CASSANDRA *pricks again.*)

AGAMEMNON: Oh my! I'm struck another bloody blow!

CASSANDRA: Up you get! And I too. Quick now, Clytemnestra, the axe! Three seconds to spare.

(AGAMEMNON *and* CASSANDRA *close their eyes and endeavor to become pallid. They with* CLYTEMNESTRA *and the axe are eccyclemed out of the front door.* CLYTEMNESTRA *converses with the chorus, and with the help of* AEGISTHUS *the play is concluded. The chorus, proud of their prophetic power, disperse to their homes. The eccyclema returns, and the front door is barred.* AGAMEMNON *sits up.*)

AGAMEMNON: What an experience. Far more confined than the wooden horse. And all my clothes wet, and the axe has scratched the paint off the bath.

CASSANDRA: Be thankful you are alive.

CLYTEMNESTRA: You too, miss, for that. Pray, how are we

to keep up appearances before the servants when you are both supposed to be dead?

AEGISTHUS: They must pretend to be ghosts, of course. Flit about noiselessly and all that.

AGAMEMNON: A cheerful prospect.

CLYTEMNESTRA: And pray how are we to get through the Choephori?

AEGISTHUS (*nervously*): Well, for my part, I don't see why we should have it at all.

CLYTEMNESTRA: You appear to have lost your taste for the dramatic. I have shut Electra up. Orestes is paying a visit to a friend.

CASSANDRA: Well, let's have a good time now. Otototoi popoi da!

(*Her attempts at merriment fall flat.* CLYTEMNESTRA *procures writing materials.*)

AGAMEMNON: Really now, this play might have been written by Euripides.

CLYTEMNESTRA: Or by Dr. V*rr*ll.

(*An advertisement from a monumental mason drops into the letter box. The scene closes in hopeless gloom on the four endeavoring to compile a letter to Orestes.*)

1900

A Tragic Interior, 2

BEING A FURTHER ATTEMPT TO ASSIST THE EARNEST
STUDENT OF AESCHYLUS, BY MEANS OF AN
INTERPRETATION OF THE CHOEPHORI

SCENE: *Interior of the palace at Mycenae as before, with the exception that the bath has been removed and the carpet cut into strips and laid.* ELECTRA *is discovered sitting, engaged in crocheting an egg and arrow border for an antimacassar. At the opposite end of the room are* AGAMEMNON *and* CASSANDRA, *habited as ghosts, nervously watching for an opportunity to retire.*

ELECTRA: They certainly look very solid. For my part I don't believe in ghosts. Antigone was saying the same to me when I was stopping with her—says they are never bothered at all. But I said "that very much depends how good your family is"— and of course those Cadmus people are nothing much. Fancy Antigone getting engaged. How any one could! That Chrysothemis is going to the wedding. I wonder why I am never asked again.

I'm certain that board squeaked. I mean to see if that is papa or no. Papsy!

(AGAMEMNON *jumps and is about to answer when he is saved by the entrance of* CLYTEMNESTRA.)

CLYTEMNESTRA: Electra! how could you speak so irrever-ently to your father's ghost?

ELECTRA: I believe it's papa.

CLYTEMNESTRA: Do not argue, dear. I came to say that I want you to pour a libation for me on your father's tomb. I had a bad night and am rather tired. You can take the maids, but you must be back quick as I want them in the house. Go and put on your things.

ELECTRA (*sotto voice*): Pour your old libations for yourself!

CLYTEMNESTRA: What do you say, dear? Speak distinctly. And put up your work at *once*. I do not wish to speak again.

(*Exit* ELECTRA *grumbling*.)

AGAMEMNON: Pray, will this continue much longer?

CLYTEMNESTRA: Now dear, do be patient: you don't sup-pose I want you to be uncomfortable. You oughtn't to be in the front room, though, so much; Electra's getting suspicious. The shrubbery's a far more suitable place. As for you, Cassandra, I positively forbade you to come into our part; why are you here?

CASSANDRA: I cannot stand the servants' quarters, or the coach house. They all shriek when they see me; I'm sick to death of nervous people.

AGAMEMNON: Yes, indeed; and funeral offerings are very in-sufficient food, and as for the tomb—there's pounds and pounds of money spent on it, and not a soul inside. I never saw such a muddle in my life, and I daren't even sit down on a cushion, in case one of the maids comes by and sees I've left an impression.

CLYTEMNESTRA: And I'm sick to death with your grum-bling. You'll please to go at once both of you. No one's about.

You can climb up under the pediment and sit on the hot water cistern. I told the maids to leave the door open to warm the house. (*To* AGAMEMNON.) You see dear, that I'm only reasonable. If the chorus found out that they had prophesied incorrectly, and you weren't dead, there would be a rebellion.

AGAMEMNON: When a woman——

CLYTEMNESTRA: Now, dear, go before you're rude.

(*Exit* AGAMEMNON, CASSANDRA. *After an interval enter* ELECTRA, *dressed in black, and the maids bearing libations.*)

ELECTRA: Mother, my clothes don't fit and I don't want to go.

CLYTEMNESTRA: More grumbling! Electra, when you are discontented remember that it is much worse for your mother. You and the maids going means the house being put out for the day. Be more considerate. And go.

(*The big front door is opened, and* ELECTRA *and the procession pass out.* CLYTEMNESTRA *shuts it after them. She then lies down on a couch, hearing snatches of chorus now and then, but happily unconscious of the thrilling recognition between* ORESTES *and* ELECTRA *that is taking place outside. At last there comes a loud bang on the door. She hastily jumps up.*)

CLYTEMNESTRA: What an hour to call!

A VOICE (*without, nervous, and assertive*): Don't you hear me calling? (*Bang.*) That's the second time I've knocked. (*Bang.*) And that's the third.

CLYTEMNESTRA: The man must be mad. (*To footman who has just entered.*) Quick, the door!

FOOTMAN: One minute, sir, one minute if you please! (*He parleys with the visitors and returns.*) Please m'm it's two gentlemen who want to rest.

CLYTEMNESTRA: How absurd! I suppose they must come,

but the town is quite close. (*She goes out, and presently re-turns with* ORESTES *and* PYLADES *disguised*.)

CLYTEMNESTRA: Please make yourself comfortable. This is very sudden news you tell me about Orestes' death. Will you excuse me for a little? (*To footman*.) See that the gentlemen have all they want.

(*Exit through front door. Enter the nurse, weeping and gar-rulous after her kind. Having assured* ORESTES *that there "never was such a baby as Orestes, and that she should know him again wherever she met him, alive or dead," she is induced to go out to be consoled by the chorus and to inform* AEGISTHUS. *The footman suggests first a bath, then a change of raiment, which are both declined, for obvious reasons. Finally he de-parts*.)

(*A long silence*.)

PYLADES: So far so good. (ORESTES *does not answer*.) We've been jolly lucky up to now. (*No answer*.) For heaven's sake man make a remark now and then. You're so puffed up with your beastly destiny, that you won't open your lips to ordinary mortals.

ORESTES: I did not seek a destiny. My mission is not of my choosing. I cannot help living a higher life than my fellows.

PYLADES: You never liked your old father—always thought him a fool—and always said that Clytemnestra had a lot of go. And now just because she couldn't stand him either, you're going to kill her. I call it rank folly.

ORESTES: You would. I do not blame you for it.

PYLADES: And your appalling sister—you never could stand her, and there you go hanging round one another's necks, and a lot of screaming women dance round you and say you are the instrument of the gods, and you say, by Jove so I am, and——

ORESTES: You mean well, but your talk vexes me. I wish to think.

PYLADES: Think! You're always thinking. That's where all the trouble comes from. You've simply ruined yourself. If you begin to think, everything goes wrong.

ORESTES: To murder my mother and my cousin——

PYLADES: ——once removed——

ORESTES: ——and beyond that——darkness and madness ——Erinyes——

PYLADES: That part's sheer nonsense. Do be cheerful, think —think for instance how lucky that your nurse didn't recognize you, and didn't——

(*The door suddenly opens and the* NURSE *rushes in and embraces* ORESTES.)

NURSE: I said to myself—as I was speaking to you—"I don't know why, but I'm all of a turn," and then—I go out and find —that it is you after all.—Ah, you can't deceive an old nurse!

ORESTES: Pylades—remove her from me.

(PYLADES *induces the* NURSE *to retire, which she does, promising secrecy in a loud voice, and disappears, still talking volubly, to the servants' quarters. She has scarcely gone when* AEGISTHUS *enters by the front door.*)

PYLADES: Make for just over that buckle he's got on.

AEGISTHUS: How do you do? Very glad to see you both. But are you not hot in your cloaks? I'll ring the bell and tell the footman to take them and give you baths. (*Rings bell.*)

PYLADES: Oh, thank you, no; that is to say—(*To* ORESTES.) Hurry up; you are not going to funk it.

ORESTES: This house has an ill name for baths.

AEGISTHUS: Pardon me—no; we take them quite as often as other people.

ORESTES (*hysterically*): Ah! too often—the bath—the bloody bath—in which you killed my father. See (*tears off disguise*) I am Orestes—and I have come to slay you and avenge my father's death!

AEGISTHUS: Ee-ee! Otototoi!

(ORESTES *draws his sword. Enter footman who shrieks with terror and rushes out to tell the chorus that* AEGISTHUS *is dead.*)

AEGISTHUS (*dodging round the eccyclema*): Give me time—time—your father lives——Oh! let me explain——

ORESTES: Ay, his spirit is living in me. (AEGISTHUS *trips up in a ruck of the carpet.*) Ah! the carpet up which my sire walked to his doom! (*Holds him down.*)

AEGISTHUS: Oh, time!——He didn't——You shall see him —speak to him—hear his voice!

ORESTES: His voice is ever sounding in my ears!

A VOICE (*distant at first, but gradually getting nearer*): I don't care if there is a rebellion, I'll stand it no longer. It's all right for you, Cassandra, who rather like queer positions, but a man of my size can't be for two hours between the hot water cistern and the roof! I never knew before that any one could combine extravagance and discomfort—but Clytemnestra can —look at the tomb! The very next person I meet I shall speak to and touch and say who I am.

PYLADES: Hold there a minute!

(*Enter* AGAMEMNON *and* CASSANDRA.)

AGAMEMNON: Yes—you there, whoever you are—I'm Agamemnon, who wasn't murdered at all! Do you hear me? (*Stamps on the ground.*) Do you feel me? (*Slaps* ORESTES *on the back.*)

ORESTES: Good gods—and Apollo—It's my father!

AGAMEMNON: Hullo, Orestes, you back. Why on earth are you skirling up the carpet? And who's that on the floor?

PYLADES: There seems a fat lot of destiny here!

(*Everyone begins to talk at once. Matters are finally explained.*)

ORESTES: Then I must go and tell them outside that Agamemnon isn't dead and I have not killed Aegisthus.

AEGISTHUS (*brushing himself*): Which will be a little—er—flat. But it'll teach you not to take yourself seriously, which is an important lesson for a young man.

CASSANDRA: Do nothing of the sort! Say you've killed him, meet Clytemnestra and bring her in to be killed. Then don't kill her, then go and say that you have. Then the chorus will be satisfied, and go away and then we'll settle what to do.

ORESTES: I must say that's a good idea. Thank you very much.

AGAMEMNON: Yes. And Aegisthus can be a ghost. And Clytemnestra too.

(*Exit* ORESTES *to inform the chorus.*)

PYLADES: I'm afraid he's awfully cut up, but it'll do him good. What I've suffered since he thought his father was dead and he had a mission, no one'll ever know.

(*Enter* ORESTES, *dragging* CLYTEMNESTRA *who is genuinely terrified, but recovers as soon as she sees the large company.*)

CASSANDRA: Eccyclema as before. Aegisthus and Clytemnestra as corpses, Orestes with a sword.

ORESTES: And when we get outside I get off.

CASSANDRA: And go mad—see the Furies and so on. Then the chorus goes and you come in.

AEGISTHUS: And then?

CASSANDRA: I can't plan everything.

(*Her directions are obeyed. The loaded eccyclema goes out, drops* ORESTES, *and returns. The company remain, listening to the closing scene of* ORESTES *and the chorus.*)

AEGISTHUS: The great advantage of Furies is that they are generally invisible. If he just pretends to see them the chorus will be thoroughly contented.

AGAMEMNON: I dare say I'm old-fashioned, but I never yet knew anything but discomfort come of pretending. Oh! listen to him. I don't like to hear him go on like that. It isn't right. No. It isn't right.

CASSANDRA: It seems quite natural when you're used to it. I couldn't have done it better myself.

PYLADES: It's the kind of thing that just suits him.

CLYTEMNESTRA: Let me look out of the window, will you? He'll be done now, I should think. How he shrieks! (*She climbs on to a table to see out of the window.*)

AGAMEMNON: It isn't right.

AEGISTHUS (*nervously*): Shut up you old dodderer.

AGAMEMNON: It isn't——

CLYTEMNESTRA (*at the window*): Papai!

ALL: What's the matter? What? What do you see?

CLYTEMNESTRA: Apapapapai!

CASSANDRA (*in full song*): Otototoi popoi da!

(*There is a rush of feet outside, the great door is burst open and* ORESTES *flies in, pursued by a band of* FURIES *with snaky locks. Round the room they go, overturning furniture, including Clytemnestra's table, and rush out, disappearing up the Delphi road,* ORESTES *first, then the* FURIES, *then* PYLADES *at a respectful distance behind.*)

AEGISTHUS: Those—those weren't the genuine article were

they? Ow! (*he stamps on a small pale blue snake that has been detached, and is wriggling over the carpet.*)

CASSANDRA: We must go after them. Go and order——

CLYTEMNESTRA: Hold your tongue: no more of your plans, please.

(*Enter* ELECTRA *who has hitherto remained outside.*)

ELECTRA: Well, mamma, you have made a mess. But think what a disappointment for me to find you here!

AGAMEMNON: It wasn't right. I knew it wasn't right. For once in a way I had my senses!

(*The curtain falls on a scene of confusion and strife.*)

1901

Strivings after Historical Style

WITH APOLOGIES TO A CERTAIN SERIES OF
OXFORD TEXTBOOKS

1. Dramatic

But this castle in the air was to have a rude awakening. Rising to the occasion from a bed of sickness, the young king blew to arms. A hardly contested battle decided fortunes of the day, and the insolent invader bit the dust of the projects he had so magnificently conceived. Baffled and thwarted where he deemed himself most secure, he was compelled to conclude an ignominious peace, and retired with diminished territory to the execrations of an infuriated nation and an exhausted treasury, whose life blood he had so lavishly squandered in furtherance of his chimerical designs.

2. Personal

Albert was at this time thirty-eight years of age. In appearance he was of medium height, inclined to corpulence, and subject to fits of internal depression. In spite of an elaborate education he read with difficulty, and it was seldom that he could be induced to sign his own name. He was not without affection, or totally devoid of generosity, but the vicious surroundings of his earlier years went far to eradicate such sparks of promise as afterwards appeared. He was, moreover, a martyr to gout, and excessively partial to boiled venison.

But in spite of these natural shortcomings he had a belief in his destiny that went far to overcome what would have appalled a more confident man, and girt with it he went forth among the nations, conquering and to conquer. Such was the man who was to dominate Europe for the next thirty years.

3. Critical

The fruits of this policy were long in unfolding, but their arrival was none the less inevitable. As is so often the case, it was not the generation that sowed but the generation that reaped, that was to suffer for the mistakes of their forerunners. A discontented populace, an apathetic church, a turbulent and licentious nobility, and above all an impoverished exchequer, each added their quota to the general downfall. In her foreign affairs, moreover, France had committed the fatal error of staking too many pawns upon the chessboard of nations. One false step is, to a great extent, the parent of another, and her enemies were but hatching the eggs that she herself had laid forty years before.

4. *Cosmic*

The great movement rolled on, submerging alike kingdoms, principalities, and powers in its relentless course. Old institutions toppled on all sides with a headlong crash, or were carried away bottom upwards into the outer darkness. The land was full of the shrieks of the drowning and the corpses of the drowned.

To some imaginative minds it seemed almost as if the days of the Flood were coming again; but who would say when the waters would abate from off the face of the earth? Here and there those jackals in human form, who are the disgrace of every cataclysm, were callously casting their bread upon the troubled waves, but as a rule the disaster was too overwhelming to think of individual aggrandisement. It was a terrible reckoning for the luxury and indolence of the past hundred years, but it was none the less inevitable and effective; for such was the corrupt state of Europe that by fire and by fire alone would she be renewed.

1901

A Day Off

Now and then either one's self or the other half of creation takes a day off, and on such a day there is nothing that cannot happen. The rule of Cause and Effect, with all its advantages and disadvantages, breaks down, and we have a provisional government—it may be a Restoration—under which events follow a newer and more suggestive sequence. On such a day the sun puts the fire out, the poker draws it up again, the sea serpent appears, the tortoise outstrips Achilles, King Canute's feet are dry, Queen Elizabeth's muddy, Sir Isaac Newton sees the apple fall upward. Words will not alliterate on such a day: *veni, vidi, vici* begin with different letters; so do Cape and Cairo, and the destinies of nations are changed. Washington lied on it, Martin Tupper died on it, Columbus tried on it to balance an egg and failed. For it is the confutation of scientists, and scientific historians, and proverbial philosophers and politicians, and most poets, and artists, and of all who have a mission or a life's work, a System or an Explanation. But the ill-conditioned greet it joyfully, for it is the harvest of journalism and the flower of life.

I will fearlessly relate how such a day came upon me in the Tyrol, last July, beginning at breakfast, where two German ladies sat all the time with their right eyes in their coffee cups. Not merely glancing down at the cups, but with their noses on the rims, and their right eyes in. They were not telling their fortunes nor trying the steam cure for ophthalmia, for the cups were empty, and the coffee stood by them on the table cooling. I offer no explanation: that is not my business. But I saw that one of the days had come when there were more things in heaven and earth than usual.

It was raining when I started, and raining up, which is particularly inconvenient, for nothing keeps dry except the outside of the umbrella. I asked the way of a German in German, and he fled, and of a German in English, and he handed me three wax matches. Then I spoke to an Italian, for the Italians understand all speech and all gestures and every unexpressed desire, and, moreover, days off are more common in Italy than in other countries. But he was a stranger in these parts, being a soldier, a Sicilian, who had a little farm at Enna, and he advised me to ask a very large toadstool, which I did. The stool part was a haystack fastened up in a dust cloth, and the stem was a human body, walking on human feet. Out of the stool came a human voice, as of a kind old lady, which told me the way and hoped that the mountains would please me, and warned me against spraining my ankle, and scolded me for traveling "cosi soletto," which means "alonekin," whatever that may mean.

So I ascended the valley towards the precipices of the Pelmo, which were grey and frothy, as if one had covered them with lather. And I reflected that never since the spring, when, while flying from a large woolly dog through the streets of a Greek village, I had distinctly seen a brood of seventeen magenta-colored chickens—never since the spring had the world and all that is in it been so irresponsible, so illogical, and so joyful. At the head of the valley was a little white church, with a big Saint Christopher painted on it, so big that you could not help seeing him, and if you see Saint Christopher you cannot help having a good time. He was painted where you saw him as you were going out of Italy; there is no need to see him as you are coming in.

The weather cleared as I ascended, and I forgot my bad night and my nasty breakfast, and the nasty lunch which I carried among my pyjamas—consisting of a petard of bread and two eggs, under-done and over-kept. I forgot I had forgotten the salt, I forgot all the discipline of life, and amongst other things I forgot the directions given me by the toadstool. I was close underneath the Pelmo: the humanities of the valley were far behind, and nature had assumed an air of self-conscious majesty. The mountain was horrific, minatory, unscalable; over its precipices a torrent leapt with studied indifference, and was spanned below by a fallen pine. Oh, that fallen pine! Who will raise it up? For it has fallen on the picture postcards and the colored photographs, and the oleographs, and the lithographs, and all the host of souvenirs, and now it has fallen on a torrent also, and for that reason the torrent is spanned!

The whole scene was so picturesque, so solitary, so eminently wunderschönable, that I was not surprised to come upon a new hotel, pleasantly situated in its own grounds and commanding an extensive view. It was not aggressive, being rather of a nature of a resort—a low building round a courtyard—and the whole thing said "En Pension." As I approached it I saw some pigs. I got nearer and saw more pigs. I entered the courtyard and it was full of pigs. I looked in at one of the doors and out ran a pig. I looked in at another door and a pig asked me to let it pass. I went on to the terrace and there were pigs looking at the view and discussing the management, and how it compared with other pensions, and what one ought to tip on leaving, and two or three of them had just concealed a Fallen Pine in sepia. There were single pigs and pigs in pairs, and families taken at a reduction, and they all looked at me without seeing me, as the better sort of tourists do.

I left that pension without a word, and then came a surprise, for lying straight across the upward path was a boy asleep. I have never seen such sleep; he might have slept since the be-ginning of weariness, and it is not I who will rouse him to ask the way. For if he wakes, one of two terrible things must hap-pen; he will either become a pig or remain a boy. So he may be sleeping there still, with the sun on his face, and the mud and the leaves in his hair, and the generations of pigs waxing and waning by his side.

An hour further up I came to one of those rare places which are equally unattractive to the tourist, the historian, and the esthete—a place where nature was so solitary that she did not even mention her solitude. There were no trees, no rocks, no view, though it was near the top of the pass, no interesting Alpine flora, nothing but sky and grass and wild onion, grow-ing by the side of stagnant water. (The source of a stream is often stagnant.) In the midst of the silence, which spoke neither of life nor of death, but of eternal simplicity, was a small wooden shrine, full of lighted candles. Who lit them, and for whose advantage, are further problems for the inquiring

mind. I only know that so long as I watched—and I was there
some time—not one of them went out, though the flames
trembled in the wind and paled before the midday sun.

The same adventure happened to Sir Bors, I think, just before he killed a dragon and two false knights. But to me the
lighted shrine signified the end of the interlude, for a few miles
over the pass I met some soldiers, and in the course of conversation they let out that things were going on as usual. So
though many other pleasant incidents happened to me that day,
they happened because of some reason, and were pleasures
which are well recognized and generally popular; as, for example, if you speak kindly to a cow, and hold her out your
hand, she will take it in her strong warm mouth and lick off
the salt; or again, if you are tired with walking, and eat a
little and drink a good deal, you will not mind where you lie
down to sleep, nor who sees you. Such things happen daily,
and result from normal conditions, but I do not chronicle them
now; nor shall I relate how I saw the white Ampezzo road
swarming with two-horse carriages, wherein sat ladies and
gentlemen, driving up and down; nor how by following the
road I came to the Austrian frontier, and the language of Ach
and Ja. For after all, the day off had been very short—scarcely
a five-hour day; I saw the German ladies at seven and by twelve
o'clock I had passed the shrine.

"But really now! Why, of course, those ladies at breakfast—
how like Germans!—were looking into the cups to find the
trademark. And shrines are common all over abroad, and the
peasants there burn candles because they know no better. Now
for your magenta chickens—or take the rain which 'rained up';
well, if you were on a hill, and there was a cloud down in the
valley, what is to prevent the cloud rising and finding its own

level, like a barometer for example—and so producing the effect? And so on with the other things. Of course your 'enchanted pension' was a big farm, and the 'sleeping prince' was there to watch the pigs. Or take the toadstool—Well, hay in the Tyrol is always carried on women's backs. So there is your wonderful day quite right after all."

"Thank you . . . . But the magenta—?"

"Oh, how funny you are over those chickens! Did—did you pop salt on their tails?"

She—for I recognize her voice—departs with a merry smile, and as soon as she is round the corner, taps her forehead. But let her walk the right way and the right day from the Val Florentina towards the Pusterthal. And if she will run from a dog through the streets of Gremka in Elis, she shall infallibly behold seventeen magenta-colored hens.

1904

An Allegory

This contribution was sent in without a title. We have done our best, but feel doubtful.—Editors

A CANOE: River! River!

A PUNT: The river never answers. What do you want?

CANOE: Anyone to play with. I am so bored. Tell your boys to push you over to this side.

PUNT: They are all asleep, having moored me nicely. Tell yours to bring you over to me.

CANOE: They are asleep too. What is to be done?

MOTOR LAUNCH: Pompha . . . Pompha . . . Pompha . . .

CANOE: Now we can manage it . . . Oh how glad I am to be with you. We'll have a real good talk and probe things. I'm not one to skim over a subject, like an Isis boat. One ought to research, surely.

PUNT: Surely, and last year I went—

FALLING BLOSSOMS OF THE CHESTNUT: How d'ye do, how d'ye do, how d'ye do!

An Allegory

CANOE: Oh look, I must catch a blossom. I'll be back in a moment.

PUNT: Canoes have no steadiness of purpose.

BLOSSOMS OF THE CHESTNUT FLOATING AWAY: Farewell, farewell . . .

CANOE: I couldn't catch one.

PUNT: No matter. Like yourself, they are ephemeral. (*To another punt*) Good morrow, sister.

THE PUNT'S SISTER: Good morrow afternoon.

PUNT: Sister, you have no sense of style, but being a relative I say nothing. Grapple yourself to me. I was about to tell this canoe that last year I researched—

A CUSHION: Plish! There! I knew I should fall in. How perfectly delicious.

ALL THE CANOES: Tee hee hee, tee hee hee.

PUNT POLE (*pulling the cushion out*): Lie there in the sun, and get dry, scatterbrains.

THE CUSHION: Pog.

THE PUNT: I was going to say that I have been through the lock in Nines week, and seen the races.

THE PUNT'S SISTER: Well, so have I, and so has this young gentleman. I saw him there—in fact, I'm afraid I upset him coming back.

CANOE: Have I? Did you? I can't remember anything.

THE PUNT (*under way at last*): I have seen the Nines and think nothing of them. They hire eight large boys and a small one to sit in them, and yet they always have some accident. Not one of them has yet reached the Backs, and just opposite me two collided with each other and were obliged to draw up to the bank at once. More haste, less speed, I say. Still one must float and let float, I suppose.

THE PUNT'S SISTER: Ah, Emily, you never spoke a truer word.

THE PUNT: Yes, we can't all be punts.

DOUBLE SCULLER: None of us were once. Punts were unknown up here in my father's day.

PUNT: Indeed! Then how does your father account for the causeway, specially constructed for punting in midstream and existing from the prehistoric period?

DOUBLE SCULLER: I must be getting on to the Orchard.

CANOE: Where's that?

DOUBLE SCULLER: Upper river.

CANOE: What's that?

PUNT: There are three rivers—the upper, the lower, and this. Fish do say that the upper river comes out of the earth and the lower goes into the sea, but nothing of the sort ever happened in my time.

CANOE: What's the sea?

DOUBLE SCULLER: The sea—barges sometimes mention it.

PUNT: How like a barge.

CANOE: And what's the earth?

MOWN GRASS FROM SCHOLARS' PIECE: My position is—where Pragmatism is so dishonest is—oh, of course, if that's your attitude!—Hall Lunch—Why shouldn't they camp in the chapel?—Hall Lunch—I like a tune I can tap to—I know what I like—I don't like what I know—Hall Lunch—The acting was so awful, so Perfectly Appalling, that I simply Scree-ee-ee-eamed. And every one else said "How good!"

CANOE: Oh what cultivated grass! I must gather some up and see if it won't stuff a cushion.

MOWN GRASS FLOATING AWAY: Farewell, farewell.

CANOE: I couldn't gather any. Let's make a raft instead, and all float after it down stream.

ALL THE CANOES: Oh, do let's!

PUNT: What do you say, Margery? Shall we join the young people?

TRACTION ENGINE (*stopping on the bridge*): Humph!

CANOE: Who's that?

TRACTION ENGINE: Humph! What have we here? Every one happy? This'll never do.

PUNT: It's a traction engine. It's reality, it's the hard facts of life. Oh what a lucky chance that it happened to be passing.

TRACTION ENGINE: I shall pass often enough in the future.

PUNT: A futurist! Better and better.

TRACTION ENGINE: I see much amiss here. I see trees that must be lopped and turf that must be scarred out of recognition. I see buildings that ought never to have been built, or, if built, ought never to be put to the purposes for which they were originally intended. I shall destroy them.

PUNT: How perfectly splendid of you.

TRACTION ENGINE: I am not splendid. Don't idealize me. I come to remind you of the filth of the lower reaches and the monotony of the sea, of the winds, not heroic, that blow ships further and further from joy. I am strong but not splendid, smoky but not picturesque, clumsy, but there are no graceful little jokes to be made about me, there is nothing laughable or charming that will avert me. I am the squalor of experience. I shall come.

ALL THE BOATS: Oh how absolutely splendid! That's exactly what we want. Better than the Union or the University Sermon even. One is so in danger of getting narrow and academic. I only hope that the paddles and boat hooks have been attentive —they are apt to wander at times.

TRACTION ENGINE: River! I cannot waste smoke over cockle shells. River! River!

PUNT: The river answers no one.

TRACTION ENGINE: He must answer me. Every one must. He is compelled to by the Universal Law.

(*Silence.*)

THE BOATS: Oh River, do make an exception in the Traction Engine's favor. His attitude is so splendidly interesting.

(*Silence.*)

TRACTION ENGINE: Humph! Well, we shall see. There's a bad time coming, and I have done my best to warn you. Humph (*going off diminuendo*). Humph, humph, humph . . .

PUNT: He's perfectly right. We ought to be clad in iron.

CANOE: I know. Let's all go and have it done. It's the only way to steer through life. Let's—(*he capsizes*). Don't mind me. I'm just as happy upside down—happier in fact.

MORE BLOSSOMS FALLING FROM THE CHESTNUT: How dy'e do, how dy'e do, farewell, how dy'e do.

1912

BOURGEOIS VALUES VERSUS INSPIRATION

After his Mediterranean travels, Forster in the spring of 1905 went to Nassenheide, the country estate of Elizabeth, Countess von Arnim (*Elizabeth and her German Garden*) in the depths of Pomerania. His reason for going there was to act as English tutor to Elizabeth's children. The estate was not a great distance from Stettin, now Szczecin, on the Polish side of the present border with Germany near the mouth of the Oder. It was presumably while at Nassenheide or shortly after leaving there that Forster visited Rostock and Wismar. It is curious that from his youthful travels he should have chosen as the subject for an essay this pair of small German cities on the Baltic. The reason, I think, is Forster's underlying preoccupation with bourgeois values. He feels some of their appeal, but he is fascinated more by the extreme and unrelenting hold they have on others. When that hold is ancient or removed, he contemplates it with equanimity. When it is near and pressing, he analyzes it with amazed comprehension.

Rostock and Wismar are at a distance. They are ancient—the gable of the Wädekin Hotel dates from 1363; they are historical; and they are bourgeois, true to their commercial past, so the lard factory where the pigs of Rostock are rendered down is "a fair patrician mansion," adorned with wise remarks like *Watch and Pray*. Only the Alte Schule, built about 1300, restored in 1880, and housing a collection of Wismar antiquities, achieves a unique beauty.

If Rostock and Wismar seem an odd choice of subject for a young traveller, *Some Literary Eccentrics* by John Fyvie is an even more surprising choice for a first book review. Yet there can be no doubt of Forster's lively interest. He understands and values the category of eccentric, and wants to have it accurately applied. He quotes several passages to demonstrate that Fyvie is wrong to include Landor but argues that he might properly have added George Borrow, whose *Lavengro* is discussed with reference to the apple-woman, Stonehenge, and Isopel Berners.

The eccentric, like the child, has imagination. He is moved by the spirit of adventure. He defies routine by looking right through it. "The crank is irrational; he has no wild objection to the universe but only a wild objection to some isolated point in it. . . ." But the eccentric "at every turn sees through our smug civilization to the barbarity and licentiousness on which it is founded." The eccentric exposes the pretentions of bourgeois society. For that reason he interests Forster.

Bourgeois society may also bear witness against itself. Forster calls his essay on J. H. Walsh's *A Manual of Domestic Economy* "Mr. Walsh's Secret History of the Victorian Movement" because the truth about the "movement" is not to be found in the double standard for men and women or in the shoddy sexual escapades of the Victorian gentleman but rather in the routine of domestic economy. The secret history concerns the behind-doors character of the Victorian household. There we encounter the young matron pressing, cajoling, and deceiving her husband into sending their daughters to an expensive boarding school, and the young matron is none other than Agnes Pembroke in a new disguise. After such a beginning, one is prepared for the worst. That worst is a world of inanimate things. The people who move through it neither make history nor make suitable subjects for literature. For them, personal relations are nothing, passion and beauty are nothing. "And so, step by step, the house is built up, and the world built out."

During the period when he was himself writing fiction Forster had little to say about the creative process and the art of composition. For this reason, the short anonymous essay on the theme of "Inspiration" published in 1912 is of special interest because it gives a circumstantial description of the experience of writing.

Forster said in an interview with David Jones, recorded for BBC television and published in *The Listener* on Forster's eightieth birthday, 1 January 1959, that he enjoyed writing. "I have never found it a trial or an ordeal of suffering. Some writers do." Nor did he find it an occasion for excessive effort. His vivid account of inspiration could only have been written by someone who experienced the process. There is no reason to question the implication that at least until 1912 this was his usual experience of creation. He begins slowly, feeling used up, then comes the queer catastrophe, the mind—so to speak—flips over, the underside comes to the top and takes over, he writes rapidly, and— what is most odd—he feels more himself than usual.

Such a state need not imply genius. A shallow writer may be inspired, his poor little mind may "turn turtle." But the mind being shallow, the result will be worthless. In saying this Forster demonstrates his honesty. Most theories of inspiration are useless because they make the definition hinge on the quality of the product and not on the process by which the product is arrived at. Forster is right to insist that inspiration does not cease to be itself just because the product is less than inspired.

The shallow writer is no doubt a slave to the values of bourgeois convention. Forster is fearful of such values and he is fascinated by them too, for they must be transcended if the act of creation is to be worthwhile.

Rostock and Wismar

The heart does not beat quicker at the names of Rostock and Wismar, nor does the finger find them instinctively on the map. They slumber in one of Europe's backwaters—too far east, or north, or something—where even Baedeker gets drowsy, and sows imaginary tram lines along the deserted streets. The lover of the Baltic style of architecture will visit them; and so will he who studies the rise and fall of the Hanseatic League. But the really nice person will only take them on the way to Stralsund; and why should he go there? The country is flat, the sea shallow, the fourth-class railway carriages far from comfortable; and the Baltic style itself has been compared in fretful moments to a Gruyère cheese.

Rostock, with a reputation for bustle, lies eight miles from the mouth of the Warnow. It is a test town. If the tourist is happy here, and can love its huge pallid churches, he will be happy elsewhere. The center of interest is the Neue Markt, every house in which has a gable. Here is the inn of *The Sun* (admirable), the inn of *The Moon* (almost too quaint), the inn of *Russia* (fashionable but dear: three marks for a bed), the decadent art-shop full of Toteninsels, the manly art-shop, full of prancing Majesties, and, loitering in front of these, undergraduates, for Rostock is a University town. The gable gains by repetition: two go for nothing, ten for very little. But the Neue Markt must contain dozens; and therefore, grey as it is, prosaic as are its details, it is picturesque.

Either art-shop sells picture post-cards of the Grand Duke of Mecklenburg-Schwerin, whose palace is hard by. His chest is broad, but not as broad as Majesty's; his medals and his moustache will never come as thick, nor his war horse prance so perpendicularly. All this is as it should be; but it makes the young fellow look headachy and sad. He would like to be first in his own town. He would like to have a nicer palace. He would rather it did not carry you back to the Westbourne Grove. He is grieved when you hurry away from it to the margarine factory and exclaim: "Now here is something worth seeing at last." For the pigs of Rostock become margarine in a fair patrician mansion, pleasingly proportioned, delicately carved, and adorned with *Vigila et Ora*, and other wise re-marks. Do not censure them for this. They had to go some-where; and in Rostock you find an old house quicker than a new one. Moreover, margarine is a Hanseatic article—or would be if the Hansa League still existed. Those Baltic mer-chants loved pigs, and herrings, and beer, and all that stoutens man's body, or makes his heart glad in a northern way. They ate, and grew fat, and were not ashamed. They knocked the King of Denmark over when he tried to catch their herrings. The Holy Roman Emperor strolled northward; and they knocked him over too. And at last, outside their pew in the church of St. Nicholas at Stralsund, instead of carving *Vigila et Ora*, they carved this:

> He who's no merchant, stop without,
> Or else I'll hit him on the snout.

Ponder these things, and consider which is incongruous: the Grand Duke or the margarine.

Sentiment is vindicated; but the fact remains that there is very little to see in Rostock—much that is old, but little that is beautiful. When the merchants made a great conscious effort (as at Lübeck, where they were determined to go one better than the bishop, and built the Marien Kirche in consequence) —they succeeded. But they never builded better than they knew. They never stray into immortality, like the Italians. They ate their dinners and won their battles. But they were seldom anxious over beauty, and never stumbled on it unawares.

Perhaps there was more anxiety at Wismar. There is certainly more charm. It has not the pleasant situation of Rostock, nor has it the same profusion of old houses. But the churches are splendid; and even the absence of water is a gain, for it leads to water-works. Water-works are common enough. But they were not so common in the sixteenth century; and that is the date of the Wismar building. It is quite small, and, standing as it does in the corner of the market place, might easily be ignored, or mistaken for a newspaper kiosk. The core of it consists of a mysterious mass, ribbed and twisted—presumably the cistern, but such a cistern as no plumber saw in his wildest dreams. This is encircled by an arcade and gratings, with Renaissance sculpture at the angles, and a long Latin poem for a frieze. How the cistern worked, if at all, and how many gallons, if any, it contained, are interesting questions for the enquiring mind. The Latin poem does not attack them, being occupied with the sanitary authorities and their pursuit of the reluctant nymph. The situation is quite Ovidian. First this went wrong, then that: it seemed as if they would never catch her, or only catch her muddy. Towards the last couplet she yields, and the "Wismarii Patres"

> *Bring (with the help of God) fresh water that is not brackish,*
> *Bring it in quite little pipes, all from the lake of Schwerin.*

These water-works are nicely seen from the *Old Swede,* a fifteenth-century restaurant hard by. Or one can eat round the corner, in the *Wädekin Hotel,* whose gable dates from 1363. After a heavy dinner, one moves across the market place to look at the splendid group of buildings that adjoins it on the west. This group contain two churches of cathedral size, a palace in the style of the Italian Renaissance, and, most wonderful of all, the Alte Schule. Here is a pageant of warm color which shifts from ruddy brown to pink, a frank avowal of material in which the very restorations have dignity. Crude new bricks, the bricks of our Surrey suburbs, look strangely beautiful when set in the midst of bricks that were crude and new some hundreds of years ago. There is no nicety of contour: a tower will try to be a spire, and then blunder back into a tower again. There is no hint of the city's personality, of her Presiding Genius: one town, if sensible, is very like another; and it is not likely that a Wismarian father of twenty stone was severed by any spiritual gulf from a father of the same weight in Rostock. There is only brick. But, whereas the Rostock brick was pallid, and built churches the color of King's

Cross station, the brick of Wismar is red, and builds her into glory that is everlasting, because it can be for ever renewed.

The palace (not of brick) would, after all, be better in Italy; and as for the churches, there are finer in Lübeck, though even Lübeck does not mass them in such splendor. But the Alte Schule is unique.

Mathematically described, the Alte Schule is a rhomboidal parallelepiped of black and red bricks; irreverently described, it is like a long narrow cardboard box, which a naughty child has sat squashy at the corners; reverently described, it is a hollow slice of fairy land, wherein should pace a queen, looking out through fairy windows upon a dull, rectangular world. It has the strange distinction of fantasy—stranger than ever in the midst of so many solid churches, solid houses, and four-square jokes—a fantasy which no restoration can destroy, for it depends, not on humorsome details, but on the building's very ground plan. Long, narrow, askew, with frequent windows on either side, and a tiny, stair-like gable at the end, it is as dainty as a jest in the music of Mozart, and as impossible to describe in writing. The Baltic stylist at Wismar, or it may be the spirit that presided over the trend of Wismar's streets, has produced a thing of beauty that is just a little unlike any other beautiful thing in the world.

From Wismar the railway, following the course of the quite little pipes, goes southward to Schwerin. But Schwerin is no bourgeois town; and its glories are another, and possibly a greater matter.

1906

Literary Eccentrics:
A Review

Some Literary Eccentrics BY JOHN FYVIE

From the highway we call Standard Literature two bypaths diverge. The one leads into a chaotic country, where all things are to be found, but where nothing is in its place—the country of our daily lives. There is passion; there is incident; there is also beauty. But the spirit of Art has never entered, and the conflict of Tragedy and Comedy remains without dignity— they pelt one another with facts—and without result. The traveller who climbs a mountain here for the sake of the view will as likely as not find the summit occupied by a suburban picnic party. He alters his mood and joins them, and immediately the hostess falls down dead, struck by some horrible disease. Again he alters: he will have no moods but will take things exactly as they come. And he learns in due time that Mr. Smith of Surbiton is a man of like passions with himself. Further research proves that the same will be true of Mr. Brown of Balham, and that Mr. Robinson of Raynes Park—

though one must not be too hasty—is probably in a similar plight. It is all very interesting, but the traveller learns nothing that he might not have guessed. He returns—if he does return, for this country has its own pernicious charm—as ignorant of the things that really matter as when he set out.

It is otherwise with the bypath that enters the country of Eccentricity. It does not profess to take us to the things that really matter. It does not profess to take us anywhere. We pass by the hippogriffs and the mock turtles and the skeleton inscribed "This skeleton was once Charles Henley, Esquire," and the twenty-six dictionaries (each divided into several subdictionaries) which Mr. Babbage, a philosopher, compiled to save his time when he wanted to "square" the word Dean:

$$\begin{array}{cccc} D & e & a & n \\ e & a & s & e \\ a & s & k & s \\ n & e & s & t \end{array}$$

The dean asks an easy nest. Similarly with the other church dignitaries—except "Bishops," whom he could not square. And, sooner or later, the path ends in a blind alley. It would be terrible if it didn't. We return good-humoredly to the highway, and find that after all we have not wandered so very far from it.

Mr. Fyvie, a guide to this country, has all the qualifications for his post—a pleasant voice, a quick eye, and above all a conviction that the post is no ignoble one: "for eccentricity has always abounded when and where strength of character abounded." And he knows the highway well, as one of his profession should. With his canons of eccentricity the reader may sometimes differ. It is strange to include so great a name as Hazlitt. George Wither, though not great, is not odd. And surely Landor belongs to a serener company?

> They who survive the wreck of ages are by no means, as a body, the worthiest of our admiration. It is in these wrecks as in those of the sea—the best things are not always saved. Hen-coops and empty barrels bob upon the surface under a serene and smiling sky, when the graven or depicted images of the gods are scattered on invisible rocks, and when those who most resemble them in knowledge and beneficence are devoured by cold monsters below.

> When Friendship has taken the place of Love, she ought to make his absence as little a cause for regret as possible; and it is gracious in her to imitate his demeanour and his words.

> There are no fields of amaranth on this side of the grave; there are no voices, O Rhodopè, that are not soon mute, however tuneful; there is no name, with whatever emphasis of passionate love repeated, of which the echo is not faint at last.

To passages like these Mr. Fyvie pays full tribute, and it is true that the man who wrote them also wrote cross letters and did tiresome things. But if the incongruous is so decisive a criterion, then must we count as Literary Eccentrics the poet who scribbled his poems on the backs of old envelopes, or the poet who dictated his to a reluctant daughter. Nor is Landor's humor as contemptible as Mr. Fyvie would have us believe. Helen taking swimming lessons, Lucian badgering Timotheus, Alexander trying to marry a snake, raise smiles that are not directed at the humorist.

But most of the Eccentrics in the book are fair game. They comprise a king, a millionaire, a "calculating" philosopher, and a Unitarian novelist. Some of them never married, others had better have done likewise, others trained up young girls to be worthy of them. And one—the Unitarian—in a novel that professes to be biographical, declares that he has had seven anti-Trinitarian wives, of whom the majority were swept off by epidemics of smallpox. Each lady was beautiful, each knew algebra and sometimes Hebrew; at the death of each he sat with his eyes shut for three days or for four days or for ten. He survived them all, and then took to the ocean in a small sloop. After nine years he bought "a flowery retreat" with the proceeds of their fortunes; for they had all been rich.

This Unitarian, Thomas Amory—though the book is called *John Buncle, Esq.*—is a type of the true eccentric. Such a man is content neither with fiction nor with life. A novel is unreal to him, an autobiography dull. He will not say "my hero had seven wives," nor will he say, "I have had one wife, and there she sits." For all his strength of character some little fleck in his brain makes him brood too much on the wonderful things that ought to happen in this world, and do not. He would like, himself, to be a work of art, and so, when we meet him, we are at once annoyed and charmed. If he is also an artist, as Borrow was, the charm prevails, and we find the entrance of that narrow creek that separates the land of experience from the mainland. As we coast up it, the shores are so near together and we touch so frequently at either, that we forget they are not united and never will unite, and that all the waters of the sea deepen the channel daily. In our childhood such voyages were frequent. We saw the Tritons and the Sirens with our spiritual eye, though we did not know their names. The stars sang tunes to each other, and our spiritual ears listened. With our spiritual fists we knocked down policemen and told the nurse afterwards, which was un-wise. For she gave us thimble-pie, and as the years passed it seemed safer to have a hero who should experience the glories that would not come to us, and perform the deeds that we could not do. Perhaps it was just as well. We might, of course, have turned into Lavengro, and met on Salisbury Plain the son of the apple-woman we had known on London Bridge. We might have seen through the mists of the morning, "a small grove of blighted trunks of oaks, barked and grey": Stonehenge. We might have taught Isopel Berners Armenian in the dingle. But we were more likely to turn into Mr. John Buncle, and the nurse knew it.

Here then is the type: Trelawney's *Adventures of a Younger Son* might furnish a third example of it. The centers of daily life and art are far from each other, and our course is para-bolic if we attempt to revolve round both of them. How wild is the parabola described by Mr. Thomas Day, the author of *Sandford and Merton!*

His famous book is sane enough, and he was too honest to pretend to adventures that he had never met with. But his life is a pageant of eccentricity, for he regarded it also as a book—an orderly treatise in the style of Rousseau. Man is equal. Education can do everything. We must improve the race. Therefore he selected two little girls from charity schools, intending to bring them up with the virtues of Arria, Portia, and Cornelia, and to marry one of them. A lady friend re-gretfully notes his failure. "When he dropped melting sealing-wax upon her arms she did not endure it heroically; nor when he fired pistols at her petticoats, which she believed to be charged with balls, could she help starting aside or suppress her screams." One girl married a friend of Day's: the other married a linen-draper.

Literary Eccentrics: A Review

Just as education can do everything for a human being, so kindness is to do everything for an animal. Why break in a colt which has learnt to feed out of your hand? Day rode this colt, it threw him, and that was the end of his treatise. In the same year the French Revolution broke out; a memorable year for Rousseau.

Day, who pretended his life was a book, and Amory who pretended a book was his life, are perhaps the two most interesting eccentrics in a very interesting selection. According to their lights they were consistent. They are not to be classed with the crank, who may be quite conventional on ninety-nine occasions, and quite dull on the hundredth. The crank is irrational; he has no wild objection to the universe but only a wild objection to some isolated point in it—to the meat in it, to the wine, to the habit of rejoicing at Christmas. In the suburb where these words are written, a pamphlet on the latter topic is issued yearly, and falls through the letter box about the time one is packing up the toys. We learn, ere it is too late, that Christmas is a heathen festival—Roman, Babylonian, worse—and that he who sold, he who bought, and he who receives this gutta-percha lion will suffer a like condemnation. If the pamphleteer can only grow warm over this, he is a crank, and study of him is not profitable. But he may be something far greater—a man who at every turn sees through our smug civilization to the barbarity and licentiousness on which it is founded. It is not normal to see through so much: such a man is eccentric. But now we read his pamphlet with respect, though of course it does not stop us packing up the lion.

In the region of the abnormal, things shade into each other very gently, and the cranky eccentric is not unlike the eccentric crank. Yet the former is akin to genius, the latter to madness, and it is with the former that Mr. Fyvie is concerned. He does not include people merely because they are tiresome; indeed, as has been hinted above, he sometimes goes to the opposite extreme. Who drives dull oxen will himself be dull—and there is scarcely a dull paragraph in his volume. It may be recommended to all, but more particularly to those whom certain grave Teutons have tempted down the other bypath, to flounder in the life we miscall real. Let us hope that he will follow it with a volume of matrons—including Mrs. Shelley, Mrs. Radcliffe, and Mrs. Aphra Behn.

1906

Mr. Walsh's Secret History of the Victorian Movement

The book is of modern appearance. It bears the imprint of a well-known firm; it was published scarcely thirty years ago. Nor does its title promise entertainment. *A Manual of Domestic Economy; suited to Families spending from £150 to £1500 a year. Including directions for the management of the Nursery and Sick Room, and the preparation and administration of Domestic Remedies.* This comprehensive but homely task is undertaken by a Mr. J. H. Walsh, F.R.C.S., "assisted in various departments by a committee of ladies," and we are further promised "Coloured Plates by Kronheim." But one of these, representing a fernery, lies opposite the title page, and there is something in the arrangement of these ferns—nay in their very botany—that should tempt the reader onward. That species is extinct today. Not for love or money could one buy anything quite so coarse and quite so green. One saw them last in the civilization of Clapham or Torquay, or in the operating room of some provincial dentist. Rochester might have bought them for Jane Eyre, Cynthia Kirkpatrick or Griselda Grantly or Tito Melema might have forgotten to water them. For we have before us not a manual of Domestic Economy but a manual of Victorianism.

The compiler has in mind a young husband and wife. Their manners are genteel, their tastes solid, their income—if one may judge by the recipes he gives them for puddings, most of which swing off with "take a dozen eggs and a pint of cream" —comes nearer to £1500 a year than £150. The husband, though a manly fellow, is inexperienced about the house. And the wife, though modest and clinging, is equally ignorant, and alas!—a little sly. She has expensive tastes, and coaxes the husband to give her what he cannot afford. As early as page 2 —and there are 800 pages in the book—the following dialogue takes place between them. Its humor, which is that of the Curtain Lecture, rings faintly today. But it is worth reading for other reasons.

> "My dear, do you know that Mrs.———has just sent both her daughters to Madame———for a year?"
>
> "No, my love, I was not aware of it."
>
> "Well, George, don't you think that Emily and Laura ought to have the same advantages, or they will appear awkward when they come out, which you know will be about the same time."
>
> "But my dear Eliza, what an enormous bill I shall have to pay."
>
> "Oh George, how can you consider such a trifle, when your daughters' welfare and future station are at stake? Besides, it is only for a year."

Eliza seems to have a strong case, and one is tempted to exclaim: "Oh, hang it all, let Emily and Laura go." But Mr.

Walsh knows better. "And so the poor father is led on to enter upon an annual expenditure of some hundreds, for the mother has omitted to state that she fully intends them to remain two years instead of one, and then to be succeeded by the next batch of girls."

This will never do. How are we to have puddings with twelve eggs in, if we send our girls to Madame ———? Comfort must precede education, and on these lines the Manual of Victorianism is compiled. Step by step, Mr. Walsh takes his young couple through life. He builds them a house in Book 2, "on a site free from vegetable emanations." He fills it with mahogany furniture in Book 3. In Book 4 he engages a staff of servants to cook in Book 6 the food that he has ordered in Book 5. Passing on through nursery and stable, he speaks of Social duties and of the principles of Carving. He makes Strong Meat-jelly for Weak persons (people with him are always persons), he makes the "Most of a chicken for an invalid." He censures Homeopathy, cures Thrush, Croup, and Indigestion, but refuses to name a remedy for Tartar Emetic on the ground that it could only be taken as poison deliberately "against which horrible practice the directions of this book are not intended." The work ends quietly, with instructions for the capture of a flea.

There is so much that one finds it difficult to begin, and the difficulty is increased by Mr. Walsh's style. It is not like anything else in literature. Many a writer is broken-backed, but his back breaks in a new place, and his sentences crawl and writhe and return upon themselves by convolutions hitherto unsuspected. Take for instance, the paragraph on skimmed milk. "Where cows are kept, a jug of Skimmed Milk is a valuable present, and always a very acceptable one where there are children; while in a gentleman's house it is only fit for pig's wash, or at all events it is used for that purpose wherever cows are kept sufficient to make butter for the family." It is clear that charity is contemplated, and that the poor are, under certain circumstances, to occupy the position of the pig. But what those circumstances are, and whether the two sets of cows are the same cows, or have changed their identity while cantering through the sentence—all this is too difficult, and it is best to conclude that the heart is in its right place, and to pass on. The paragraph occurs in a section headed "The Rich Man's Superfluities," and its meanness and naïveté are alike Victorian: the donor of today if not more generous, is more discreet. He would not suddenly exclaim "If so, many a cottage which is now rarely gladdened by the sight of animal food would be made comfortable at times if not always so," or assert that "hundreds of poor children would be glad of such a pudding," the said pudding being made of the crumbs saved from the cloth during the week. The note of the book is one of robust isolation. George and Eliza dwell in their well-appointed house, eating and drinking enormously, and at times shovelling their superfluities out of doors. That idea of comradeship, which we are gaining through intellectual unrest, that idea of society as a whole and a fluid whole which permeates the literature of today, would have seemed to them fantastic and faintly improper. Here are the rich, there the poor, and an occasional crumb pudding is sufficient bond between them.

Isolation, however robust, has its drawbacks, and these appear in the section "On Social Intercourse between equals." A well-fed family, when confronted with another well-fed family, becomes shy, and even Mr. Walsh cannot tabulate the situation as he would wish. He is particularly puzzled about

Blood Relations. Should they adhere to the usual rules of society? Or may they meet when and where they like, "being
guided by no laws but those of kindliness?" He is uncertain,
and so was Miss Austen, who has given the question imperish-
able form in her cameo of the Musgrove family. The Mus-
groves, it will be remembered, combined the disadvantages of
both plans. When Mary had an invitation from the Great
House she went because she felt she must; when no invitation
came she was offended, and went to show that she did not
mind. Here too the question is left open, a certain relaxation
of etiquette being permitted but by no means prescribed. "Beyond Blood Relations, I am strongly inclined to doubt the advantage of any intimacy carried so far as to dispense with the
ordinary terms." This is startling; it condemns every friendship
that one has had or is likely to have. Did Mr. Walsh ever care
for anybody himself, one is tempted to ask. Did he ever drop
into another medical student's rooms? One doubts it. Or perhaps his committee of ladies are writing here. They are surely
responsible for the section "After the birth of a baby," which
is refined to the point of obscurity. On the whole it seems
wiser to enquire through the servant than in person. But "After
the marriage of a daughter" admits of no doubt. Eliza must
call herself within two days, and will probably be rewarded
by cake and wine, "a practice however not invariable, but
governed by local rules." In attending such a reunion as a
private breakfast party "all that is necessary is to go in morning
costume," whereas evening parties are of so many grades that
"very little can be said about them." In giving parties at home,
we reach firmer ground, and the colored plate representing a
"table laid for dinner in the Russian mode" is perhaps the
finest example of a Kronheim extant. It is laid for eighteen.

The center piece is a sort of font, containing ferns from the fernery, and flanked by glass troughs with corrugated sides. These are full of camelias. Beyond them are water jugs, such as we now place in bedrooms, each standing on a plaque of magenta-colored plush, and attended by two chalices, two Dresden ornaments, four dishes of dessert and two bedroom water bottles. Passing on, we come to another fern, red this time in a terra cotta pot, and a pink iced cake is by its side. Add eighteen serviettes, containing eighteen large pieces of bread, and place at each corner of the table a cruet that looks like a medieval town. The Russian dinner is then complete, and is preferred by Mr. Walsh to the "heavier English style," though it should only be attempted with the aid of four efficient waiters "which in London may always be had at 10s. 6d. each." These, after handing the dishes and mentioning the names thereof, "lest from ignorance of their appearance they may be unwittingly rejected," will remove the side slips, lay dessert, bring in more wine and coffee, and finally announce tea, "when their duties are over until the gentlemen join the ladies, when they simply clear away."

Servants, whether in the Russian or any other style, appear as the natural enemies of gentlefolk. It is the age of basement kitchens that so haunts the imagination of Mr. Wells. "The servant," we are told, "is expected as a matter of course to be honest, sober, diligent, civil, and clean," but with sublime candor Mr. Walsh adds "the course to be pursued by the employer is not however always so clear." Like company, they are a troublesome matter to him. Half-inanimate himself, he is only happy when dealing with inanimate things. For these he has endless sympathy. To mushrooms alone he consecrates ten pages of print and six colored plates, and the only human being to whom he makes sympathetic reference is a certain Mr. Worthington Smith, "who is able to testify that he has partaken of every known variety of edible mushrooms with only one mishap (very nearly fatal however), but his immunities should not be made an example to others without their acquiring an equal amount of knowledge, which however he is always ready to impart, being an enthusiast in this particular study." Which of the edible mushrooms is almost fatal? Without telling us, the author passes on to anchovies, of which he approves "when not personated by sardines," and to nuts, which receive summary dismissal. "Though relished by all classes, they require the stomach of an ostrich to digest them, and should never be eaten in large quantities." The monster who "ate a peck of filberts at a sitting with impunity" is an exceptional case, and "no one should presume to imitate so bad an example." Meat is of course in favor, and when hashed beef is not followed by roast mutton, hashed mutton is followed by roast beef. These with potatoes—very large and wet; one can imagine them—and vegetable marrow—a "delicious vegetable," one can imagine that too—and cabbage, form the basis of the midday meal, and for breakfast we have had the edible mushrooms. It is odd how foods fall into bad company. The mushroom today is continental in its associations—almost demimondaine. One classes it with the omelette, which no moral person can make properly, or with macaroni, which no moral person can eat properly. Yet the mushroom was Victorian, and swam unashamed in torrents of grey hot water once; or lay stranded, a relict, on sodden rounds of toast; there used to be these two ways of cooking mushrooms. Mr. Walsh is alive to their importance, and to his six colored plates the reader is urged to refer, whenever his memory of the epoch grows dim.

As for furniture. It is all that the food implies—most substantial, and calculated to strain the servants annually, when
they move it for the spring cleaning. "In the ranks of life for
which this book is intended, certain woods are devoted to certain purposes and rooms. Thus mahogany and oak are suitable
for the hall, in the dining room mahogany prevails; Spanish
when the purse admits of it, and if not Honduras." For the
drawing-room he recommends, in addition to a walnut suite, as
many kettle-drum tables as possible, edged with fringe or with
lace over a satin fall. Lace on a plush drop for the mantle piece.
Shields on the walls, covered with plush. Water colors may be
introduced, especially when the frames are open, so that plush
may peep through from behind. Then we are conducted to the
fernery, as to something new. And so, step by step, the house is
built up, and the world built out.

The book merits notice. It is the work of a man—or of a
committee—who had a complete view of life, and imply that
view even in a recipe for a rice pudding. The audience it assumes regarded comfort as everything, personal relations as
nothing, passion and beauty as nothing. They do not make history as historians understand it. They do not appear in the
great novelists much, for literature even in satire should seek
higher game. But most of us have known and perhaps still know
a few of them in daily life. At all events they bought the Manual, for it went through several editions, the last of which is
scarcely thirty years old today. This suggests a somewhat serious conclusion. Victorianism may not be an era at all. It may
be a spirit, biding its time.

1911

Inspiration

Most of us, either as reader or writer must have taken part in the following conversation:—

READER: It is a great pleasure to meet you. I have admired your books so much; do you mind talking about them?

WRITER: Oh, thank you, I don't think so.—No.

READER: Because I wanted to ask you. How do you set about them? How do they come? Do you plan out a book beforehand? Or do you make it up as you go along?

WRITER: I can't quite remember. A little of both perhaps.

READER: I see. You start with a plan, but leave yourself quite free to alter it as the story develops.

WRITER: That does sound an awfully good way. I wonder.

READER: Won't you tell me? Well, I mustn't pry into the secrets of your craft.

WRITER: Oh please—we've no secrets.

READER: Then tell me this: Which do you conceive first; the characters or the plot?

WRITER: Er—r—a little of both perhaps—er—er—

READER (*afterwards*): Yes, I've met him at last. A disappointment; a very great disappointment.

It is indeed a disappointment. Reader and writer part with mutual annoyance. Why can't the writer explain? Why doesn't the reader guess? But instead of blaming one another, they would do better to blame the age in which they live. For their conversation is peculiarly modern. It never occurred in the past. Then, if the writer was questioned, he would reply quite simply and cheerfully, "Apollo inspired me." The reader answered, "Praised be Apollo!" and all was well. Both parties assumed the intervention of a god, who, duly invoked, poured something into the worshipper that human converse cannot produce, and made him a channel for exciting and extraordinary words. They believed in inspiration.

Today we have dethroned Apollo. But it may be questioned whether we have put any adequate theory in his place. Science —as usual—is not quite ready. She has one or two more facts about psychology and physiology to master before she can ascend Parnassus and explain exactly how books are written. And while she is mastering these facts, and the one or two hundred other facts to which they will lead her, the reader gets at cross purposes with the writer, and the writer says "Er—er—." Is it possible to forestall science and to give some answer from our own experience?

Experiences vary, but most writers when they compose seem to go through some such process as follows. They start pretty calm, promising their wives they will not let the fire out or be late for lunch. They write a few sentences very slowly and feel constricted and used up. Then a queer catastrophe happens in side them. The mind, as it were, turns turtle, sometimes with rapidity, and a hidden part of it comes to the top and controls the pen. Quicker and quicker the writer works, his head grows hot, he looks far from handsome, he spoils the lunch and lets out the fire. He is not exactly "rapt"; on the contrary he feels more himself than usual, and lives in a state which he is convinced should be his normal one, though it isn't. On returning to his normal state, he reads over what he has written. It surprises him. He couldn't do it again. He can't explain to the reader how it was done. He can't remember whether plot or character was considered first, whether the work was conceived as a whole or bit by bit. If he started with a plan it is all forgotten and faded, just as our anticipations about a new place or person fade as soon as we have had the experience of seeing that place or person. The reality has swallowed it up. It is a reality outside his ordinary self. He has created it but contains it no longer; to use the hackneyed comparison, his relation to it is that of a parent to a child. And this, by the way, accounts for a phenomenon which often repels the reader; writers are capable of perusing their own works with interest and even with admiration. No doubt it is absurd of them to do this, but it is the absurdity of a fond father who rejoices in the extension of his individuality, and trusts that it will survive when he is gone. Of all forms of conceit, it is the least narrowing.

Here, then, is the process, termed by the ancients "inspiration," and one wishes that the term was still in use, for it is far nearer the truth than most accounts. In modern usage, inspiration is still allowed to poets and a few historians, but the smaller fry, such as novelists, are denied it. How unfair! If one writer can be inspired, are we not all inspired, every one of us?

The quality of our inspiration—that is another matter: Apollo always was unreliable. But are we not all capable of getting into a state where we put down words that we shouldn't put down ordinarily? And is not this capability the first step towards producing good work? When one recalls the anecdotes about great writers—how Jane Austen composed in the hubbub of the rectory drawing-room, how Balzac saw from his summerhouse the Comédie Humaine disentangling and entangling against the shrubs that surrounded him, how Coleridge (the extreme case) prolonged into waking his vision of Kubla Khan—it is tempting to conclude that they all went through the same process, diverse as were the results to which it brought them, and most tempting to conclude that we, too, can go through that process, with results however bad.

For—to repeat—inspiration need not imply genius. The vain shallow writer is also inspired, and perhaps with the greater facility. He too can put down words when his poor little mind has turned turtle, and can declare afterwards that they are good words. There is a story of a man who, like Coleridge, dreamt a poem of superhuman splendor. It was not cumbersome like Kubla Khan, but consisted of a single immortal stanza, which he managed to write down and preserve for literature. When he was quite awake he read the little gem. It ran as follows:

> *Walker with one eye,*
> *Walker with two.*
> *Something to live for,*
> *Nothing to do.*

Are not many of our awakenings similar? The inspiration seemed splendid at the time, but criticism must relegate it to the wastepaper basket. It is pure balderdash. There is just this comfort: we mayn't get far with it, but we shouldn't get anywhere without it. Perseverance, benevolence, culture, and all the other qualities that pose as good writing, are worthless if they are not rooted in the underside of the mind.

1912

FOR THE
WORKING MEN'S
COLLEGE

The Working Men's College, London, was founded in the middle of the nineteenth century, its object to open to the working man an education in "human studies" and a social life not unlike that of the older universities. Though it grew out of the Christian Socialist movement, an origin which Forster could not fully approve, its immediate educational aims commanded his sympathy as a liberal intellectual.

The papers Forster published in *The Working Men's College Journal* between 1907 and 1914 deserve to be grouped together. With the exception of "The Beauty of Life," they were written to be delivered as talks, and they were intended for a general audience with limited formal education. Forster was a good man for an audience of this kind. He could be plain and casual without sounding affected or without talking down.

He was also a decisive thinker. If the subject required moral judgment or pertained to his self-interest in relation to the interests of others, he arrived at a firm idea. But with respect to "Pessimism in Literature," a subject of the deepest concern to him, he shows a decided ambivalence which reflects his personal situation. He takes part in the pessimistic spirit of the age; his sympathies as a liberal are naturally with the disturbing modern writers and thinkers. Yet his creative impulse moves toward comedy and the theme of salvation. Much of the complexity and ambiguity of Forster's writing arises from this interplay between the pessimistic tendencies of the age and the positive tendencies of his own temperament. Sometimes the effect is disruptive to the point where art gives way to the strain. One suspects that is why *The Longest Journey* seems unsatisfactory to many readers. Its radical yoking together of separation and death on the one side and salvation on the other reflects too faithfully the contradictory tensions of Forster's response to life at the beginning of the twentieth century.

The essay on "Dante" stresses the love defined by Virgil in Canto XV of the *Purgatorio* where he admonishes against the plague of worldly desire and enjoins a higher love which the more it is divided the more it grows. The essay also stresses Dante's conviction that harmony may prevail in the universe without abolishing variety. The contrasting forces that make for likeness and difference "are reconciled in the orbits of the stars." This idea of a celestial harmony fascinates Forster who, in *The Longest Journey,* "The Machine Stops," and "The Point of It" employs the constellation of Orion as a reconciling symbol of man's strength and heroic nature.

Forster is deeply moved by Dante's commitment to a higher love and to a harmony which does not preclude variety, yet fundamentally his response is ambivalent. Dante is too unbending in his attitude to the commonplace, too callous as he looks through people to a higher goal beyond. His medieval remoteness, his unqualified attachment to celestial things, and his spiritual elitism deprive him of human warmth.

When Forster was asked by the editor of *The Working Men's College Journal* to write an article on the beauty of life as manifest in all things, he turned for his ideal not to Dante but to Walt Whitman. He begins his paper by quoting *Leaves of Grass,* 31, and ends with the opening of part three of "A Song for Occupations." In between he approaches the subject of an earlier paper: "One might define the average educated man as optimist by instinct, pessimist by conviction." To the average modern man "life is not all gold, as Whitman would have it; it is not even strung on a golden thread, as the great Victorian poets would have it, but it is pure gold in parts—it contains scraps of inexpressible beauty." Forster advises a reading of Whitman, one of those rare men who can decipher beauty in all things. But lesser men, like himself, must be content with scraps of beauty.

One of the common characteristics of the first three papers from *The Working Men's College Journal* is Forster's ambivalence. In each case he is of a divided mind: between optimism of temperament and pessimism of conviction; between the beauty, love, and grandeur of Dante's poetry and the spiritual elitism of the man which makes even his poetry chilling; and between the universal beauty of life conceived by the great writer and the scraps of beauty for which ordinary men must settle. But no such ambivalence is to be found in "The Functions of Literature in War-time." That is because the essay is about a division within the nation, and Forster's goal is to take a strong stand on one side, the side of reason and restraint. The cheapness he opposes is largely taken for granted because it is the daily reality he and his listeners live with. It is typified for Forster by Harold Begbie, popular poet, novelist, and professional journalist. Forster's antipathy to journalism is profound. "The literature of the moment is really represented by a mind the calibre of Harold Begbie's. Let us leave it with him and him with it, and turn to the literature of the past."

The writers of the past are our spiritual trustees. They help us to abstain from the hysteria of fear and hatred and tribal religion. Forster's language is Platonic. It is a language found also in his fiction when he is deeply moved. Behind the words, however, his position remains fundamentally humanist. "The individual writer may believe that his race is the chosen, but Literature . . . declares that beauty and truth and goodness exist apart from the tribe, apart even from the Nation, and that their only earthly dwelling is the soul of man." The paradox is characteristic. Literature transcends the individual, but the values it upholds have their only earthly dwelling within the individual. However divided in mind Forster may be about the more pragmatic issues of modern pessimism, Dante's elitism, and the prospect of finding beauty in all things, he remains unshaken in his commitment to those values which he conceives as having permanence in man's nature and in his literature.

Pessimism in Literature

In every subject for discussion there are two questions, which must be kept carefully apart—the question of *opinion* and the question of *fact*. And of these questions, the question of fact must be discussed first, for if the fact has not taken place, we can have no opinion about it, favorable or unfavorable. Before we discuss the recent appearance of the sea serpent, we must be sure that the sea serpent has appeared. Before we discuss the policy of the government, we must be sure that the government has a policy. Before we discuss the German emperor's perfidious declaration of war, the annihilation of the British fleet, and the landing of a German army corps in East Anglia—well, before we get excited, we had better buy *The Tribune* as well as the *Daily Mail*. And so this evening, before we discuss the pessimism in modern literature, let us be sure that modern litera-

Paper read to the Working Men's College Old Students' Club on 1 December 1906, concerning the question, "Is the Pessimism in Modern Literature to be deplored?"

ture is, to an appreciable extent, pessimistic. To an appreciable extent. Not entirely. That we cannot and do not want to prove. The pessimism *in* literature, not the pessimism *of* literature, is the question of fact before us, and having decided that, we can pass to the question of opinion, and discuss how far this pessimism is good, how far bad.

Now the question of fact is surely not very difficult to decide. However we define pessimism, we can easily find something in modern literature that will illustrate our definition. Not once but many times may we read in modern books that time flies, that man deteriorates, that virtue is not rewarded, that innocent actions have appalling consequences, that there is nothing new, nothing true under the sun. Literature, thank goodness, also tells us other things. But it most certainly tells us these things. I would even go further and say that its general tendency is pessimistic, and that optimism is the exception.

Consider those three men who have, for good or for evil, obtained a European reputation, and who are imitated, not only in their own countries, but all over the continent. I refer to the Frenchman Zola, the Norwegian Ibsen, and the Russian Tolstoy.

Zola is the most cheerful of the three. By the side of his companions, he appears almost hilarious. He finds the world horrible, but he does believe that it can be made better. Pessimists have called him an optimist. No one has applied this epithet to Ibsen, who finds the world horrible, and believes that it will remain horrible. Ibsen has no panacea for society. People call him a teacher, but I should like to know what he teaches. Not that we should love one another; he thinks that disastrous. Not that we should have ideals: that is even worse. If we tell the truth, he scolds us; if we don't tell the truth, he scolds us. Whether we walk or talk or work or play, Ibsen gets his knife into us. He finds us all diseased, all incurable, and his interest in humanity is that of a vivisectionist in a mangy dog.

Of Tolstoy, the third of this gloomy trio, one must speak in a different tone. Perhaps there is not a man alive who loves humanity more. But he too finds the world horrible, and be' lieves that it will remain horrible. His cure is simple but alarm' ing: annihilation. Let the human race cease to propagate itself. Let it die out, by its own desire. Then—according to Tolstoy —the Will of God will be accomplished, and humanity, having solved the problem allotted to it, will enter upon its spiritual reward. Tolstoy is a far more interesting man than either Ibsen or Zola. He is a great artist, with a feeling for beauty, and even with a sense of humor. But at the back of it all lies a profound pessimism—a belief that our life on earth is a hopeless tangle, and that all who transmit life are guilty of a crime.

Such are the three men who have obtained European repu' tation—at all events in the region of the novel and the drama— the region in which I am most interested and from which most of my examples will this evening be drawn. They are men of diverse temperaments, but they all have this belief, that the world, as it now exists, is a perfectly horrible place. Their enormous sale and their enormous reputation are sufficient proof that there is pessimism in literature, at all events in conti' nental literature. Let us turn to the literature of England.

In politics, and in practical matters, England has generally been the teacher of Europe. We have given her the example of parliamentary government. We have given her the revolution of 1688. More recently, we have given her the *Encyclopaedia Britannica*. But in the domain of literature—from which I ex' clude *The Times* and all its works—the case is exactly reversed.

Europe teaches England. For good or for evil, we lag behind the continent. We get most of our ideas second hand. We make splendid use of them when we do get them, but they are imported: occasionally they are dumped. Shakespeare may be the highest product of the Renaissance, but the Renaissance was made in Italy. Shelley may be a prophet of revolution, but the ideas that inspired him were made in France. And so the ideas that inspire or worry us today are made, some of them in Germany, but nearly all of them out of England. One might compare Europe to a ship and England to a little boat, tugged in its wake. It is a very splendid little boat, but it does not come first. It follows the ship through all weathers and into all seas. The ship today has sailed into the grey waters of pessimism, and the little boat follows it.

We have in England no one great man whose name rises naturally to our lips, as Tolstoy rises to the lips of a Russian. We have no leader of acknowledged superiority, and it is more difficult to generalize about our literature, and to decide whether it leans towards optimism or pessimism. Yet, if we compare the novelists of today with the novelists of fifty years ago, we can surely make a generalization of a kind. The older generation had a lightness of spirit, a robustness of outlook, that is apparently denied to the younger. Compare Charles Dickens, Charles Reade, Tom Hughes, and Anthony Trollope, with R. L. Stevenson, George Gissing, Thomas Hardy, Henry James. The latter writers have a quality in them that may be called morbid. They are quicker to register discomfort than joy. They are obsessed with the sadness of life—Gissing with the sadness of social conditions, Stevenson with the sadness of ill health, Henry James with the sadness of personal relations, Thomas Hardy, with the general sadness of everything. In some way or another, nearly every modern writer lets us hear the note of sorrow. Take such a writer as Bernard Shaw. We call him a humorist, and no doubt he does make us laugh at the time. But when we come away, we don't know why we were laughing. We feel terribly depressed. There is none of the radi- ant afterglow that we feel when we have finished a novel of Dickens or seen a comedy of Shakespeare. In our literature there sounds that undernote, like the toll of a subterranean bell, "The world is a horrible place! The world is a horrible place!" As I said before, we hear other things. But we do hear this thing. We do hear pessimism. The question of fact—that pes- simism exists, and to an appreciable degree—is surely not to be disputed. Let us turn from it to the question of opinion. Is this pessimism to be deplored?

And now I must come into the open. Hitherto I have con- cealed my own opinion. I have been proving what no one is likely to dispute—an agreeable task, and one on which the orator gladly lingers. Indeed, I have known orators who linger on nothing else and prove by overwhelming arguments that the earth is round and that the sun never sets on the British pos- sessions. Amidst deafening applause, they resume their seats, and a vote of confidence in Mr. Chamberlain's fiscal policy is proposed, seconded, and carried unanimously. I have nothing to do with these crafty politicians. I am concerned with litera- ture, a comparatively straightforward subject, and I will come into the open and say boldly that this pessimism is *not* to be deplored. There *is* something to be said for it. There *are* rea- sons, and noble reasons, for the output of unhappy books. To call them insane, or diseased, or continental rubbish, is in my opinion pernicious as well as inaccurate. They are *not* to be dismissed with a shrug of the shoulders.

Now, at the first glance, the case against pessimism seems overwhelming. Do we not all sympathize with the old lady who exclaimed "Buy a modern novel? No thank you. If I want to cry, I can do it without spending 4s. 6d." Why should we spend money on the chance of being made unhappy? Nor is the old lady the only spokesman. People who think, people who love beauty, people who have wide knowledge of the world, join in her protest. They are angry with all these unhappy books. They are angry with the noisy author who tells them that it cannot be helped and that they ought to be unhappy. Is there not happiness in daily life, happiness sure and certain? Then why should the author neglect it? Why, when we ask him for wine, or at all events for fresh water, should he hand us a cup of bitter tears, and declare that these are the results of his chemistry, these the quintessence of life—that the many-flavored world distills at last into no sweeter drink than this? How tempting it is to say "The author is worse than a public nuisance. He is a liar. For we know for certain that life is full of the most glorious things."

And so it is. We are perfectly right about life. But between life and books there is one great difference—a difference that is too often neglected—a difference on which my chief argument will be based. It is simply this. The *end* is of supreme importance in a book. The *end* is not of supreme importance in life. We do not judge a man by the words that he gasps on his death bed. But we do judge a book by the words that are written on the last page. The popular criticisms of a book, "It was so sad: the last page nearly made me cry," or "It is so nice: they all get married in the end," are very good criticisms, as far as they go. The instinct to peep at the last page and see whether the hero gets her or not, is a good instinct in a way. A book that ends feebly, leaves a bad taste in the mouth, or—to put the point in choicer language—a book that ends feebly has failed as an artistic whole. A book with a strong ending leaves a good taste behind. We forgive it many previous faults. I think one cannot be too emphatic over this question of the end.

This being so, let us ask ourselves—A man today, if he writes a novel, how will he end it? "Happily, of course," the optimist replies. Very well. In what kind of happiness? What happy incident will he select from life? The optimist hums and haws. He says, "Why, my dear man—life's full of happy incidents." We answer, "Exactly. Now choose one that will do for the end of a book." He hums and haws again. He is fond of a hundred things—of music, of football, of his friends—yet none of these things quite do for the end of a book. And sooner or later, he will give the old, old answer, *marriage*. Let the book end with a happy marriage. Let the lovers be united, to the sound of wedding bells.

A hundred years ago, or fifty years ago, this would have seemed a very good answer. But our social feelings are altering very rapidly. We of today know that whatever marriage is, it is not an end. We know that it is rather a beginning, and that the lovers enter upon life's real problems when those wedding bells are silent. Our better education, and the better education of women has taught us this. The early Victorian woman was regarded as a bundle of goods. She passed from the possession of her father to that of her husband. Marriage was a final event for her: beyond it, she was expected to find no new development, no new emotion. And so the early Victorian novelist might reasonably end his book with a marriage. The social feeling of the period approved him. But the woman of today is quite another person. She is by no means a bundle of goods. She may throw herself flat on the floor of the House of Commons and resemble a bundle, but she only does it to give more trouble to the police. She may marry, but her marriage is most certainly not an *end*, either for herself or for her husband. Their courtship was but a prelude: their wedding is but the raising of the curtain for the play. The drama of their problems, their developments, their mutual interaction, is all to come. And how can the novelist of today, knowing this, end his novel with a marriage?

We have thus driven the optimist from a most important stronghold. We have proved to him—not that marriage is unhappy, but that marriage will not do for the ending of a book. We have *not* attacked his view of life, but we have attacked his view of literature. He goes back to his music and his football and his friends, and thither we follow him. But as a literary critic we do not follow him. Instead, we turn to that despised creature the pessimist, and say "How would *you* end a book?" And the pessimist replies, quite simply and satisfactorily, "By some scene of separation."

It seems to me that the modern author, if he is conscientious and artistic, is bound to listen to this advice. He may not be a pessimist himself. But he wants to end his book on a note of permanence, and where shall he find it? Remember that he is a modern author, and therefore saturated with the idea of evolution. He has not merely been taught that all things change. He has breathed it in, as men have breathed it in at no other age. He may be neither scientist nor philosopher. He may even protest. But he has breathed it in and he must breathe it out again. Where shall such a man find rest with honor? Scarcely in a happy ending.

It is useless to tell him that happiness exists. That is not the point. Of course it exists, frequent and intense. He would be the last to deny it. But is it permanent? Is there any happy situation on earth that does not contain the seeds of decay, or at all events of transformation? The modern mind is, in this respect, horribly acute, and perceives that the glorious, happy things are not the things that last. And therefore, for an ending, the modern author must go elsewhere, or leave his work unfinished. Separation—that is the end that really satisfies him—not simply the separation that comes through death, but the more tragic separation of people who part before they need, or who part because they have seen each other too closely. Here is something that does last—the note of permanence on which his soul was set. He has labored sincerely; he has told a story not untrue to life; he has said the last word about his characters, for he leaves them in a situation where they can never meet each other any more. Such a book as *The Wings of the Dove* has, for all its obscurity, a clear and most artistic ending. The man and woman in it, after many tests, attain to perfect knowledge of each other, and that knowledge entails eternal separation. Whether they marry or not—perhaps they do; it is left doubtful—they are divided by a chasm which no tenderness can ever bridge. Were there a bridge—there was no ending. For if you once admit that these people can meet again, you admit the possibility, from Henry James's point of view, the certainty of a change in their relations. The living change continually. Only those who are dead, or dead to each other, are unalterable.

Separation, then, is the end that best pleases the novelist or dramatist of today—the erection of a barrier, spiritual or physical, between the people in his book. Separation is the incident that he selects from life, and therefore we conclude, quite unjustly, that he sees in life nothing but separation. The truth is that modern art has not succeeded in depicting all modern life. It has tried, it would like to, but it cannot. If the critic of the future says, "How sad the twentieth century books were," he will be right. But if he goes on to say, "How sad people must have been in the twentieth century," he will be wrong. For a man and an author have different aims. The author looks for what is permanent, even if it is sad; the man looks for what is cheerful, and noble, and gracious, even if it is transitory. This, to my mind, is the root of the whole contention. The author and the public are not nearly as different as they suppose. The same joys and sorrows are submitted to both. But their aims are different. They focus differently, and though their results are diverse, they are not contradictory.

It is the most important point that I am trying to make, and I will illustrate it by two examples. The first example shall be that of a place that we all know—Box Hill; the second that of a man of whom we have all heard—Julius Caesar. They are rather an incongruous couple, but they will help us to get clear on this point.

Consider Box Hill. In spite of the Aunt Sallys and cocoa nut shies on the top, it is still a delightful place. But what will Box Hill be like in a few hundred years? Why, it will be part of London. The roads to it will be lined with sky scrapers and screaming with motor cars. The view from it will survey uninteresting houses, and the air machines, as they whistle over head, will shower down the catalogues of the *Times* Mammoth Universal Providing Stores. In a few million years even the *Times* will have died, and Box Hill, in company with the rest of Europe, will have vanished underneath the polar ice cap. Again a few million years, and Box Hill, if it has any visible existence, will exist as a shooting star in some other planetary system, and perhaps give rise to evening discussions in the debating societies of the Milky Way. Now the next person who writes an epic poem on Box Hill—I leave the field unoccupied —is bound to allude to these deplorable facts, and his poem will be a sad poem, a pessimistic poem. But the majority of us are not epic poets. We are tourists. We are photographers. We are members of the Lubbock Field Club, a most optimistic institution. I have met the Lubbock Field Club when it hadn't half a daisy root between it, and yet it was in the highest spirits. What do all of us care for the final doom of Box Hill? We regard it not as a subject for a book, but as part of our lives; not as a place to write about, but as a place to be happy upon.

And now for my second example—that meritorious character, Julius Caesar. Julius Caesar has been treated in two ways— as a character in history and as a subject for a book. The historian treats him somewhat as follows, "Julius Caesar conquered Gaul, and wrote an account of his campaigns there. He overthrew the Roman Republic, but was an enlightened, amiable, and noble man, to whom the world owes much. In B.C. 44, he was murdered by a little group of reactionaries, and his work devolved upon Octavius, his adopted son," etc. Here our attention is not focussed on the end of Caesar. He was murdered. It is one fact out of many. He did much good before the murder, and much of the good lived after him. But the dramatist does focus our attention on the end. To him the life and works of Julius Caesar are but a prelude to the appalling catastrophe of his death.

> *O mighty Caesar! Dost thou lie so low?*
> *Are all thy conquests, glories, triumphs, spoils,*
> *Shrunk to this little measure? Fare thee well.*

Of course, the conquests of Caesar have not shrunk to that little measure. They survive, in altered forms, at this very day, and they will survive until the coming of the polar ice cap. But this is history, not Shakespeare: a fact of life, not necessarily a truth of art. The end of Julius Caesar, like the end of Box Hill, is to a practical man not the most important thing about him.

Now, it may be objected that if all this is true, it is true always, and has no special connection with modern books; that sad endings, if they are the best, will be the best in every age— not merely in the twentieth century. I do not think so. For though the facts of human nature are constant, the spirit of humanity is not, but alters age by age, perhaps year by year, and, like some restless child, continually groups the facts anew. Now it pushes the sad facts to the front, now the sorrowful; today it has pushed to the front the fact that all things perish, the fact of evolution. What new and more inspiring combinations it may find, no man can say; that it will find a new combination is surely inevitable, and happy the artist who records it. The artist of today, if he records nothing cheerful, can at all events find consolation in sincerity. His pessimism results, not from wrongheadedness, not from spiritual blindness, but from an honest attempt to interpret the spirit of the age. Whether it is worth interpreting—that is a question too enormous. But he has to choose between sad art and no art—between doing as well as he can and doing nothing—and for my own part I am glad that he does as well as he can.

Perhaps we do not often realize how very far this pessimism extends in modern work—especially in what we term comedy. The sentimental comedy of J. M. Barrie, the tit-for-tat comedy of Ellen Thorneycroft Fowler, the cynical comedy of Pinero— all pay their ultimate homage to something that is certainly not a laugh. We are so keenly—if you like, so morbidly—alive to sorrow and suffering, that human action seems impossible without them, and laughter impossible unless there is someone to laugh *at*—someone whom the laughter would pain if he knew of it. Even in life, practical jokes are rather shocking. The world grows so frightfully cultured and kind that old gentlemen who slip upon orange peel are no longer what they were. Even in life—and in books much more so. Yet we have still memorials of another attitude—notably in some of the comedies of Shakespeare.

Nothing illustrates this point better that a comparison of *Twelfth Night* as it is written, and *Twelfth Night* as it is presented on the stage by modern actors. *Twelfth Night,* as written, gives the idea of a garden, owned if you like by Olivia, a tiresome person in black, but inhabited by Sir Toby Belch, Sir Andrew Aguecheek, a clown, Fabian, and Maria. These people want to laugh, just as the birds want to sing, and therefore the sun of their comedy rises—Malvolio—to provide them with unending mirth. They are frightfully unkind to him, but we feel that their unkindness does not matter; nothing matters, so long as they laugh and we laugh with them. But the modern actor—Mr. Benson, and I believe Mr. Tree—quite changes the feel of the play by demanding our pity for Malvolio. "He hath been most notoriously abused," says Olivia, and her remark, which read like a piece of delicate shading in the general brilliancy, becomes on the stage a black indictment of the comic life. He *has* been most notoriously abused, and when he dashes off, frantic, dishevelled, miserable, crying, "I'll be revenged on the whole pack of you," our hearts sink, not because he will accomplish that revenge, but because he is too impotent, too broken by cruelty and mockery ever to do so.

From Shakespeare one naturally turns to Mr. Bernard Shaw. He too has written brilliant comedy. He too has introduced characters laughing on the stage—a thing comparatively rare in modern drama. But they laugh only to be condemned. In the third act of *John Bull's Other Island,* the curtain rises upon what seems to be a delightful farce. There has been a motor accident. Mr. Broadbent, who is hoping to be returned to Parliament as member for an Irish constituency, has given a lift to a pig, the property of one of his supporters. He was in the front seat, steering; the pig, clasped by a boy, was enthroned behind. As soon as they started, the pig broke loose, jumped forward, and got its tail under the brake, Mr. Broadbent then tried to slow down, and put the brake on, hard. The result can be imagined. No one was dangerously hurt, with the exception of the pig, which—but there is no occasion to go into details. The story is told to a roomful of laughing Irishmen, and at first the audience joins in their laughter heartily. But in the corner of the room there sits a strange figure—a mad unfrocked priest, a mystic. He looks up gravely and says, "Our brother the pig." One laughs again. "This place is Hell," he continues, "for no other place would laugh when the flesh that God has made is in torment." We begin to feel ashamed. He speaks again, until, for a moment, the whole theater is in silence. How brutal we have been! How culpably thoughtless to laugh at the death terrors and death pangs of an animal!

Now Shakespeare, for all the limitations that Mr. Shaw finds in him, could probably write a funny account of a motor accident. What he could not, or would not do, is to make us ashamed of our fun. Here the modern mind has progressed—if it is a progress. It has detected the discomfort and misery that lie so frequently beneath the smiling surface of things. But what it has gained in insight it has lost in power. It can be witty and sarcastic and amusing. But it can never recall joy on a large scale—the joy of the gods.

One man has tried to recall this joy, and has failed decisively —a man whose failures and triumphs are peculiarly those of the modern world—Richard Wagner. Wagner can give us tragedy, and the disquieting passion of human love, and the sounds of the earth and the sea and the poetry of nature. What he cannot give us is the poetry of laughter—the laughter that once filled the earthly paradise of Olivia's garden. I am thinking of a scene that is intended to be perfectly joyful—to present, on a heroic scale, the cheerfulness, the high spirits, the auda-cious laughter that are so splendid and magnificent in life. The scene in question is the opening scene of *Siegfried*. In life the youthful Siegfried would be quite an agreeable person. We should like to know him—at all events we should like to think of him at a public school. "Boys will be boys," we should mur-mur, when he laughed and shouted, and bullied and jumped to and fro in the most distracting way. But the youthful Siegfried on the stage is intolerable. It is not merely that his tights are too large and his wig not tight enough, that the rocks on which he bounds are stuffed with horse hair. It is that he is a bounder in a more fatal sense—neither a hero nor a school boy, but a cad. There are some things that will not come across the foot-lights, just as there are some things that are intolerable if the footlights do not intervene. In spite of the jolliest music, the youthful Siegfried will not do, and when, in accordance with the stage directions, he "makes a long nose" our depression is complete. Wagner has failed—not because jumping and shout-ing, or even the formation of long noses, are ignoble things, but because they will not fit into the spirit of modern art. And the failure is so grave that it does much to spoil the whole of the opera. We cannot believe in Siegfried as a hero. Siegmund was a hero, because he was unhappy. Hagen is a hero, though heroically evil. But Siegfried remains to the end an upstart boy, who marries a woman ten times better than himself.

So—to recapitulate—there are three obstacles that prevent the modern artist, who wishes to write cheerfully. Firstly, he is in the grip of the modern idea of evolution, which teaches that all things alter, and that if he wants an "end" he must choose a sad one, or leave his sense of fitness unsatisfied. Here again Wagner is typical. We know from his letters that when he began the *Nibelung's Ring,* he intended to give it a happy ending. As he worked, he found that it was impossible. A work so great and so grave could in modern times only conclude in a world catastrophe. Aeschylus, two thousand years ago, could give a happy ending to his *Oresteia* and leave us with the sense of joy and salvation. Wagner, though he too ends with a motive of salvation, leaves nothing to be saved, for the powers of good have perished, as well as the powers of evil.

Here then is one obstacle. The second is connected with it; that modern tendency to see in everything some latent discomfort and sorrow. We marked that tendency in Bernard Shaw, and also in the modern actor who saw the latent discomfort in the comedy of *Twelfth Night.* This tendency is very tiresome, and hampers the artist greatly. But we can scarcely condemn it without also condemning insight, sympathy, and earnest thought. Life is not a bed of roses. Still less is it a bed with all the roses on one side of it, and all the thorns stuck into an expiring villain on the other. The writer who depicts it as such may possibly be praised for his healthy simplicity. But his own conscience will never approve him, for he knows that healthiness and simplicity are not, in all cases, identical with truth.

Here I end my paper. I will repeat from it one remark, because it sums up my chief argument. In life we seek what is gracious and noble, even if it is transitory; in books we seek what is permanent, even when it is sad. I uphold optimism in life. I do not at present uphold optimism in literature. When the optimists fall on me in the discussion and rend me, as only optimists can, let them remember that I am as anxious as anyone for cheerful books; but they must be cheerful with sincerity.

1907

Dante

As we journey through life, there are three great questions that we can ask ourselves, if we choose; three great problems that we can try to solve, if we are interested in problems. The first is: How shall I behave to the people I know—to my relatives, friends, and acquaintances? The second is: How shall I behave to the people whom I don't know, but who nevertheless exist and have claims on me—to the government, to society as a whole, to humanity as a whole? And the third question, which some people think of supreme importance, while others neglect it entirely, is this: How shall I behave to the Unknowable? What shall my attitude be towards God, or Fate, or whatever you like to call the invisible power that lies behind the world?

These three questions have existed for all men in all ages. They are inseparable from our humanity. They are no more old-fashioned than they are modern. And it is my intention this evening to call up Dante out of the darkness of six hundred

Paper read to the Working Men's College Literary Society on 21 November 1907.

years, and see what answer he gives to them. How did Dante behave to the people he knew? How did he behave to the people he didn't know? And how did he behave to the Unknowable? I think that this is the best way of approaching the great poet. It is hopeless to attempt a detailed account of him. There isn't the time. Let us just put these three questions to him, and so see what he makes of the problems that are bothering us today.

But before we begin, I must inflict one or two dates on you —only one or two, for we are not concerned with history; and I must mention the names of some of the books that Dante wrote.

Dante was born in 1265, when Henry III was King of England. He was born in Florence, which is today part of the Kingdom of Italy, but which was then an independent republic, ruling a territory of about the size of Yorkshire. We know little about his youth, the two important facts being that when quite a boy, he fell in love with a lady named Beatrice, and that when he was twenty-five years old, Beatrice died. Like most Florentines, he entered public life, and in the year 1300 (aged 34) became a member of the government—of the cabinet, if I may use the phrase. He was becoming rather a prominent person. And then the blow fell—the blow that ruined him as a politician, but made him as a poet. A great fight broke out in Florence, and Dante's side got the worst of it. He was exiled. The remainder of his life he spent wandering about Italy and Europe, trying to find some champion who would restore him to the city that he loved so much and had served so faithfully. He found no one. He failed absolutely, and died in 1321, broken-hearted.

So his life falls into two distinct portions—up to 1300,

when he is at Florence and happy; and after 1300, when he is in exile and miserable. And if you agree with most historians, and take the year 1300 as marking the end of the middle ages, it follows that Dante lived at a most important moment, when the medieval world was passing into the modern.

As for his books. When he was a young man, he wrote a book called *The New Life*, in which he described his love for Beatrice. It treats of personal relations. In it we shall find some answer to the question, "How shall I behave to the people whom I know?" Then, after he had been exiled, he wrote a book called *The Empire*. It deals with the world's government and with the destiny of our race on earth. It is a political and sociological tract. It answers the question, "How shall we behave to the people whom we don't know?" And lastly, just before he died, he wrote the *Divine Comedy*, the scene of which is laid in Hell, in Purgatory, and in Heaven; and the aim of which is to answer the question, "How shall I behave to the Unknowable?" He did write other books, but I am only going to mention these three.

As for *The New Life*. Its "plot" is easily described, and is I daresay already familiar to you from the pictures of D. G. Rossetti and H. Holiday. It opens with an account of Dante's first meeting with Beatrice, at the somewhat tender age of nine. Nine years later they meet again, and the crisis of his love comes. Beatrice greets him—gives him her salutation. Nothing more. That is the happiest moment that he ever knows on earth. "And then with her ineffable courtesy, which is now receiving its reward in Heaven, she gave me her salutation, so that in one moment I beheld all the bounds of bliss." His intimacy with Beatrice goes no further. We are not even sure whether she returned his love. The rest of the book is concerned with his emotions—how he tried to be near her and fainted in her presence; how his love gradually became more manly and more spiritual. Then Beatrice dies. He is over' whelmed with grief. There is the episode of his infidelity—he is attracted by a lady who resembles her; and then he returns to her with remorse and determines that some day he will write a poem in her honor. He fulfilled this promise at the end of his life, by writing the *Divine Comedy,* in which Beatrice is the heroine.

Even from this brief sketch, you will have gathered that *The New Life* is rather a queer little book. It is half a diary and half a novel. At one moment Dante describes what actually happened, and at another he is only describing what might have happened, or what he felt. At one moment Beatrice is an ordinary woman who has friends and relatives and goes to dinner parties—an actual woman whom he might marry, as Hamlet might marry Ophelia; and at another, she seems an inhabitant of heaven, who had strayed by accident into our sordid world. We never know what the poet is up to, and we are apt to close the book with a feeling of irritation. There has been a great deal of talk about Beatrice, but we have not learnt what she was like, nor even whether she loved him. Con' trast *The New Life* with the Sonnets of Shakespeare. In the Sonnets, though much is obscure, we do know definitely what the various characters are like. In *The New Life,* we only hear that Dante loves Beatrice. Nothing else. He gives us no hint of her personality.

Now, this is a very interesting point, and goes far to answer the question, "How did Dante behave to the people whom he knew?" His answer is, "I regard them as a means to something else"; I regard them as windows in this sordid world, through which I may get a glimpse of heaven. Hamlet loved Ophelia because she was Ophelia. Othello loved Desdemona because she was Desdemona. But Dante loved Beatrice, because she was a means to God; because the emotions with which she inspired him, took him out of daily life into the life celestial. Here is the great difference between him and Shakespeare, between medieval and modern thought; and unless we keep this difference in mind, we shall fail to understand *The New Life*, and much else that he wrote. We of today naturally ask, "Why didn't Dante marry Beatrice?" But he would have shrunk from marriage as from sacrilege. He would have regarded it as a debasement of his ideal, a concession to the animal element within him. He preferred to worship Beatrice from a distance. And as for marrying—he married someone else. His wife—Gemma Donati was her name—seems to have had no influence on her husband. She was merely his wife, the mother of his children, not a window through which he could see God. Dead, as alive, Beatrice remained the most important person he had ever met; and so when he came to write the *Divine Comedy*, he takes her as his guide through heaven. The little girl he had known from the age of nine, has become a type of celestial wisdom. She meets him on the top of Purgatory, when earthly wisdom, however noble it may be, can help him no more. She takes him into the company of the blessed, to see the saints and the martyrs, the prophets, the Virgin Mary, Christ, the supreme Deity Himself. He had loved her as a woman, and now she shows him the Love that passes all understanding, and moves the universe. *The New Life*, which he wrote when he was young, is not complete in itself. It must be considered in connection with the *Divine Comedy*, which he wrote just before he died.

But I want to say a little more about this habit of regarding our fellow creatures as windows, through which we may see God—a habit, you must remember, that was not confined to Dante, but was typical of his age. At first sight, there is some' thing sublime in it. It makes a man behave with reverence and courtesy to a woman; he disciplines his body and soul, that he may be worthy of the high thoughts to which she leads him. It inspires him to work: it may inspire a whole life, as it did Dante's, and so give us the *Divine Comedy*. But, is it a true compliment to the woman herself? I am not going to answer this question, but I want to suggest it to you. Which seems to pay the truer homage—Dante looking through Beatrice, or Othello looking at Desdemona; Dante narrating the return of his lady to the angels, or King Lear with Cordelia dead in his arms?

Another point. Hitherto I have been concerned with the people whom Dante liked very much—with the woman, in fact, whom he loved most in the world. But how did he behave to people whom he did not much like, or only knew slightly— to his "bowing acquaintance," if I may use the phrase? Much as we do? No. Much worse. I do not wish to praise our own times overmuch, but this particular point brings out our strength and Dante's weakness. He was anxious for sublime thoughts; and if his acquaintances did not inspire him, he had no further interest in them, and treated them with discourtesy. He soared higher than we can; but he could sink lower. Here is an episode from *The New Life*, which will make clear what I mean.

One day, Dante was staring at Beatrice as she sat in church. Between them sat another lady, who, being in the direct line of the poet's glance, naturally concluded that he was staring at her. Dante determined to profit by her mistake. He was desirous of keeping his love for Beatrice a secret. People knew that he was in love—he had already said so in a poem—but they did not know with whom. "What a good plan," he thought, "if I pretend to be in love with this lady, and so throw gossips on the wrong track. I shall be able to sigh and look pale, and yet no breath of scandal will touch Beatrice." In pursuit of this ingenious plan, he paid a certain amount of attention to the new lady, and wrote her a few poems. All went well, until she had occasion to leave Florence, and so placed the poet in an awkward position. He ought to have been overwhelmed with grief at her departure, but he did not care a straw. The lady was perfectly welcome to leave Florence, and to stop away from it for ever. His spirits remained admirable, but how was he to justify them to her and to her friends? I must again commend his ingenuity. He wrote her another poem, in which he said that his grief at losing her was so tremendous that he showed no outward signs of it at all. So the lady went, in full belief that the young poet loved her; and not long afterwards he found another lady, and began playing the same game with her. He wrote so many poems to this second lady, and sighed to her so much, that he embarrassed the poor creature, and the matter came round to the ears of Beatrice. Beatrice was much annoyed. She seems to have had no idea that Dante loved her, and that these ladies were simply shields to conceal his love. She only saw that here was a young man who was persecuting a girl by undue attentions, and on that ground she withdrew her salutation from him. In modern phraseology she "cut" him, and surely he deserved it.

Now, the earnest student of Dante—who is sometimes rather an alarming person—will accuse me of flippancy on this point.

He will say, and truly, that secrecy and subterfuge in love was a literary tradition of the time. True. Yet such a tradition shows a real defect in the minds of the men who adopted it. Let us suppose that Dante did invent the story. The fact remains that he is not the least ashamed of it, and has no notion that he is depicting himself as a "cad." Beatrice is the only woman to whom he owes loyalty—Beatrice, who leads his thoughts heavenwards. He can be false to all others, if he is thus enabled to be true to her. What duties has he to these other ladies? They cannot give him the keys of heaven. What duties has he to people whom he does not passionately love or intimately know? None. And here, I think, is the real defect in his noble character: he cannot be fair to the commonplace.

We of today—and I count Shakespeare one of us—try, however unsuccessfully, to look *at* people, not through them. We see our acquaintances as a throng of living creatures, some of whom are tedious, others unpleasing, others positively repugnant, but all of whom are living creatures, not to be injured wantonly. But Dante, in *The New Life*, looked through people; and through most of them he saw nothing, and through one of them he saw God. Why should he trouble over the dull majority? Those sublime visions of his, to which none of us can attain, seem to entail these unmanly lapses, to which none of us, I hope, will sink. His answer to the question, "How shall I behave to the people whom I know?" is quite clear, but not, I think, quite satisfactory.

Up to now, we have been examining his personal relations. Now let us examine his relations to humanity, and find out how he behaved to the people whom he did not know. I want to make it clear that I am turning to another aspect of him, for otherwise you will think I am contradicting all that I have just said. In a few minutes I shall be praising his tolerance, his rectitude, his magnanimity—qualities that I have just denied to him. But between a man's behavior to the people he knows and the people he doesn't know, there is often a wide gulf. Milton was tolerant when he wrote the *Areopagitica*, but it did not prevent him bullying his daughters. Carlyle was mag' nanimous when he wrote the *French Revolution,* yet he grum' bled to Mrs. Carlyle when the cock crew or the study chimney smoked. And so Dante, though he did not behave well to people who bored him, would have laid down his life for humanity as a whole. He loved humanity as it was never loved again until the eighteenth century. His books are all written to make people better; his life was one effort to guide the human assemblage into happiness and peace. His was no arm' chair devotion; he suffered for his ideals, he remained in exile for them; on their account he died. History has few spectacles more inspiring than Dante's public life. He is to be classed in the little band of men who were absolutely unselfish, and of that band he is by far the most talented member. If a man is unselfish and a genius, he has a very sure claim on immortality. Dante was both, and perhaps his position is unique in the history of the world.

He loved humanity. Then how did he propose to help it? He tells us in the second of his great books, *The Empire.* But be' fore we examine *The Empire,* I must make rather a long digres' sion, for if I do not, the book will puzzle us completely. I must point out a second great difference between medieval and modern thought.

Man consists of body and soul. So the middle ages thought, and so we think today. We agree with them. We believe that a material element and a spiritual element go to make us up. All religion, all philosophy, all science, acknowledges the fact. There are within us these two things. But—and here comes the difference—the middle ages thought that between the body and the soul one can draw a distinct line, that it is possible to say which of our actions is material, which spiritual. Body and soul, they thought, are as distinct as the land and the sea, or the earth and the sky, or the night and the day. Matter on this side; spirit on that, and no connection between them. Each has its own duties, its own functions, its own laws.

Now I need hardly point out to you how different our attitude is today. He is a rash man who would assert where the body ends and where the soul begins. Some things are certainly material, just as the sky is certainly dark at midnight. Some things are certainly spiritual, just as the sky is certainly bright at noon. But between the two certainties there intervene the infinite gradations of twilight and dawn. Look at the sky in the evening. Can you be positive whether it is light or dark? Look at an invalid. Can you be positive whether it is his body or soul that is diseased? Most modern thinkers realize that the barrier eludes definition. It is there, but you cannot put your finger on it, be you theologian or biologist. It is there, but it is impalpable; and the wisest of our age, Goethe for example, and Walt Whitman, have not attempted to find it, but have essayed the more human task of harmonizing the realms that it divides. Not so the men of the middle ages, to whom we will now return. They desired not to harmonize the body and the soul, but to find out where one stopped and where the other began. Matter on this side: spirit on that, and no connection between them. On the one side, Adam, in whom all die; on the other, Christ, in whom all shall be made alive. Both body and soul are made by God, but he has destined the body for mortality and corruption, and the soul he has destined for immortality. He has linked them together for a little space, to journey through this life in unwilling partnership. But their goals are different.

And having these beliefs, the men of the middle ages naturally turned for help to the greatest event in their past history. Surely Christ, during his ministry on earth, would have told them what to do. In this important question of the division between matter and spirit, surely he would have left them some example, some guide? And surely he had. When the disciples asked him whether they should pay tribute to the Roman tax collector, he had answered, "Render unto Caesar the things that are Caesar's, and unto God the things that are God's." Render unto Caesar the things of the body, and unto God the things of the soul. In other words, Christ had acknowledged the civil power, and Christians must do the same. It is to the government that we must look to guide us in material affairs.

So far, there is nothing fantastic in the medieval attitude. But they carried their reasoning further, and so plunged into fantasy. They concluded that Christ by the mere mention of Caesar had given divine approval to the Roman Empire, and appointed it as the peculiar guardian of men upon earth. They reflected that Christ had consented in his infancy to be numbered in the census of the Emperor Augustus; that the Apostle St. Paul had boasted he was a Roman citizen, and had appealed from the Jewish law courts to the judgment seat of Nero. The feeling grew that the Roman Empire had a divine mission to govern men's bodies all over the world; and that the Roman Emperor, though he might not know it, was ruling as the agent of God.

This in itself is a strange enough notion. But stranger is to come. When the Roman Empire was destroyed by the barbarians, there sprang up in course of time a *fictitious substitute* called the Holy Roman Empire, which was supposed to carry on its divine mission. As a matter of fact, it did nothing of the sort; you may sum it up as a gigantic fraud. The old Empire really had ruled the world; the Holy Roman Empire only ruled central Europe. The old Empire really had been Roman; the Holy Roman Empire, in spite of its name, was Teutonic. The old Empire may have been pagan, but it brought peace upon earth. The Holy Roman Empire may have been Christian, but it brought little but war. It is a fraud, and yet it is important, because it appealed to that medieval belief in a sharp division between the body and the soul. Here was the Emperor, God's agent in governing men's bodies. And here was the Pope—for now the Pope comes forward—God's agent in governing men's souls. The Emperor would say to a man "do this," and he would do it. The Pope would say "think this," and a man would think it. Emperor and Pope would together illustrate Christ's precept, "Render unto Caesar the things that are Caesar's, and unto God the things that are God's." Here my digression ends. Let me sum it up in tabular form. Medieval thought divides a man into (i) the body, which dies, and which while it lives must take its orders from the Emperor; and (ii) the soul, which is immortal, and which while it remains on earth must take its orders from the Pope. And now let us return to Dante.

Perhaps you will ask, "Why have we ever left him? What have these fantastic ideas to do with the great Florentine poet?" My answer is, that though you and I do not believe in the Holy Roman Empire, Dante did; and that it seemed to him the visible

channel of God's grace, and the only means of helping humanity on earth. If you said to Dante, "This Holy Roman Empire
—it isn't a bit what you say it is. The Emperor's a German
princeling; he daren't even come to Italy; he is not even a good
man; the whole affair's nothing but a pretence"—if you said
this, Dante would reply. "The Holy Roman Empire is ordained
by God." If you continued, "But the Emperor and Pope have
even quarrelled;" he would reply, "The Emperor and the Pope
have both erred, but the institution, the Holy Roman Empire,
is ordained by God." Dante was not a socialist. Far from it.
But his attitude can be compared to that of some socialists of
today. He would not tinker at existing affairs, in the hope of
improving them gradually. He must have a theory, and put it
into practice at once, no matter how inopportune the moment
was. He would save men through the Holy Roman Empire.
Some socialists would save them through equality. The Holy
Roman Empire was a dream; yet he spoke of it as ordained by
God: equality, so far, is a dream, yet socialists speak of it as a
natural right. Not for a moment am I blaming these passionate
beliefs in a brighter future. But they are beliefs, not facts. They
are not justified by history; and the men who hold them occasionally ignore the present and misread the past. So Dante
did; so, I sometimes think, do certain socialists now.

Well, grant Dante his Holy Roman Empire. What is he
going to do with it? I will quote from his treatise, *The Empire,*
the force of whose title you will now see. Granting that the
Emperor is supreme, how will he lead us into earthly felicity?
In the first place, he will give us peace.

"It is by leisure," he says, "that each man grows sensible
and wise; and as it is for one man, so it is for all men: only
by universal peace can humanity advance to its goal. When
the shepherds watched their flocks by night, they heard not of

riches, nor pleasure, nor honor, nor health, nor strength, nor beauty: but of peace; for the celestial soldiery proclaimed Glory to God in the highest, and on earth Peace and Goodwill towards men."

There is nothing medieval or out of date in this. Dante's words are as true today as when he wrote them. He never speaks of the beauties of war, like Ruskin or Rudyard Kipling. He has fought in battles himself, he knows what they are like. Peace is the only educational atmosphere for humanity; and peace can only be ensured by an international power, who shall keep the nations from flying at each other's throats. He called this power the Emperor, we call it the Hague Conference; but he, like ourselves, saw the necessity of an arbitrator, to whose decision the jingo capitalist and the jingo demagogue must bow, and under whose far-reaching power the myriads of the earth shall dwell together in unity.

And this brings me to his next point. When the Emperor has given us peace, what are we to do with it? We are to dwell together *in unity*; we are to realize the potentialities of the human race *as a whole*. Dante had a firm belief—you can call it right or wrong—that the whole is greater than the sum of its parts; that humanity is greater than the individuals who go to make it up; and that God would receive with a peculiar joy the praise of a united world. The belief verges into mysticism, but you may find it, though in different words, in writers of today, such as Tolstoy and Walt Whitman. Just as the city expresses something that the individual cannot express, just as the nation expresses something beyond the scope of the city; so humanity, were it ever united by peace, would express some-thing far beyond the scope of either, and re-enter the terrestrial paradise, which was lost at the primal disunion. The terrestrial

paradise is Dante's phrase for the highest earthly bliss, and the
Emperor will guide us to it. Of the celestial paradise, in which
humanity returns to God and has knowledge of the unknowable, he will speak later.

And by the side of this common goal, Dante admits an individual goal. He believes in national and local life; his Emperor
is not to introduce a gray cosmopolitanism. Mankind united
is not to mean that men are dull. The Emperor is to suppress
war, not personality. Our bodies are not to be absorbed into a
machine on earth, any more than our souls will be absorbed
into a machine in heaven. Even in the next life we shall retain
our personality, so why should we lose it in this? It was harmony, not monotony, at which Dante aimed; and I wish I
could say the same for the social reformers of today. These,
excellent as they are, seem to see no path between monotony
and war—between the bloodiness of Mr. Rudyard Kipling and
the greyness of Mr. Sidney Webb. It is only the poet who
points upwards, and offers humanity the example of the stars.
Men, like stars, differ from each other in brilliancy. Let them
also imitate the stars' harmonious motion.

> Happy, O men, were ye,
> If but your souls were swayed
> By love, as heaven is swayed

—sings the Latin poet, whom Dante quotes. Mankind shall
attain salvation through harmony; and the love of humanity,
like the love of Beatrice, has led us to the love of God.

It may interest you to know that this is not mere "fine
writing." Dante actually suffered for these ideals, unpractical
as they may seem to you. Early in his exile, when Florence and
all Italy were distracted by war, he thought that the Emperor

of his dreams was at hand. Henry of Luxembourg, known to history as the Emperor Henry VII, invaded Italy to restore peace and to establish the Holy Roman Empire, in fact as well as in theory. He was a high-souled monarch, and for a time Dante was hopeful. The Emperor occupied Milan, and advanced southward; and the poet, with increasing excitement, worked in his interests and execrated his enemies. Florence, Dante's own city, beat the Emperor back. The expedition failed, the Emperor died, and things were even worse for Dante than they had been before. I am not dealing with his life, but this incident so clearly shows that he practiced what he preached, that it cannot be omitted. In all that Dante writes we have a feeling of security. It may be tiresome and it may be wrong, but we may be certain that he really meant it, and would have died to put it into practice.

We may take it, then, that his book *The Empire* is a practical offering to humanity, and deals with a question the interest of which is perennial, namely, the destiny of our race on earth. Dante believes that as yet we have accomplished only a fraction of what we could accomplish; that we have fallen short of the will of God—to put it in his words; or, to put it in modern words, that we are only at the beginning of our evolution. He believes that for this accomplishment we need peace and unselfishness; and that progress begins when a man turns from the pleasures he must enjoy alone to the pleasures that he can share with his fellows.

> *True love hath this, differing from gold or clay,*
> *That to divide is not to take away*

—wrote Shelley, 500 years afterwards, directly echoing Dante's words. Repeatedly does Dante warn us against greed, against setting our desires where companionship is one with loss; that is to say, against too great desire for personal possessions. Don't label him as a socialist. He has a profound respect for property and rank; it is harmony, not equality at which he aims; and the evils against which he fought are political rather than economic. But compare him to the socialists in this: he has a passionate belief that things are not all right as they are, and that all is *not* for the best in the best of all possible worlds. The best would come when the divergent types of men acknowledge some element that makes them one, when national life is combined with international peace. This state of material happiness Dante figures by the earthly paradise, where Adam and Eve dwelt before greed and selfishness had entered; and hither, he tells us, we shall be led by the Emperor, appointed for that purpose by God. Here of course the glorious fabric of his aspiration falls. There never was such a person as Dante's Emperor, and there never will be. The Hague Conference, feeble as it is, has more international power than Henry of Luxembourg, or the other German potentates for whose coming the poet so ardently longed. The machinery through which he would achieve his Utopia is impossible; but the Utopia remains as not only one of the most beautiful schemes of the kind, but also as one of the wisest. It would be hard to find a more just discrimination be-tween the forces that make men alike and the forces that make men different—between the centripetal power that may lead to monotony, and the centrifugal power that may lead to war. These powers are reconciled in the orbits of the stars; and Dante's first and last word to us is that we should imitate the celestial harmony.

I have spent so much time examining Dante's attitude towards men, that I must be comparatively brief over the

question that he deemed all important—his attitude towards
God. To him this question is supreme; the things that he knew
seemed of little importance, when compared with the Unknowable. Beatrice and the Holy Roman Empire were not ends in
themselves, but alike means, by which he could approach the
Divine. And thus the *Divine Comedy* is in every sense the
greatest book that he wrote—not only because it contains
his best poetry, but because it is about the subject that he
thought greatest, our behavior to the Unknowable. The *Divine
Comedy*, like the *Pilgrim's Progress*, takes the form of a journey
to God. Dante imagines himself as travelling through the three
spiritual kingdoms of Hell, Purgatory, and Heaven, until he
actually sees the Love that lies behind the Universe and moves
the stars—until he actually knows the Unknowable.

[*Mr. Forster here explained, by means of a diagram, the imaginative
journey which Dante describes in his book.*]

Perhaps the quickest way of getting some idea of the *Divine
Comedy* is to realize Dante's conception of the universe, and
of that I now propose to give a short account. In his mind,
cosmography and theology were closely connected; he believed that one could step out of the material world into the
spiritual, as we believe that we can step out of one room into
another; hell was really under his feet, heaven was really over
his head among the stars. He is perfectly definite; it is even
possible to draw a diagram of the universe as he conceived it.

His conception, then, was as follows: In the middle of all
things he placed the earth. He believed that the earth was
round, but he also believed that it was motionless, and that
the sun and the stars revolved round it. He conceived of Hell
as a great funnel extending to the earth's center, and at the

center he placed the Devil. On the opposite side of the earth, *i.e.*, in the Southern Hemisphere, he thought there was a great mountain—Purgatory—where those souls who would ulti' mately go to Heaven purged away their sins. Heaven con' sisted of ten circles, the first eight being ruled by the sun, the moon, the five planets, and the fixed stars; the ninth being the *primum mobile,* or moving heaven, which communicated mo' tion to the heavens inside it, and so caused them to revolve round the earth; and the tenth, or Empyrean, being outside time and space altogether, and the abode of reality and of God.

Such was the framework on which he built the *Divine Comedy*—quite definite, and he is equally definite as to time. He imagines himself entering Hell on Good Friday, rising from the dead on Easter Sunday, as did Christ, and entering Purga' tory; entering Heaven on Easter Tuesday, and concluding his vision on the Friday after Easter. The action takes a week. As for the date: it is supposed to be the year 1300—the year that modern historians fix as the end of the middle ages. Of course the book itself was written some time after 1300, and thus Dante often refers to events that had actually happened, such as the death of Henry VII, under the guise of prophecy.

As Good Friday approaches then, Dante imagines himself on the surface of the earth, pursued by three wild beasts, who typify the sins of luxury, avarice, and pride. From these beasts he is rescued by the Latin poet, Virgil, who had been sent to his help by a "lady from heaven," *i.e.*, by Beatrice, and who tells him that only by entering the gates of Hell will he get free. The two poets accordingly enter Hell, whose funnel is divided into nine circles, which increase in torment as they decrease in size. This is the most famous part of the poem, and the dramatic episodes of Paolo and Francesca, of Farinata degli Uberti, and of Count Ugolino, are known to thousands who have never followed Dante through the less exciting realms of Purgatory and Heaven. The horror of Hell reaches its climax in the apparition of the Devil, a monster with three mouths, in each of which he champs a sinner. The center mouth holds, as we might expect, Judas Iscariot, but the contents of the other two mouths are somewhat surprising. The sufferers are Brutus and Cassius. We are bewildered until we reflect that Brutus and Cassius murdered Julius Caesar, the founder of the Empire, just as Judas Iscariot murdered Christ, the founder of the Church; and that Dante would desire to punish those who did not render unto Caesar the things that were Caesar's, quite as severely as those who did not render unto God the things that are God's.

A grotesque episode succeeds. The poets, who have now approached the center of gravity, take hold of the Devil and begin to climb down his legs; presently they pass the center of gravity, and find themselves climbing *up* his legs, towards his feet, and after a toilsome ascent, reach the surface of the earth at a point exactly opposite to that at which they went in.

The second part of the poem now commences. Dante and Virgil find themselves standing at the foot of the mountain of Purgatory, which is washed by the waters of the Southern Ocean. It is dark; then the sun rises, and over the sea a ship approaches, full of redeemed souls who land in the dewy meadows and hasten to their purgation. From the smoke of Hell, Dante has passed to the purity of an earthly morning; and if I had to describe the atmosphere of Purgatory in one word, I think I would say "cleanliness." Not "rapture," or "knowledge," or "love"; those will be found in Heaven—just the state of cleanliness, through which we must pass before other sensations are possible.

Purgatory consists of seven terraces, on each of which souls undergo an expiation appropriate to their sin. On the summit of the mountain, the highest point on the terrestrial globe, lies the earthly paradise, the goal of our highest earthly effort. You will remember Dante's allusion to it in *The Empire*. And here Virgil can go no further. He is not a Christian, and cannot guide his friend to the higher mysteries. In a scene of great pathos, the two poets part, and Virgil goes back to his place in Hell, not to the circles of torment, but to a border region reserved for those gentle heathen who have died without the knowledge of Christ. Now Dante sees a great procession, typifying harmony of the Empire and the Church. In the procession is a shrouded figure who finally unveils herself; it is Beatrice. Thus the whole of Dante's life is, as it were, joining up; the promise he made in *The New Life* is fulfilled; the teachings of *The Empire* is illustrated by the procession; and the Poet, who has no more concern with material affairs, leaves the earth altogether and, with Beatrice as his guide, rises through the encircling belt of fire to Heaven.

We have come to the third part of the poem. Those readers who chiefly admire Dante's dramatic power will find this, the climax of the *Divine Comedy*, disappointing; in the realm of bliss we are concerned with sensations rather than with personalities. But those who have followed the poet's spiritual yearnings with due attention and with sympathy will find here a sublime fulfillment, and will perhaps think that the "Heaven" contains the most wonderful words ever written by the hand of man. Dante's account of spiritual happiness and of God has a curious effect on one, which I can only describe as "authorita-tive"; it seems as if he really did know, as if he has really been outside time and space, and has come back to us with news. To quote his teacher, Aristotle, he has really made "the impossible credible." I have already described the ten heavenly spheres through which he and Beatrice pass, and I will not say more about them now; the poem concludes with a hymn to the Virgin Mary, who in her turn intercedes for him with God. God appears to him as Light; but at the last moment Dante's gaze is strengthened; he sees something even more vivid than light. Three rainbow circles glow against the radiance of Eternity, and in the center of one of them is the image of a human face.

The vision closes. Dante returns to the earth. He has seen the Love that lies behind the universe and moves the stars.

Here my paper ends. I am afraid that you will find it a little remote, a little hard to follow in parts. There are several reasons for this, one being that it is not a good paper. A second reason, less painful to myself, must also be taken into account, and I will lay it before you, as a conclusion. Briefly put, it is this: Dante tries to look at human affairs with the eyes of God. His standpoint is not in this world. He views us from an immense height, as a man views a plain from a mountain. We, down on the plain, have our own notions of what the plain is like, and at times we reject Dante's description of it as false. We feel that by his very elevation he is not qualified to judge; and that he knows no more about us than we know about the canals in Mars. Here we are wrong. Dante knows a great deal about us. He was himself a soldier, a politician, a scholar, and a lover, and he never forgets his experiences. We are wrong, and yet it is natural that we should find him hard to follow, for his standpoint is not one that we find congenial today. Shakespeare stands among us. Though he has walked into Paradise with Queen Katharine, and into Hell with Macbeth, he has also walked with Falstaff into the taverns of Eastcheap. Though Shakespeare is a sublime poet, he is also a jolly good fellow; and if he walked into this room this evening, we should be very glad to see him. But Dante stands with unwavering feet upon the Empyrean, proclaiming the will of God; and though his words are full of love and beauty, they gather a certain terror as they pass through the interspaces, and they fall with a certain strangeness upon our ears. We enjoy reading Dante. But if *he* walked into the room this evening, we should make all haste to walk out of it.

1908

The Beauty of Life

The subject of this article—a magnificent subject—was suggested by the editor.* "Would it not be possible," he wrote,
"to illustrate the beauty and the wonder of life, to show that
they are always manifest wheresoever and howsoever life and
force are manifested?" But unfortunately it is a subject that
could only be treated by a poet—by a poet who was at the
same time a man of action; whose enthusiasm had stood the
test of hard facts; whose vision of things as they ought to be
had been confirmed and strengthened by his experience of
things as they are—by such a poet as Walt Whitman.

> I believe a leaf of grass is no less than the journey-work
>   of the stars,
> And the pismire is equally perfect, and a grain of sand,
>   and the egg of the wren,
> And the tree toad is a chef-d'oeuvre for the highest,
> And the running blackberry would adorn the parlors of
>   heaven.

* The editor of The Working Men's College Journal.

Whitman knew what life was. He was not praising its beauty from an arm-chair. He had been through all that makes it hideous to most men—poverty, the battlefield, the hospitals —and yet could believe that life, whether as a whole or in detail, was perfect, that beauty is manifest wherever life is manifested. He could glorify the absurd and the repulsive; he could catalogue the parts of a machine from sheer joy that a machine has so many parts; he could sing not only of farming and fishing, but also of "leather-dressing, coach-making, boiler-making, rope-twisting, distilling, sign-painting, lime-burning, cotton-picking, electro-plating, electro-typing, stereo-typing"; one of the lines in one of his poems runs thus! He went the "whole hog" in fact, and he ought to be writing this article.

But most of us have to be content with a less vigorous attitude. We may follow the whole-hogger at moments, and no doubt it is our fault and not his when we don't follow him; but we cannot follow him always. We may agree that the egg of the wren is perfect, that the running blackberry would adorn the parlors of heaven; but what about the pismire and the tree toad? Do they seem equally perfect? Farming is wonderful because it probes the mystery of the earth; fishing, because it probes the sea. But what about "electro-plating, electro-typing, stereo-typing"? To most of us life seems partly beautiful, partly ugly; partly wonderful, partly dull; there is sunshine in it, but there are also clouds, and we cannot always see that the clouds have silver linings. What are we to do? How is the average man to make the best of what he does see? For it is no good him pretending to see what he doesn't.

One might define the average educated man as optimist by instinct, pessimist by conviction. Few of us are thorough optimists; we have seen too much misery to declare glibly, that all is for the best in the best of all possible worlds. Nations arming to the teeth; the growing cleavage between rich and poor; these symptoms, after nineteen hundred years of Christianity, are not calculated to comfort an intelligent person. But we are not thorough pessimists either. We are absolutely certain, though we cannot prove it, that life is beautiful. Fine weather—to take what may seem a small example; fine weather during the whole of a day; the whole city cheered by blue sky and sunshine. What a marvellous blessing that is! The thorough pessimist may reply, that city weather is more often wet, and that a fine day is only a scrap in the midst of squalor. Possibly. But it is a scrap that glows like a jewel. If we hope for a great deal of beauty in life, we may be disappointed; nature has not cut her stuff thus; she cannot be bothered about us to this extent. But we may hope for *intensity* of beauty; that is absolutely certain, and never, since the beginning of time, has a man gone through life without moments of overwhelming joy. Perhaps, Mr. X., you will contradict this. But can you contradict it from your own experience? Can you sincerely say, "Never since I was born have I had one moment of overwhelming joy?" Don't reply, "I've been happy, but think of poor Mr. Y." It's no answer; for if Mr. Y. is questioned, he too will assuredly reply, "I've been happy," perhaps adding, "but think of poor Mr. X."

Here then is what one may call the irreducible minimum, the inalienable dowry of humanity: Beauty in scraps. It may seem a little thing after the comprehensive ecstasies of Whitman, but it is certain; it is for all men in all times, and we couldn't avoid it even if we wanted to. The beauty of the fine day amid dingy weather; the beauty of the unselfish action amid selfishness; the beauty of friendship amidst indifference: we cannot go through life without experiencing these things, they are as certain as the air in the lungs. Some people have luck, and get more happiness than others, but every one gets some-thing. And therefore, however pessimistic we are in our con-victions, however sure we are that civilization is going to the dogs on account of those abominable—(here insert the name of the political party that you most dislike)—; we yet remain optimists by instinct; we personally have had glorious times, and may have them again.

That is the position, as it appears to the average modern man. To him life is not all gold, as Whitman would have it; it is not even strung on a golden thread, as the great Victorian poets would have it, but it is pure gold in parts—it contains scraps of inexpressible beauty. And it is in his power to make a great deal of the scraps. He can, in the first place, practice cheerfulness. He can dwell on the wonderful moments of his existence, rather than on the dull hours that too often separate those moments. He can realize that quality is more precious than quantity. He can—to put it in plain English—stop grum-bling. Grumbling is the very devil. It pretends that the whole of life is dull, and that the wonderful moments are not worth considering. Dante, a man of the soundest sense, puts grumblers deep into Hell. They lie at the bottom of a dirty pond, and their words bubble to the surface saying, "Once we were sullen in the sweet sunlit air. Now we are sullen in the mud." Of course grumbling springs from a very real outside evil—from all the undoubted sorrow that there is in the world, and that no optimism can explain away. But it always flows far from its source. It pretends that the whole world is sorrow, a view that is as false as it is depressing; and if we sometimes resent the shallow optimist, who calls "peace" where there is no

peace, we may equally resent the shallow grumbler, who complains of war before war is declared, and who is either re-
gretting the disasters of the past or expecting disaster in the
future. To such a man, life can have no beauty. He can never
open his eyes and look at the present, which may be full of
sweet air and sunlight. If it is night, he cannot remember that
the sun set yesterday and may rise tomorrow. He goes through
existence pretending that he is at the bottom of a mud pond,
as indeed he is, but it is a pond of his own digging. One must
distinguish between such a man and the pessimist. The pessimist denies that life as a whole is beautiful, but he never denies
the existence of beauty. Great men have been pessimists: Lu-
cretius, Michelangelo, Cromwell, Thomas Hardy. But the
grumbler denies everything, and no grumbler ever became a
great man; he would not think it worth while.

If cheerfulness is one great help towards seeing the beauty in
life, courage is certainly another. The average man needs to be
just a little braver. He loses so much happiness through what
might be termed "minor cowardices." Why are we so afraid of
doing the "wrong thing," of wearing the "wrong clothes," of
knowing the "wrong people," of pronouncing the names of
artists or musicians wrongly? What in the name of Beauty does
it matter? Why don't we trust ourselves more and the con-
ventions less? If we first of all dress ourselves appropriately and
fashionably, and then fill our minds with fashionable thoughts,
and then go out in search of Romance with a fashionable and
appropriate friend, is it likely that we shall find Romance? Is
it likely that Life will give herself away to us, unless we also
give ourselves away? There are occasions when one must be
conventional—one's bread and butter often depends upon it;
but there are occasions when one need not be, and on those oc-

casions life opens her wonder-house. That is why one's happiest moments usually come on holidays. It is not that the surroundings are different. It is that we are different. We have not to pretend that we are valuable members of society—that if it wasn't for us, electro-plating, electro-typing, stereo-typing, and the rest would come to an end. We have not to impress people by our ability or taste. We have merely to be ourselves, and like what we like. A little courage does the trick. The world is touched at once with a magical glow; the sea, the sky, the mountains, our fellow-creatures, are all transfigured, and we return to work with unforgettable memories.

To sum up. A few great men—mostly poets—have found life absolutely beautiful, in all its aspects. Other great men have found it threaded, as it were, on a beautiful chain. But the average man finds that it is beautiful in parts only, and it is his attitude that is touched upon in this article. No definition of the Beauty of Life is offered, because it is "this to me and that to thee." Some people find it reflected in pictures and poems; others, going to life direct, find it in human intercourse or in scenery; while a few have even found it in the higher truths of mathematics. But everyone, except the grumbler and perhaps the coward, finds it somewhere; and if the article contains anything, it contains a few tips which may make beauty easier to find. Be cheerful. Be courageous. Don't bother too much about "developing the esthetic sense," as books term it, for if the heart and the brain are kept clean, the esthetic sense will develop of itself. In your spare time, never study a subject that bores you, however important other people tell you it is; but choose out of the subjects that don't bore you, the subject that seems to you most important, and study that. You may say, "Oh, yes, it's jolly easy to preach like this." But it's also jolly easy to practice. The above precepts contain nothing heroical, nothing that need disturb our daily existence or diminish our salaries. They aren't difficult, they are just a few tips that may help us to see the wonders, physical and spiritual, by which we are surrounded. Modern civilization does not lead us away from Romance, but it does try to lead us past it, and we have to keep awake. We must insist on going to look round the corner now and then, even if other people think us a little queer, for as likely as not something beautiful lies round the corner. And if we insist, we may have a reward that is even greater than we expected, and see for a moment with the eyes of a poet —may see the universe, not merely beautiful in scraps, but beautiful everywhere and for ever.

> *The sun and stars that float in the open air,*
> *The apple-shaped earth and we upon it, surely the drift*
>   *of them is something grand.*
> *I do not know what it is except that it is grand, and*
>   *that it is happiness.*

One final tip; read Walt Whitman. He is the true optimist —not the professional optimist who shuts his eyes and shirks, and whose palliatives do more harm than good, but one who has seen and suffered much and yet rejoices. He is not a philosopher or a theologian; he cannot answer the ultimate question, and tell us what life is. But he is absolutely certain that it is grand, that it is happiness, and that "wherever life and force are manifested, beauty is manifested."

1911

The Functions of Literature in War-Time

Let me begin by anticipating an objection. It is generally said that war is not the time for reading books: we ought to be doing something else—either serving at the front or fighting that other battle against poverty on which our existence as a nation equally depends. With that objection I agree. War is not a time for reading books, and I am not suggesting that any-one should read them. I am going to justify literature along an-other line, and suggest that we should not read, but remember what we've read, re-think, re-feel. There is a great danger that people like ourselves may be ashamed of our peaceful and lei-sured past, and try to shovel it out of sight. The past has gone, it is true, and nothing resembling it will ever return in our life-time. But we can still re-think it and re-feel, and by so doing

Paper read to the Working Men's College Old Students' Club on 13 February 1915.

176

can face the present. Books do not cease to exist because we have no time to read them. We Old Students have—most luckily—been granted time in the past, and I know that I am speaking this evening to friends who have not only read, but read properly; who, like myself, have faith in the inspired utterances of great men, and believe that books are not merely the solace of a peaceful hour or the occasion for cultured talk, but spiritual possessions that survive in the hour of war. How are we to use those possessions best? That is the subject of my remarks—not "What shall we read?" but "What shall we remember?" I may be a bit preachy, I'm afraid, but in the discussion you can preach at me, and get back a bit of your own; and, at all events, we shan't have left all the preaching to the parson, which is something.

Now just a word on the sort of literature that one is supposed to read at the present moment—the pamphlets, books, poems, etc., that deal more or less with the war. I am not speaking of the press. One must ignore the press in any serious discussion. The newspapers have behaved as one knew they would behave. They have taken advantage of the crisis to lower their tone even further; they have grown more sensational, more hysterical, more heedless than ever of the truth; they have pretended with even more than their old impudence that they voice what is best in the nation. It is natural that they should behave like this: they are commercial undertakings, and must act accordingly; but we—we who want to keep decent, we who want England to keep going spiritually as well as physically—we also must act accordingly, and ignore whatever they say. I don't, then, think of the press when speaking of current literature: I speak of the more reputable literary products—signed pamphlets, poems, etc.—which proceed from men of more or less eminence, and try to tell us what we should think or feel about the war.

Well, for my own part I don't find those are of much use either, because they are inspired not by emotion, but by excite-ment. Little good comes out of excitement. It's a function of the nerves, not of the heart, and most of our writers have yielded to it. They have followed where one hoped they would have led. They echo one's own little sensations instead of trans-forming them. When we go to them, we find just our own feverish minds, and one goes to literature for something bigger. There are exceptions. Shaw's Manifesto in the first place. I have not read all of it. I could not. But despite its egoism and conceit, despite its heartless, tinny quality, it has the great merit of being a discussion; and at a moment like this, when there is a foolish instinct to stifle discussion for fear it encourages the Germans, a man like Shaw is more valuable than usual. And of far higher value are Clutton Brock's *Thoughts on the War,* a little book of noble patriotism and noble humanity, Professor Dicey's *How We Ought to Feel about the War,* G. Lowes Dickinson's *The War and a Way Out,* and Romain Rolland's *Above the Battlefield*; while in poetry we have Masefield's sin-cere and beautiful elegy, "August, 1914," and Albert Allen's "Labour War Chants." Writers such as these are inspired by emotion, not excitement. They feel as keenly as any of us, but on a higher level; they have purged their work from selfishness and vulgarity, and consequently can help us. But they are ex-ceptions. The literature of the moment is really represented by a mind the calibre of Harold Begbie's. Let us leave it with him and him with it, and turn to the literature of the past.

The books we have read in the past influence life in two

ways—directly and indirectly. The direct influence is not important. You can, of course, extract a code of behavior from the books you read, and have your favorite quotations and favorite characters. There is no harm in doing this, but you are getting nothing that you did not possess before. If you seek peace, you can find arguments in books for peace, and if you seek not peace but a sword, you can find arguments for the sword. If you are a humanitarian you can quote "One touch of Nature makes the whole world kin," and if you are cynic you can complete the quotation. You will find just what you want. That is to say, the direct influence of literature on your conduct will be slight. You'd have been the same person anyhow.

It is otherwise with the indirect influence. That can be immense, and I would appeal to it now. Indirectly, literature can help us to be noble and gentle and brave, and this not by any particular passage, but by its general impression. To take an example. At the conclusion of *Othello* what impression remains? A sense of fine poetry? Partly. A sense of pity for Desdemona, and of indignation against Iago? Partly. But much more a general sense that we have been in a world much greater than our own. A world of greatness, the world of the spirit, that helps us to endure danger and ingratitude and answer a lie with the truth; the world that we look for also in religion—that is what literature offers to those who have read her aright; that is her indirect influence upon life. It matters not what our favorite writers are. I should begin my own list with Shakespeare, Wordsworth, and Dostoevsky, but it doesn't matter. Whatever we have read, the *general sense of greatness* remains, and it was never more needed than it is today.

In the first place it helps us not to hate the Germans too much. Literature does not teach us that war is either right or wrong—these are questions outside her competence—but she does teach us that hatred and revenge are wrong, because they cloud the spirit. It is not easy to love one's enemies—for my own part I find it impossible—but one needn't be proud of not loving them, and she does exhort us to that much. Love is an emotion, hatred an excitement, and she is against excitement all along the line. If war were only death, there would be little to say against it, for we must all die, and preferably die young; but war is also hatred, a narrowing of the spirit. The soldier seldom hates; his job doesn't give him the time, and he has, from the technical point of view, an interest and even a sympathy with the fellow opposite; the soldier can come out of his trench on Christmas Day. But though the soldier does not hate, the stay-at-home does. From the clubs and drawing-rooms, and, above all, from the press pours a torrent of hatred which scarcely any eminent man has had the courage to rebuke. Literature does rebuke it. Her position is impregnable. She is neither pro-German nor anti-German, because the great men who built her up all died before this world-trouble began, and have become our spiritual trustees. Her thousand voices—the voices of Shakespeare, Wordsworth, Dostoevsky, and of whomever else you will—blend into one voice which says, "Do not hate: hatred clouds the spirit." And I can't see why we should be the worse Englishmen for listening to this, or why, if we must hate, we should not at least be a bit ashamed of doing it. I know it has been said, "Only a good hater knows how to love," but the man who said this, wherever and whenever he lived, was a German professor. It's the voice of pedantry speaking—not literature.

After hatred, fear. There never has been a time when one's own little life and one's own little income were of less importance, and yet there never was a time when the gusts of ignoble fear blew harder. Ten nations are at war, with misery certain for the poor in all of them, whoever wins: the young men who ought to be the fathers of the next generation are killing one another all over Europe; and yet I can find time to be afraid whether *my* dividends will pay or whether a bomb from a Zeppelin will hit *me*. Probably other Old Students have never been thus afraid, and if they have I am sure that they have found an effective reply. In my own case I have replied by thinking of the immensity of man's soul as embodied in literature—an immensity that armies cannot embody and cannot destroy. It then seems to me not so much shameful to be a coward as silly. The real thing existed before I came into the world, and will continue after my important departure. Then what is there to be afraid of? You may remember how Lord Tennyson cured himself of fear. He used to be shy and timid, especially when entering a drawing-room, and he cured himself by thinking of the great star nebula in the constellation of Orion. My remedy is analogous. By another route, it recalls us to the contemplation of greatness, and, that once achieved, there is no room for fear; you go on with your job instead.

So much for hatred and fear. A third point. Literature is detached. As soon as a writer dies, he ceases to have an axe to grind. All that is temporary and selfish, all that is excitable in his work, becomes meaningless and is forgotten, and the pure emotion survives. To his contemporaries he may have been a jingo or a pacifist, an Anglo-Saxon or a Teuton, a Parthian, or Mede, or Elamite, or dweller in Mesopotamia; but to us he only shows forth the wonderful works of God. The Germans have tried to annex Shakespeare. I applaud the attempt—it does credit to their taste—but they might as well annex the great nebula in Orion, for Shakespeare lives neither in Germany nor in England now, but in the heart of any person who cares for him. Again, we at the outbreak of war tried to banish Beethoven and Wagner from our concert halls. We could do that, but we could not stop them from playing inside our heads whenever some chance sound reawoke their immortality. Literature is the commerce of immortals with mortals, and it is on this side that it connects with religion. You know as well as I do how, in a war like this, there is always a danger we should degrade our conceptions of the Divine, and lower it into a merely national deity—in fact, into a tribal god. We can see this danger at work all through history, from the Jews onward; its worst exhibition was lately, in the Kaiser's celebrated telegram about the Crown Prince—"Our good German God has supported him magnificently." We in England haven't gone as far as the Kaiser yet; we haven't spoken of "our good British God," and I pray we never may. But even in England tribal religion is a real danger, and literature is a useful corrective against it. Literature knows nothing of a Chosen Race, that disastrous fallacy that has produced so much self-righteousness and cruelty. The individual writer may believe that his race is the chosen, but literature—the voice into which the thousand voices blend, the voice I am asking you to listen for now—declares that beauty and truth and goodness exist apart from the tribe, apart even from the nation, and that their only earthly dwelling is the soul of man.

Such seem to me her three main functions in war-time. She helps us to abstain from fear, from hatred, from tribal religion. As far as our passions permit, let us do this. Let us not brood over German atrocities, or squeal about spies, real and imaginary. There are atrocities, there are spies. Nobody doubts it. But

let us not concentrate lovingly and persistently on these subjects. It is true the *Jugend* has published the "Hymn of Hate,"
but that is no excuse for quoting it in English pulpits. It is true
that German professors have fabricated an absurd abstraction
that they call England, but we shall not right things by getting
English professors to fabricate another abstraction and call it
Germany. Against all such hysteria the voice of the immortal
dead protests, their personal yearnings are stilled and so they
can help us, as the living cannot; their hatreds and fears are
over, their lust for possessions quelled, they have become one
with Urania, the Muse of the Divine Song, who has given them
—not happiness, but peace; not Germany or England, but an
empire beyond the grave.

1915

INDIA

Forster has said that Syed Ross Masood, whom he first met in 1907, woke him up from his suburban and academic life by showing him another civilization and another continent. (He had previously been wakened up in 1902 and 1903 by Italy and Greece.) In a fine memorial essay of 1937, reprinted in *Two Cheers for Democracy,* Forster goes on to say of Masood: "My . . . debt to him is incalculable. . . . He made everything real and exciting as soon as he began to talk, and seventeen years later when I wrote *A Passage to India,* I dedicated it to him out of gratitude as well as out of love, for it would never have been written without him."

Neither would it have been written without a visit to India. The visit coincided with that of Goldsworthy Lowes Dickinson, the Cambridge don with whom Forster established a lifelong friendship. Forster records that Dickinson joined him on 11 October 1912 at Port Said for the voyage to Bombay. In *The Hill of Devi,* Forster describes his arrival at Dewas (twenty-three miles from Indore) on Christmas Day, 1912. He stayed only a week, but became friends with the Rajah of Dewas Senior (the tiny kingdom divided between a Senior and Junior branch of the family) whom he met again in Delhi on 6 March 1913.

They spent three days together. Eight years later in the spring of 1921 Forster again went out to India—to act for a few months as secretary to the Rajah.

Forster had a draft of the first half of his Indian novel finished by the end of 1914. How it would have developed had he gone on to complete it at that time, we do not know. It appears from the manuscripts that he was unable to settle on a right treatment of the expedition to the Marabar. Whatever the cause, he set the book aside until his second visit to India. While he was working on the first draft and even after he gave it up, he published a variety of articles and reviews on Indian topics between December 1913 and April 1915. They vary in importance, but as a group they are of exceptional value in understanding *A Passage to India*.

The opening essay on the Indian railway is a lively and charming piece of writing which displays Forster's thoughtfulness, his sympathy, his eye for the rich detail of life, and his complete freedom from feelings of racial superiority. It shows too how India captivated him with its exuberance and variety.

"The Age of Misery" gives Forster a chance to survey the history of India and India's indifference to history. The most valuable part of the review is the vivid sense it gives of how Alexander and the Greeks failed to touch India because she was not interested in the dust of facts. In *A Passage to India* a similar impression is conveyed when Fielding looks at the muddle and confusion of the vast subcontinent from a vantage point in Europe. His application of Mediterranean norms is irrelevant to the modern India of Forster's novel, just as the civilization of ancient Greece was irrelevant to the India of that day.

The history of British involvement in India is long and complex. It began in trade, turned to imperial conquest, and ended in 1947 with the granting of independence to India and Pakistan. Effective control of India by the British is usually dated from their victory at the battle of Plassey in 1757. The country was run by the East India Company but with a governor general appointed by the British parliament. A hundred years later after the Indian Mutiny of 1857–1858, Britain abolished the trading company and took over direct rule. Those who ran India now became civil servants.

This is the background to "The Indian Boom," a review of a bad little book about Bengali village life but in reality a brief history of how India has been reported and interpreted to the English stay-at-home. Of most interest is Forster's comment on reporting in the last half of the nineteenth century when the reader's guides were often Anglo-Indian ladies, "and their theme the disaster of intermarriage; that disaster obsessed and obsesses them, and the novels that exhibit it read as though written on an elephant's back, high above the actualities of the bazaar." The plot of Forster's own novel, with its interracial assault, is a wicked extension of that obsession.

"The Indian Mind" is a nicely turned piece of polite invective at the expense of an author alienated from his native land. As authentic guides to the Indian mind, Forster would probably give first place to two Indians, the Hindu writer Rabindranath Tagore and the Mohammedan poet, Iqbal of Lahore, about whom Forster published an essay in 1946, now collected in *Two Cheers for Democracy*. The two writers are singled out for honorable mention in "The Indian Boom."

Following them, Sir Alfred Lyall might well come next in Forster's estimation. In "The Indian Boom" he speaks of Lyall as the last, and perhaps the greatest, of the fine old type of Anglo-Indian officials who were "cultivated, leisured, and sympathetic to the country they had made their home." "A Great Anglo-Indian" Forster calls his review of Lyall's *Studies in Literature and History*. The book is not important but Forster is fired with enthusiasm by the subject of Lyall himself.

Forster was interested in saints, like Santa Deodata in *Where Angels Fear to Tread* and Catherine of Siena whom he speaks of more than once. It is not their Christianity that attracts him but the nature of their experience. One of Forster's most extended comments on the saintly life is his review of the autobiography of Devendranath Tagore. "The Elder Tagore" was the father of Rabindranath Tagore, the most famous modern Indian writer at this time. Tagore is described by Forster as an unorthodox saint whose belief "denies that God is identical with man, or that he can ever become incarnate as a man, thus striking at the two chief tenets of Hindu orthodoxy. . . ." This orthodoxy, which Forster was later to represent in Professor Godbole, is explained in two important reviews about unimportant books.

In "The Gods of India" Forster asks: "Where shall a man find guidance?" Readers have asked the same question of *A Passage to India.*
And Forster's answer is the same: "Guidance there is, but not towards
a goal that has ever seemed important to the Westerner. And the
promise is not that a man shall see God, but that he shall be God."
In *A Passage to India,* however, we are told that India is not a promise
but an appeal; we are given to understand that in Godbole's song the
call to Krishna of "Come, come, come, come" is never answered, but
remains an appeal; and at the end of Chapter XXXVI, as the climactic
point of the religious festival is reached and the village of Gokul on
its tray is about to be carried into the waves and drowned, we read
that the singers were "preparing to throw God away, God Himself,
(not that God can be thrown) into the storm. Thus was He thrown
year after year, and were others thrown . . . scapegoats, husks, emblems
of passage; a passage not easy, not now, not here, not to be appre-
hended except when it is unattainable: the God to be thrown was an
emblem of that." Rational attempts to interpret the novel must founder
at this point. What Forster is saying is clear from "The Gods of India." The tray with the doll-like gods on it may tilt. "Krishna and Siva
slither into the void. Nothing is more remarkable than the way in
which Hinduism will suddenly dethrone its highest conceptions, nor is
anything more natural, because it is athirst for the inconceivable. Whatever can be stated must be temporary." Only the unattainable and inconceivable escape the laws of time and space, only they are a promise
of something beyond the temporary.

"The Mission of Hinduism" is Forster's most wide-ranging commentary on the nature of Hinduism. It stresses the point that the hundred Indias are one India. This concept of a mystical unity in multi-
plicity is an extension of the idea found in the Dante paper, that the
stars are individual in their brightness but harmonious in their inter-
relations. When Forster found that Hinduism accommodated the con-
tradiction that "I am different from everybody else" and "I am the same
as everybody else," when he found that it accommodated the hundred Indias and the one India, he was instantly sympathetic. As a result he put this aspect of Hinduism to work in *A Passage to India.*
That is why the novel can sustain an immense amount of muddle and

disorder without the total fabric of the narrative being ruptured or destroyed. Hinduism on the one side and the vast confusion of India on the other made it possible for Forster to express, with clarity of insight and richness of detail, the supreme paradox of the One and the Many.

Iron Horses in India

When the European enters his first Indian railway carriage, he feels himself in a moving palace, so many are the luxuries that surround him. There are sofa beds, racks, hooks, washing apparatus, electric lights, a white lincrusta ceiling from which electric fans depend, and there are windows of which no Westerner has ever dreamed—shutters to keep out the glare, wire screens to keep out the flies, blue-grey glass to keep out everything. Meals are served on the train, or else the train stops while they can be eaten, gay little timetables and maps of India hang framed in the embossed wallpaper. Housed in such comfort, might one not travel for ever?

First impressions wear off, and there are few who keep this wholehearted enthusiasm. For one thing, no place is a palace when filled too full of furniture, and—except at Bombay, where it is not to be done without bribing the ticket inspectors —every passenger brings all his luggage into the carriage. The tourist is the worst sinner in this respect, but an old-fashioned Indian gentleman well on the travel, or a large Eurasian family each with a plant in a pot, can give even the tourist points. A trunk is a trunk, an object of known dimensions, but what of a bundle of bedding which, when undone, swells to twice its previous size and cannot be done up again? Or who can cope with a round little brass vase which turns over at a jolt of the train and deluges the floor with water? Or with fourteen rolling melons? All day and all night the luggage piles up, and the journey that began in a palace is apt to end in a boxroom.

Nor do the appliances always work. The windows jam, the tap sends an empty sigh instead of water into the washing basin, and the sofas grow strangely rigid when one tries to sleep on them. There are usually four—two each side of the compartment, running parallel to the windows, and two above these, which are unhooked at will from the wall. It is a choice between evils. The lower sofas are easier to get into, but the upper are less easy to fall out of, because the chains that secure them to the ceiling also secure one's prostrate form from jolting over the edge. The lower are out of reach of the electric light, while the upper can't open the windows. In the lower, people may wake you through sitting on you by mistake, but if you are in the upper they may, equally by mistake, remove your luggage without waking you at all. It is difficult; but in no case should one choose the fifth sofa that is provided in some second class carriages, midway between the lower two, and that combines all the evils of upper and lower—away from the lights and the windows and the racks, short, insecure, exposed to every avalanche of luggage and inrush of dust.

There is furthermore the trial of unpunctuality. One must censure lightly here: no Indian train rivals the South Eastern.

But it is unpunctual, and in a way peculiarly its own. It starts up to time, and is generally up to time at the terminus. But between whiles all sorts of things happen. Sometimes it is detained by matters of state: the local rajah who was going to join it has not turned up, and it waits half an hour for him; or an important sahib is talking to another sahib on the platform: he doesn't see why he should be punctual when the rajah wasn't, and the train waits for him too. Or passengers forget to get in, or those who are in forget to get out, and the train stops again while they alight screaming; or it stops for social reasons, so that the guard may chat with his friends, or the engine driver wash his face in the fountain. Later and later it gets, missing all the connections at wayside junctions. What does it care? It will arrive at its terminus punctually. When three-quarters of its course are over, it leaps forward, heedless of sharp curves or of monkeys and pariah dogs sitting on the lines; heedless of passengers who are trying to sleep inside. On it rushes, dashing down hill in the dawn, and the Company note with pleasure in their Way Book that the Ujjain—Bhopal Mixed was again up to time.

There are four classes in the Indian Railways. First class passengers are usually Europeans: Indians who travel first generally engaging a special carriage. The second class is patronized by both Europeans and Indians, and it is here that occur the "unpleasantnesses" of which one hears so much, and which are, happily, so infrequent. Much has been written on this subject; but it has been written round a few cases and worked up by the press; as a rule the two races travel together in a harmony which it requires fools on both sides to disturb.

Between second and third classes comes the "intermediate," frequented by Eurasians, and only attached to a few trains.

The backbone of the railway system in India, as in England, is the third class. It is the only class that pays. First is run at a loss. Since first class fares are double second, and six or eight times as much as third, it may be surmised that the third class traffic, to pay, must be enormous. And it is. The waiting room —a large open shed—is packed before the arrival of every train. The door is unlocked, out the passengers rush, their luggage on their heads and their babies on their hips, and they storm into the long carriages, which are full already; sometimes they are repulsed: the compartment can hold no more. The train goes on without them, every window gesticulating. After a few laments they go back to the shed to wait for the next.

It was said that the Indian would not travel; that he was timid, conservative, and that he would be defiled by associating with passengers of lower caste. But caste, in some ways so stubborn, is pliable in others, and timidity has yielded to the desire for excitement and a little fun. When a certain branch line in the United Provinces was being constructed, it was at first possible to procure labor without paying any wages at all; the coolies were carried up free in trucks to the railhead, and this contented them. They worked all day, were carried back to their villages in the evening, and recounted their treat to relatives round the fire all night. Even now this enthusiasm survives; the third class carriage, though crowded, is happy; the passengers are as happy as if they were in a museum, and this is saying much. The Indian loves museums; families walk through them hand in hand, not looking at anything in particular, but pleased with the atmosphere of wonders that surrounds them. And a train is even more wonderful than a museum, because it moves.

Some observers declare that in the end the railway system will break down caste. It is true that the Hindu often relaxes

a little; he should buy all his food at a special refreshment room
—such as is provided at some stations—but he is inclined to
consider that fried sweets are not really food and may on a
journey be bought anywhere, and that a bottle of soda water
may be quickly quaffed without grievous sin. All the same, it
may be argued that the railways will do more for Hinduism
than they will against it. They have greatly increased the popu-
larity of the religious fairs. Formerly pilgrims walked to the
holy places, or even measured their length along the roads.
Now they go in the comparative comfort of a cattle truck, and
their numbers grow yearly. Of the two and a half million souls
who converged on Allahabad for the bathing fair of 1912,
nearly all must have come by train. What are bottles of soda
water compared to this?

And as the Indian train goes forward, traversing an immense monotony and bearing every variety of class, race, and
creed within its sunbaked walls, it may serve as a symbol of
India herself. She jolts and jars and puts the brake on, but,
roused from her ancient stillness by science, she does move, and
though one must not press the simile—(for the train arrives ultimately, whereas India has not arrived so far nor even learnt
the name of her destination)—there is nevertheless truth in it.
The first class—white skinned and aloof—the second and intermediate where the two races mingle—the third class many-
colored, brightly clothed, and innumerable as the sand—the
train has brought them together after so many centuries and is
dragging them towards one goal. Palace and boxroom and truck
have this in common: they do move.

1913

The Age of Misery

Ancient India BY E. J. RAPSON

There are four ages, teaches the Hindu, of which the historical is the most miserable and the last. These four make up one Great Period of about five million years, while one thousand Great Periods make up one single day in the life of Brahma. Facts are a sign of decay in the world's fabric. They are like dust crumbling out of the palace walls which Brahma, after the thousand Periods that are his night, will rebuild. We cannot conceive of the joy and the beauty of that palace, because facts have silted in through our senses and blocked the soul. Some day the palace will fall, and we with it; and when it is rebuilt we shall be re-created too. For we are the palace and the palace is we, and when the soul glances hither and thither among the falling masonry it is really looking for the soul.

Some such notion, however silly he may think it, should be present in the mind of the Westerner who attempts to study the pre-Mohammedan civilizations of India. Left to his own precon-

ceptions, he will be bewildered or bored. He must nòt expect a
sweeping narrative, or vivid portraitures—there is no material
out of which they can be constructed—nor political philos'
ophies such as inform the chronicles of Florence or Greece. He
is studying something that has never interested the Indian, and
this must be his main interest. History to the Indian is a pattern
in the fallen dust, and such a monograph as Professor Rapson's
would seem a childish fabric woven out of old inscriptions and
books whose true purport was holiness, out of old coins and
cross references, out of the ignorant exclamations of visitors,
Greek or Chinese. All this material (he would feel) has been
wrested from its proper place. Arranged as it is, it reveals noth'
ing about the palace walls, and it exhibits the dawn not of prog'
ress, but of misery. The West may call such an arrangement
scientific. The Indian knows very well that it is not. And it is
only by remembering his profound indifference to his own past
that we can study it intelligently.

The layman must take the scholarship of Professor Rapson's
book for granted, but he may be allowed to praise its lucidity
and balance. There are three main points of interest in the early
history of India—namely, the development of a priestly reli'
gion, the growth and decay of a great empire—the Maurya—
round Patna, and the arrival of the Greeks. All three are admir'
ably presented here, and connections between them ingeniously
established. It is by establishing connections that the early his'
tory of the Indian countries has been recovered. Information
was always available, but it was dateless and half mythological.
Not until the "Sandrokottos" of the Greek historians was iden'
tified with Chandragupta, the Maurya founder, was a sheet
anchor thrown to steady chronology.

Of the three points, the religious is the most important, and

half the book is devoted to it. When the curtain lifts (circa
B.C. 1000) religion and morality are at one. Caste does not
exist, the power of the priest is slight, sin means the transgres-
sion of some universal law. In the later Vedic books a change
has come, and the India we know now has been born, complex,
priestly, superstitious. The protests follow—the *Upanishads*
with their remedy of esotericism, the two great epics composed
in the interests of the warrior class, the two religious reforms of
Jainism and Buddhism. When the curtain falls (circa Anno
Domini) the victory of priestcraft is still doubtful. It is accomplished during the medieval period, of which it is to be hoped
that Professor Rapson may one day give us an account as read-
able.

Religion dominates India. The Maurya Empire is famous not
for its extent or duration, though both were remarkable, but for
the edicts of Asoka. A convert to Buddhism, Asoka erected
pillars of stone on which spiritual maxims are inscribed. He
glorifies not himself, nor even his particular creed, but "duty"
(dharma), and announces that an empire can only endure
while governors and governed have the sense of duty in their
souls. He does not prescribe unanimity. Souls are different, and
it is wrong to exalt one's own sense of duty at the expense of
someone else's. But in all men the sense is latent, and it is more
glorious to acquire duty than any earthly kingdom. The one
material conquest Asoka does record—that of Kalinga—is
coupled with an expression of bitter regret for the bloodshed
it entailed, and is cited to exemplify inferiority. Before an empire of this type the West must stand silent. It is easy to retort
that Asoka must have been a hypocrite, who preached religion
while he laid his own hands on the good things of this life. But
evidence of this has yet to be unearthed. We only know that he

sent missionaries all over the world, from Greece to Ceylon, to preach the eight-fold path and the need of a life beyond facts, and that he died in meditation and seclusion. After his death the empire fell gradually to pieces—"passed away," as the historian would express it. But the village communities who formed it did not pass away. They lived on unaltered to form other empires, undisturbed beneath changes of name. They live today. They may not be saintly, but they understand saints, and that such a ruler as Asoka should exist has never seemed strange to them.

In strong contrast to the Maurya power stands the coming of the Greeks. The West dwells on the episode complacently; it sees in the military tour of Alexander the Great an event of profound spiritual significance, just as it sees the origin of Indian art in the bad Greco-Buddhist sculptures of Gandhara. Professor Rapson puts all in a truer perspective. He shows that whatever Alexander might have done, he did nothing, and that it is to later immigrants that we are to attribute such Hellenism as was established along the Indus Valley. Even that died. Greece, who has immortalized the falling dust of facts, so that it hangs in enchantment for ever, can bring no life to a land that is waiting for the dust to clear away, so that the soul may contemplate the soul. Let us imagine—dates would permit us—that some wandering Athenian was present in B.C. 250 when Asoka's inscription was being carved on the rock at Girnar. Interested in everything, however barbaric or unbalanced, he would ask some bilingual friend to translate it for him. And he would hear:

> Everywhere in the realm has the King, the beloved of the Gods, provided remedies of two kinds, remedies for men and remedies for animals, and herbs, both such as are serviceable to

men and serviceable to animals, wheresoever there were none, has he everywhere caused to be procured and planted; roots also and fruits, wheresoever there were none, has he everywhere caused to be procured and planted; and on the highways has he caused wells to be dug and trees to be planted for the enjoyment of animals and men.

Asoka was a wealthy monarch, who could have paid for the Parthenon a thousand times over. But his memorial is this. For what more can a government do than alleviate in passing the misery of the age?

1914

The Indian Boom

Svarnalata: Scenes from Hindu Village Life in Bengal

BY T. N. GANGULI, TRANSLATED FROM THE BENGALI

BY D. ROY

India has reached the English imagination by different routes. To the stay-at-home of the eighteenth century "India" meant Southern India, a land of coal-black heathen, and tropical vegetation, wherein elephants trumpeted and Little Henry converted his bearer. Becky Sharp dreamt of such an India, when Jos Sedley first met her virgin gaze, but Jos came from Bengal really; the center of interest had already shifted from the extreme south. During the nineteenth century it moved up to the Imperial cities of Delhi and Agra, and another India, less fantastic but more interesting, dawned upon the stay-at-home. Sleeman—that noble and fascinating writer!—rambled with him through the States of Bundelkhund and the Kingdom of Dudh: Tod led him into the chivalrous deserts of Rajputana. His guides were Anglo-Indian officials of the fine old type, cultivated, leisured, and sympathetic to the country they had made their home; Alfred Lyall was the last of this type, and perhaps the greatest.

After the Mutiny and the transference from John Company to the Crown, a change began. The new type of official may have been as fine as the old, but he was harder worked, less independent, and less in touch with the Indian socially. He could get back more easily to England for his leave, owing to improved steamer service, and his womenfolk could come out more easily to him. Such a man was not likely to waste his time in interpreting India to the stay-at-home; indeed, he would gruffly imply that there was nothing to interpret: "India's a hole in which you've got to do your job, that's all." So it followed that our conceptions of the land grew more sterile. The glamor of the old nabobs and missionaries had gone, the kindly light of Tod and Sleeman had gone also. Our guides now were often Anglo-Indian ladies, and their theme the disaster of intermarriage; that disaster obsessed and obsesses them, and the novels that exhibit it read as though written on an elephant's back, high above the actualities of the bazaar. We were assured that there was no real religion in the country, no literature, no architecture except the Taj, and that was built by an Italian. Official enthusiasm had petered out.

With the twentieth century begins a new interpretation. It comes from many sources, which have only this in common: they are unofficial. In religion Mrs. Besant has shown us that Hinduism has a meaning, even for the West. In music, Mrs. Mann has unlocked a subtle and exquisite spirit. In art, Dr. Coomaraswamy has revealed the beauty of Rajput miniature, Mrs. Herringham has worked among the frescoes of Ajanta, Mr. Havell has celebrated forgotten sculptures and buildings, many of them admirable. And in literature India has told her own heart, through the mouth of Rabindranath Tagore. A new conception of the country has come to us in consequence. She may be puzzling, but we cannot now ignore her. Her culture, or rather cultures, have been reinterpreted.

It will be noted that the reinterpretation is mainly Hindu. Mohammedanism has figured little, and its chief living poet, Iqbal of Lahore, remains untranslated. And one might even say that it is mainly Bengali, owing to the predominance of the Tagores. Bengal, that derided province, home of Jos Sedley and Baboo Jabberjee, B.A., has achieved fame of a new kind. The sensitive native civilization of Calcutta—a civilization that is trying to adapt the West instead of adopting it—has very rightly caught the world's attention, and *Svarnalata,* the little book under review, is one of the results.

It is, unfortunately, a bad little book, which, but for the Indian boom, would scarcely have been translated. One cannot suppose it had ever honor in Bengal, for it lacks atmosphere, plot, and style, its moral reflections are hackneyed, its pathos mawkish, its characters divided into good, humorous, and bad; and, though its theme—the dissolution of a Hindu joint family —is full of capabilities, all are neglected, and no picture arises in the reader's mind. Its chief merit is unpretentiousness, and, as the following extract will show, there is some interesting material:

> In Sasibhushan's new house Gadadhar had a pretty little outer room for his own use. The floor was covered with a valuable carpet, over which was spread a costly sheet with a bolster on it. Right in front of the bolster were the hookahs in their stands, the shells of which were mounted with silver. Behind the bolster and close to the wall stood a clothes-horse on which hung two or three fine Simla cloths with coloured borders, two shirts and one

scarf. On one side of the clothes-horse, which had on its under-shelf two pair of shoes, was a walking-stick resting against the corner, and on the other side there was a rough chest made of the wood of the mango tree.

But the material is never vitalized, and Indian village life still waits for the writer who will do for it what Mr. L. S. Woolf has done for village life in Ceylon. One's only fear is that an attempt like the present will discredit others, and reaffirm official cynicism; certainly the frontispiece (which depicts a plump Babu at the deathbed of his wife) is rather hard to bear.

1915

The Indian Mind

Reflections on the Problems of India BY A. S. WADIA

The Indian who attempts to interpret his country to the Westerner is apt to become part of the mystery he offers to solve. He
is too often full of vague platitudes, of illustrations that explain
nothing, of arguments that lead nowhere, and such interpretation as he gives is unconscious. He leaves us with the sense of a
mind infinitely remote from ours—a mind patriotic and sensitive—and it may be powerful, but with little idea of logic or
facts; we retire baffled, and, indeed, exasperated.

It is with the greater relief that one turns to these essays of
Mr. Wadia. He not only writes well, but his mind moves on
the Western plane, and though its conclusions may be contro-
versial, they are never intangible. No doubt he is out of sympathy with his native land; he confesses to feeling an alien
there, and no doubt this disqualifies him as a guide to it. Religion, for instance, only interests him in its social aspect (he confines the adjective "sacred" to property), and the Indian who is

not interested in religion will never take us much beyond Bombay. Nevertheless, such help as he gives is valuable. He throws
a vivid, if dry, light on the subjects under discussion.

These subjects are four in number—Elementary Education,
which he would discourage; the Caste System, which he would
retain; Industrial Development, which he would discourage;
and the Political Future, which he hopes will remain dominantly
British. The position of women he does not touch, but one may
assume he would retain purdah also, since to relax it must loosen
the present social fabric, which, at any cost, he would preserve.
It will thus be seen that his conclusions are conservative, not to
say retrograde. He opposes the Nationalists of India and the
Humanitarian Liberals of England. He ridicules missions,
whether Hindu or Christian. He has no belief in the dignity of
man, or that social evils may be ameliorated by kindness or
thought. He hates liberty. His ideal is an autocrat, or, failing
him, a bureaucracy. Europe has deteriorated ever since the
French Revolution, and he would save India from her fate.

These conclusions are based on a philosophy. Thus spoke
Zarathustra! A Parsee by descent, Mr. Wadia has been attracted by the writings of Nietzsche, and apparently regards
them as the Zend Avesta of the modern world. He knows (one
wonders how) that there is a definite and irreducible amount
of evil in the universe, that an inevitable dualism bisects Nature, that good is completed by evil, and that evil can never be
destroyed, only shifted. Someone must scavenge: then how fu-
tile to educate the Depressed Classes; someone must rule: then
how dangerous to soften or weaken the spirit of caste. Why
will the humanitarian not realize this? Why will he not face
the fact of the all-pervading law of polarity, and see that it ap-
plies with particular force to India?

Now, Nietzsche despised not the poor, but the mediocre, and it is here that Mr. Wadia misapplies him. He brings to social distinctions an attitude that is only applicable to ethical, and assumes that the lower an Indian's caste, the lower will be his mental capacity. The assumption, other observers tell us, is wrong. They will point out stupid Brahmins and chamars of genius. Why should not the chamar of genius be allowed to rise? Mr. Wadia is prepared for this question, and replies that if he has genius he will rise unassisted. Genius "always" triumphs over environment. (One wonders again how he knows this.) "There never was a mute, inglorious Milton," and the proof is that Milton wasn't inglorious or mute! Mr. Wadia regards the question as answered, and does not see that, though he may demolish the theory of the humanitarians, his own is sapped by an optimism as puerile.

When he does criticize authority, the occasion is significant. He resents the behavior of the Anglo-Indian to the cultivated Indian. Most Indians do, and one understands their resentment, but for a Nietzschean to squeal is surely unsuitable. It is merely the law of polarity at work, but in his personal annoyance he quite forgets this. Why should the ruling caste behave with sympathy or politeness to him? What claim has he to receive a measure other than that which he metes? Surely none. The truth is that, though willing to face facts, he does demand something soft behind him, while he faces them—an armchair, or perhaps a settee, where his friend Mr. M., who was once insulted in the Byculla Club, may sit, too. This demand for a settee is universal. It is made equally by the chamars, and some of us are looking round to see whether there may not be enough stuff in the world to grant it. Our efforts amuse Mr. Wadia. He knows that there is no more stuff—he has private information on the point. There ought to be a little more behind him, but, with that exception, society is as it will be and must be, for ever.

It would be wrong, however, to part from the book upon a critical note. It is a serious, vigorous, and stimulating work, and is to be particularly recommended to those who will disagree with its conclusions. Most Indians and many Englishmen will.

1914

A Great Anglo-Indian

Studies in Literature and History BY SIR ALFRED LYALL

By profession an administrator, Lyall went out shortly before
the Mutiny, rose to be lieutenant-governor, and nearly became
viceroy. In consequence he is an important official figure, with
a niche in the Temple of History, where we may imagine him
standing with his Biography of Lord Dufferin in one hand, and
his Sketch of the British Dominion in India in the other. But he
lives in the Temple of the Muses also. The book he holds there
is *Asiatic Studies,* and though in poetry he was a frank ama-
teur, his *Verses Written in India* are likely to outlive more pre-
tentious stuff. All that he wrote is important, and his volume
under review (though merely a posthumous miscellany of articles that he contributed to magazines in his old age) is of great
interest, both for its contents and for the light it throws upon a
fascinating character. Lyall here breathes what he had always
wished to breathe—the cultivated atmosphere of London. His

honorable and active career has closed, his exile is over. He has sometimes regretted in the wilds of Berar or the vacuities of Simla that he has missed his vocation, and given to India what was meant for academe. Now a few years are granted in which he may express himself, and take his place among his literary peers.

Every sensitive mind must have regrets, but we who look on may doubt whether Lyall could have developed more fully than he did. Had he remained in England he might have read more and acquired subtler tastes, but without India he would have remained half a man. She taught him two things—to value action and to be interested in religion. He loved action, not hysterically like Stevenson, or pedagogically like Kipling, but simply because he was used to it, because it had become a natural part of his life; and he loves not action in general, but the doing of some particular thing. Hence his admiration for heroic poetry and for Byron. The heroic poet, whether medieval or Homeric, is concerned to give a true picture of his time. He is a man, singing about the sort of man whom his audience know, and he has to keep to the facts, or they will laugh. He does not describe war in general, or even a campaign, but some special scrimmage. He is far from the romantic poet of later years, who softens outlines with a haze of sentiment, and to Lyall seemed far superior, because he wrote of what he knew—it mightn't be much, but he did know it. And Byron—Byron is not heroic, Byron is rhetorical and sophisticated, but he did know a little, he had acted, he had visited the Greece and the Levant that he describes. "He broke through a limited mannerism in poetry, and led forth his readers into an unexplored region of cloudless sky and purple sea, where the serene aspect of nature could be powerfully contrasted with the shadow of death and desolation cast over it by the violence of man." And Byron's heroes, "at all events, live and die in a masculine way, without any of the wailing sensuality that infects the more harmonious poetry of a later day." Here writes the true man of action, the man, that is to say, who has had a great deal to do, and enjoyed doing it; the man who has ruled and occasionally fought in India. He has limitations as a critic, as we shall see, but when the subject of his criticism has also enjoyed doing things, he extends to him at once a generous and instinctive sympathy, and the essays on heroic poetry and on Byron are perhaps the best in the book.

Religion, the other great interest that India awoke in Lyall, figures little here. There are a couple of addresses on it at the end, but they deal chiefly with its relation to the state. Experience has taught the lieutenant-governor that fanatics are ticklish customers, and he warns the ideologues of London to handle them carefully. This scarcely takes us into the depths, and it must be remembered that Lyall's religious interest, though it could be deep, was narrow. He cared little for the aspirations of the refined; witness the scathing reference (in one of his letters) to the Brahmo Samaj. It is the primitive superstitions of Berar that move him—not, of course, to approval, but to a very real sympathy, and that inspire his finest work. It is in his Verses, not in these late essays, that Hinduism catches him, as it has caught sceptics at all times, and wrings cries of acquiescence and whispers of hope. As men grow old they seem to think of religion either always or never. Lyall inclines to the latter class, and the politeness with which he now treats Christianity argues an indifference more profound than his former diatribes: Saul has become Gallio.

Of the remaining essays, perhaps the best is that on English letter-writing. An admirable correspondent himself, he can appreciate others, especially men like Coleridge, who wrote in a less sophisticated age, before pens were curbed by the fear of publicity. "When you have to think what you say, it does not follow that you say what you think," and he traces the growth of epistolary caution in the letters of Matthew Arnold and of Dean Stanley. But there is so much that is good that one scarcely knows what to choose, and perhaps it is wiser to choose something that is not good—namely, the Essay on Swinburne— because it exhibits Lyall's limitations as a critic, and so may help us to understand him. He is most severe on Swinburne. To Byron all is permitted, because he was a man of action; to Swinburne, because he was a stay-at-home poet, nothing. He had not the right to shock his contemporaries, Sir Alfred feels, and at the first mention of *Poems and Ballads* he opens the entire Victorian armory, or shall we say, medicine-chest. *Poems and Ballads* may not be great poetry, but they are the greatest Swinburne ever wrote, and cannot be physicked out of sight, on the ground that they are "too often tainted with morbidity" or have "alienated reverent minds." What about *Don Juan*? We are invited to admire the "mature work" instead, but Swinburne did not mature, he happened not to be that type of man; he blazed out in youth, and the fuel of experience only dulled him, and Lyall, to whom experience had given so much, cannot understand this, any more than he can understand the letters of Keats. Young men like these, he feels, are indulging in emotion without facing the results; they are keeping their wild oats in a bushel; let them scatter boldly abroad, and then the trained observer can judge them. But young men do not write for the trained observer; "let him untrain himself" is their very proper retort. They write for an audience which, for good or evil, numbers few Anglo-Indians, and that Lyall should have troubled to criticize *Poems and Ballads* at all, is proof of his breadth of mind.

1915

The Elder Tagore

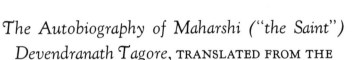

The Autobiography of Maharshi ("the Saint")
Devendranath Tagore, TRANSLATED FROM THE
BENGALI BY S. TAGORE AND I. DEVI, WITH AN
INTRODUCTION BY E. UNDERHILL

Most of us assume that religion is a duty, and we cannot realize that the saints, of every age and clime, have decided otherwise. Religion, to the saint, is not a duty, but a necessity. He is religious, not because he "ought" to be, but because an irresistible call draws him away from a world whose pomps and vanities seem silly rather than wicked. St. Francis of Assisi, St. Catherine of Siena, both illustrate this, and an illustration even better—because not overlaid by the ecclesiastical—is to be found in the autobiography of this nineteenth century Hindu.

Devendranath Tagore's father was a Calcutta merchant, and up to the age of eighteen his life was orthodox and comfortable. Then his grandmother died: they carried her down to the Ganges to breathe her last, and he waited close by, cross-legged on a mat, beneath the full moon. The burning ground was near. Suddenly he became convinced of the folly of his life, he recoiled from wealth, his mind was filled with inconceivable joy.

Next day he tried to recapture the sensation, but in vain. Only an aching memory survived, and he mourned, because he had lost all interest in society, and gained nothing in exchange. "While sitting in my drawing-room I said to those around me, 'Whoever will ask of me anything that it is in my power to give, that will I give to him.' Nobody asked me for anything except my cousin, Babu Braju, who said, 'Give me those two big mirrors, give me those pictures, give me that gold-laced dress suit.' I immediately gave him all these. But the grief in my heart remained the same."

In her learned and sympathetic introduction, Miss Underhill points out that the saint develops by stages, and that the transition from stage to stage is, to the outward observer, abrupt. Devendranath reached the second stage at the age of twenty-eight, this time through studying the Hindu scriptures. While reading the *Upanishads,* he became convinced of a purpose in nature, of a King of Kings, whose temple is the universe, and who rewards those who worship him with a joy that is indestructible as well as inconceivable. The stage of loneliness had ended. The hint given beside the Ganges was fulfilled, and the young man entered into a state of happiness so vivid and acute that the world became negligible.

He had already adopted Brahmaism. Brahmaism (not to be confused with the orthodox Brahmanism) is a Unitarian sect, whose fortunes recall those of Unitarianism in England. It is now on the decline, but in Devendranath's day had been recently founded and attracted the nobler minds of Bengal. It worships one god, under the name of Brahma. It believes that God is all good, all powerful, and cannot be expressed in images. Besides rejecting idolatry, it denies that God is identical with man, or that he can ever become incarnate as a man, thus striking at the two chief tenets of Hindu orthodoxy; and, in the form that Devendranath adopted, it also denies the Hindu doctrine of Illusion. The above summary of Brahmaism is necessarily incomplete, but the reader will see that it is not so much a creed as an attitude of mind, and would particularly appeal to a spiritual rebel.

Happy within, Devendranath had to face problems without, the chief of which came at his father's death. Was he, a Brahmaist, to perform the funeral rites in the old idolatrous way? Or was he to disgrace his family and break with society? He chose the latter. During the years that followed, he extricated himself slowly from the world. His third stage may be dated from his entry into the Himalayas. He was drawn up to their heights as the cloud is drawn by the sun. He did not go to them in order to become a recluse, or to see a vision, but, having arrived, he saw, he became. In words of crescent ecstasy, he describes the superhuman spirit of those hills, their snow, their forest fires, their thin air, their moon and stars, until— until, abruptly, tragically, the third stage of his sainthood ends, and he is compelled to enter on the fourth. He was looking at a bright mountain stream, and wondering why it should hurry to lose its purity in the plains, when suddenly a voice said within him: "Thou art that stream; go back to the world." He became ill, physically ill, at the command, but never thought of disobeying.

"Give up thy pride, and be lowly like the stream. The truth thou hast gained, the devotion and trustfulness that thou hast learnt here—go, make them known to the world."

Next day he started for Calcutta. The autobiography ends here, at the age of forty-one, but he lived to be eighty-eight, a useful and influential member of society.

What is one to make of this beautiful but extraordinary book? Can the experiences it records be paralleled by our own? They cannot; and perhaps there exists a special type of human being, who answers to a call that escapes our ears. There is no suggestion that Devendranath ever "tried" to be good, as we try; he rose because he was obliged to, so that the very substance of his spirit seems remote. One link with us he has: he was the father of Rabindranath Tagore, whose genius, delicate yet popular, has done much to interpret the saint to the average man.

"I saw that the fairies had come, whence I know not, to the pond near my house; and were playing about like swans, with cries of delight. Thus the stream of time flowed swiftly and happily on."

In such a passage as this one may catch a foretaste of *Gitan-jali,* and realize that, as far as flesh and blood go, Devendranath was of this world.

1914

The Gods of India

The Gods of India BY THE REV. E. O. MARTIN

Religion, in Protestant England, is mainly concerned with con-duct. It is an ethical code—a code with a divine sanction it is true, but applicable to daily life. We are to love our brother, whom we can see. We are to hurt no one, by word or deed. We are to be pitiful, pure minded, honest in our business, re-liable, tolerant, brave. These precepts are not incidental. They lie at the heart of the Protestant faith, and no accuracy in theology is held to excuse any neglect of them. The man, how-ever orthodox, whose life is bad, is described by his fellows as "not really a religious man," as "a hypocrite by whom God at all events will not be deceived."

The code is so spiritual and lofty, and contains such frequent references to the Unseen, that few of its adherents realize it only expresses half of the religious idea. The other half is ex-pressed in the creed of the Hindus. The Hindu is concerned not with conduct, but with vision. To realize what God is seems more important than to do what God wants. He has a constant sense of the unseen—of the powers around if he is a peasant, of the power behind if he is a philosopher, and he feels that this tangible world, with its chatter of right and wrong, subserves the intangible. He can point to a Heaven where virtue is rewarded, and to a Hell where vice is punished, but he points without enthusiasm; to realize or not to realize, that is the question that interests him. Hinduism can pull itself to supply the human demand for morality just as Protestantism at a pinch can meet the human desire for the infinite and the incomprehensible. But the effort is in neither case congenial. Left to itself each lapses—the one into mysticism, the other into ethics.

If the above distinction be correct, it will follow that the two creeds can never hope to understand one another, and certainly that is the impression one gets from Mr. Martin's book. His subject is Indian mythology, and he handles it well; no better guide for the beginner could be imagined; in turn he surveys Vedic, Puranic, and local deities, quoting freely from sacred books and modern authorities, and illustrating his remarks by photographs. But, naturally enough, he comments. Being a missionary he could scarcely do otherwise, and though anxious to be fair to "the gods and goddesses," his comments are naturally scathing. Deity after deity is summoned before the tribunal of Wesleyanism, and dismissed with no uncertain voice. Krishna stole butter as a baby, and worse later. Jagganath is a goggle-eyed log. Brahma "has an unenviable moral record," and his head was once cut off by the thumbnail of Siva's left hand. "What a scene is this for the wonder of the world!" Mr. Martin cries. Some goddesses are satanic, like Kali, others corrupt, like Radha. And as are the deities, so are some of their followers: lustful, cruel.

Is this the Hindu religion? Is it really this trayful of naughty dolls? Well, in a sense it is. One can dispute isolated points with Mr. Martin. His wholesale condemnation of Krishna worship is surely monstrous. His quotation from Lyall has been wrested to bear false witness. But, details apart, he makes his case: Hinduism is not what he can regard as "really religion," and his hatred of it is inevitable. Good and evil are blurred. The benevolent wife of Siva assumes, as Durga, the name of the demon she conquers, and, as Kali, his attributes. Demons, by their holiness and austerities, can acquire power over the gods, and are only kept out of heaven by a trick. Sex is worshipped—symbolically in Saivism and actually in some Sakti-rites. The divine is so confounded with the earthly that anyone or anything is part of God. In this chaos, where shall a man find guidance? What promise does he receive?

Guidance there is, but not towards a goal that has ever seemed important to the Westerner. And the promise is not that a man shall see God, but that he shall be God. He is God already, but imperfectly grasps the mystery. He will realize the universe as soon as he realizes himself, and pity, courage, reliability, etc., may help him or may hinder him in his quest; it depends. The deities may help him, or they may mislead, like the shows of earth; it depends, depends on the step he has taken just before.

> Is it a God or a King that comes?
>   Both are evil, and both are strong;
> With women and worshipping, dancing and drums,
>   Carry your Gods and your Kings along.
>
> When shall these phantoms flicker away
>   Like the smoke of the guns on the wind-swept hill,

The Gods of India

Like the sounds and colors of yesterday,
And the soul have rest and the air be still?

For outside the "trayful of dolls" are the hands that hold the tray, and occasionally tilt it and present the worshipper with emptiness. Krishna and Siva slither into the void. Nothing is more remarkable than the way in which Hinduism will sud-denly dethrone its highest conceptions, nor is anything more natural, because it is athirst for the inconceivable. Whatever can be stated must be temporary. "The gods and goddesses," writes Mr. Martin, "are largely self-condemned," and so, in a very profound sense, they are. They are steps towards the eter-nal. To a Protestant, such an arrangement seems scandalous, and since Mr. Martin has misapplied Lyall, one may perhaps apply him. "It is idle," he writes, "to think of ingrafting the rigid and simple faith of the Saxons upon the Hindus."

The present reviewer has been reminded of a picture that a Holy Man once explained to him at Benares. It showed the human frame, strangely partitioned. God was in the brain, the heart was a folded flower. Yoga unfolded the flower, and then the soul could set out on its quest of God. Two roads lay open to it. It could either proceed directly, by the spinal cord, or in-directly through one of the Hindu deities who were dispersed about the body. When asked which road was the best, the Holy Man replied "That by the spinal cord is quicker, but those who take it see nothing, hear nothing, feel nothing of the world. Whereas those who proceed through some deity can profit by ——" he pointed to the river, the temples, the sky, and added, "That is why I worship Siva." But Siva was not the goal.

1914

The Mission of Hinduism

———— ❧ ————

Footfalls of Indian History BY SISTER NIVEDITA
(MARGARET E. NOBLE)
Hinduism in Europe and America BY ELIZABETH A. REED

Is Hinduism a missionary religion? Since it is based upon caste, since its adherents are born, not baptized, can it take any interest in the non-Hindu? One would suppose not, and Max Müller has laid down that it is purely local, or rather racial, in its appeal, and has contrasted it with Buddhism, Christianity, and Islam, which offer the Kingdom of Heaven to all men, independent of birth. Yet, whatever Hinduism may do in theory, it has certainly proselytized in practice. It has converted the non-Aryan races of the peninsula, and may still be seen at work among the Bhils and Gonds, tincturing their simple animistic faiths with its theology. And, outside India, it has made some appeal to another simple folk—the Anglo-Saxon—as the two books now under review both testify. Sister Nivedita (Miss Noble) was a Religious of the Ramakrishna Order. Mrs. Reed, judging from internal evidence, is a Christian missionary. Each in her own way bears witness to the expansive power of Hinduism, the one by her blessings, the other by her very hearty curse.

Neither book is of high merit. Sister Nivedita is said by those who knew her to have had a great personality, but it does not come out in her writing, which is sentimental and muzzy. And Mrs. Reed gets so hot that she fails to marshal her evidence, and can scarcely convince anyone who does not agree with her beforehand. Yet both deserve attention—they are so sincere and so well informed, and their diverse conclusions throw such an interesting light on the intentions of Hinduism towards the West.

India, to Sister Nivedita, is not the only path to the truth but the most satisfactory. It is easier here to attain the Reality that all men desire. The mind that has felt the message of Benares, for instance, "can never again think of God seated on a throne, for to it the secret has been shown that Shiva is within the heart of man." And to the objection "What is India? Are there not a hundred Indias?" she replies that India once was, still essentially is, and in the future visibly shall be, One, and shall give light to those who sit in comparative darkness. Magadha (the modern Behar) is the center. There over two thousand years ago, the great Gupta Empire arose, and there Buddha taught and attained renunciation. Buddha unified Hinduism. He did not generate a new religion, as Christendom supposes. He was a preacher, like Ramakrishna in the nineteenth century; after his death India becomes spiritually, and for a time politically, one; architecturally, that unity is expressed in the Ajanta and the Elephanta caves. The book, though concerned with questions of topography and art, emphasizes this supposed unity of India; the writer has been absorbed into it herself, and feels that other Westerners, if wise, should suffer the same.

Such is her faith. How different does it appear in the pages of Mrs. Reed, who undertakes to present "a repellent picture of the unethical character of the Hindu gods, the revolting features of certain popular and esoteric rites, and the venal character of members of the sacerdotal order." She presents it without difficulty—religion in India has taken so many forms that facts can be found to support any hypothesis—and then she denounces its spread in the West, especially among American women. One wishes she would be more explicit here. To what extent has it spread incidentally, owing to the influence of Hindus who have visited us for other reasons? To what extent has it been consciously preached? If the latter, what organizations exist for disseminating it? What, if anything, has the Brahmo Samaj accomplished, what the Ramakrishna Order? What is the relation between missions that are avowedly Indian and missions that are vaguely Indian, like Theosophy? Mrs. Reed is too enthusiastic to tell us. She utters cries about scandals and the police. Her argument—and at first sight it seems unanswerable—is that all Hindu missionaries must be liars; their religion is based upon caste, so no Westerner can ever enter it; and on the masculine, so that it is useless for women; consequently they are wanting nothing but money. It is seldom that she censures by name—Vivekanda, the teacher of Sister Nivedita, is one of the exceptions—all seem to her tainted by one initial deceit. She also attacks the Sacred Books, declaring that (unlike the Bible) they reveal no conception of man's nature. But her main accusation is as above: that the Westerner and the woman are being invited to enter a church that cannot be entered, and are, therefore, being swindled.

To attempt a comment. It is true that Hinduism emphasizes the fact that we are all different. But it also emphasizes the other side of the human paradox—the fact that we are all the same, and from this side it is bound to draw missionary force. Stripped of its local trappings, of its hundred-handed gods, and monkeys and bulls and snakes, and Twice-born, it preaches with intense conviction and passion the doctrine of unity. It believes in caste, it believes in pantheism also, and these two contradictory beliefs do really correspond to two contradictory emotions that each of us can feel, namely, "I am different from everybody else," and "I am the same as everybody else." The historical unity that Sister Nivedita derives—not very convincingly—from ancient Magadha, prefigures a spiritual unity in which all races and species and sex shall one day be merged. Mrs. Reed would tell her that she, a woman and a Westerner, must be excluded from it, and that the other members of the Ramakrishna Order are laughing at her behind her back. But even if they were, they could not affect her salvation. She has found peace, has balanced to her own satisfaction the claims of the Many and the One; she is a recent, if not an important, example of the missionary power of Hinduism—a religion which (*pace* Mrs. Reed) does reveal a conception of Man's nature, and in consequence always has appealed and will appeal to souls who are technically outside its pale. It may not intend to proselytize, or may proselytize with its tongue in one of its hundred cheeks. But it gains proselytes, whatever its intentions, because it can give certain types of people what they want. It is—to this extent—a missionary power in the West, and a legitimate subject of enthusiasm to Sister Nivedita and of anxiety to Mrs. Reed.

1915

THE ARTS
AND WAR

"The Wedding," about marriage ceremonies in Morocco, is a sign of Forster's fascination with an institution he greatly distrusted. His review works up a lively comparison between marriage as a crisis in the mountains of Morocco and in the English village. He comes away from Westermarck's book with a clear idea of marriage as a *rite de passage*.

"The Rose Show" is a review of some patriotic Persian verse. In Forster's view it is very nearly a law that poems of utility, whether Persian or English, will not be poems of beauty. But in discussing the recent history of Persia (1906–1914), now known as Iran, Forster does not allow bad verse to deflect his sympathy from the indigenous population in its struggles against exploitation and conquest by great powers.

Some readers of "To Simply Feel" may find the discussion of the once renowned Ella Wheeler Wilcox and especially the references to America and the semieducated public rather hard to take. But the commentary on H. Fielding Hall's novel is amusing, and the general topic of feeling in art is of some importance. It was one of Forster's deepest convictions that emotion could not be expressed by direct imitation, whether by gesture in a painting, emotive acting in a play, or the overt assertion of emotion as a theme in fiction.

E. M. Forster

Love's Legend by Hall was the first novel Forster ever reviewed. Eight months later in "A New Novelist" he approached a writer worthier of his insight. Virginia Woolf was thirty-three years old in 1915 when she published *The Voyage Out,* her first novel. Forster was thirty-six and had already published four novels and twelve short stories. From her journals and from Leonard Woolf's autobiography, we know that Virginia Woolf at once dreaded and respected Forster's judgment. But I wonder what she made of this review? The effect is elusive as though Forster were seeking ways of getting a grip on the novel. I suspect this is because he and Virginia Woolf—though they were both members of the Bloomsbury group and had in their cultural and social background a good deal in common—failed to grasp on either side the radical way their fiction differed in aim and method. Forster, in particular, has trouble understanding Virginia Woolf's characters in *The Voyage Out.* It is not precisely, as he suggests, that they are all clever together and rather too much alike. It is that they lack typicality, the firm outlines that one expects of nineteenth century fictional personages. For Virginia Woolf's is a realism of the unique; each speech and gesture is individual. Forster misses this truth about character but grasps it in relation to action when he says that Virginia Woolf believes in adventure and knows it can only be undertaken alone. His discussion of adventure is puzzling until one realizes that it is his way of recognizing that the events of *The Voyage Out* are attached to the characters and so are unique and personal rather than typical and social.

Of course Virginia Woolf has "characters" in the Victorian sense as well. Forster even foregoes an analysis of the closing chapters to talk about them. They belong to the comic side of the novel. They are part of the world of gossip and assumed stability and vivacious indifference that cuts across the tragic and enhances it. For the tragic, as the remarks on the aloneness of adventure imply, is entirely private and individual.

Forster only half understands Virginia Woolf, but on one point he is clear. She is educated, by which he means that her mind, her critical intelligence, has penetrated all the areas of her subject she has chosen to represent. Her vision is not blinkered by emotions or illusions or compulsions. They are there but she has looked into them and made them yield to the insistent power of her mind. It is a great tribute.

The complexity and ambiguity of Forster's response to fiction, and particularly to realism, comes out again in his review of "Short Stories from Russia." After quoting a substantial passage from Tchekov's story "Agatha," he says of one of the characters: "Savka does not symbolize the Russian spirit, any more than the quiet evening where they sat symbolizes life or death or love. It is true that 'there's a meaning in everything,' but also true that each thing means itself and not something else." Tchekov, he adds, "avoids generalization, he even avoids climax, because either would seduce him from the subject—and consequently from the poetry—in hand." Each thing is itself and not a symbol, yet each has meaning and poetry. It is like having the best of both worlds, of the symbolic and the realistic. Each thing is real, yet each has an aura beyond the real. That aura, as indicated by the comments about Sologub later in the review, is engendered by the central heat of inspiration.

Some of Forster's writing published in 1915 reflects the immediate reality of World War I. The first major event in that war was the German invasion of Belgium. The violence of the onslaught and the atrocities committed by the Germans roused English public opinion. It is against this background that one must see the paper on "The Function of Literature in War-time" and the two concluding selections in this volume concerning art and social reconstruction.

In the first of these, "Tate versus Chantrey," Forster offers a lucid and devastating account of how the Tate Gallery, supposedly devoted to the best modern British art, is being inundated with clichéd academic paintings chosen by officials of the Royal Academy because they control the money from the Chantrey Bequest. It is well to remember that the Tate, built on the former site of Millbank prison and opened in 1897, is now a far more famous and secure institution than it was in 1915. That this is so is in part due to the thoughtful interest of men like Forster. Even in the midst of war he has the sense to realize that art will be needed after the fighting has ceased. Accordingly, he insists that action be taken on the Report of the National Gallery Committee and that the Tate be rescued from its anomalous position.

That nothing much came of the Report immediately will hardly surprise those familiar with things British. Indeed, the history of the Chantrey Bequest is a classic example of how things are done in the United Kingdom. In 1917 a Board of Trustees was set up for the Tate and, after complaints from this new body, the Council of the Royal Academy agreed to consult the Tate on the purchases from the Chantrey Bequest. The Tate did not, however, have a veto. In 1927 there was more trouble, and for two years no purchases were made. In 1949 the Royal Academy exhibited the entire collection purchased through the Bequest. Both sides aired their views, and in the upshot, the Tate won fifty percent representation on the selection committee and an effective veto. In 1956, however, the power of veto was abolished as con-travening Sir Francis Chantrey's will. After that, by agreement, the Tate took only the works it wanted, and the Royal Academy disposed of the residue as it saw fit, on a loan basis. An excellent example of British muddle and compromise.

"Reconstruction in the Marne and the Meuse" is an honest and well-constructed account of work done by the Society of Friends to aid the French villages overrun, devastated, and then deserted by the invading German army. Forster's interest in the Society was undoubtedly stimulated by the fact it was international in outlook and pacifist in sentiment. His survey of the reports of the Society's work stresses—as always—civilization and love. It is a quiet statement, typical of Forster.

The Wedding

Marriage Ceremonies in Morocco

BY EDWARD WESTERMARCK

When the ceremony in the village church is over, without a hitch, when the gentleman has not kept the lady waiting in the porch, nor the best man mislaid the ring, when the register has been signed neatly and the rice—not too much rice; too much rice is vulgar—has not made the horses shy; when the bride-groom has managed to make his little speech, and the bride to sever the stony icing on the wedding cake; when the happy pair are safely off to Windermere or Como, and the relations of either have been rude to the relations of neither; then the survivors, as if conscious of some great danger passed, are apt to exclaim, in chorus, "Oh, how well it has all gone off! Oh, how thankful I am!"

What was the danger? Why the gratitude? Why should society become abnormal whenever two of its members are in love? It is a far cry from the village church to the sea beaches and mountains of Morocco, yet in those desolations some answer to the questions may be found. Professor Westermarck's book, which he offers as a supplement to his *History of Human Marriage,* is not only marked by the learning and openness of mind for which his great name is guarantee, but contains mat-ter that should entertain and instruct the general reader. He has travelled Morocco for six years, penetrating into districts where his legation refused him protection, and he was depen-dent on a Moorish friend. Some fascinating information is the result, and though he warns us against rash analogies, it is tempting to compare that information with the facts that are familiar to us all in England.

The Berber and Arab tribes of Northwest Africa appear to have retained marriage customs and marriage emotions that rea-son has modified elsewhere. They are not simple; only reason brings simplicity. They are primitive, but complex, like the savages from whom we are ourselves descended, and even if their ceremonies throw light on ours, they imply darkness, not light, in the nature of man.

The dominant emotion in their lives is fear. The universe is full of evil spirits—of jinns, who were created before Adam, and of *bas,* a disembodied power that slips hither and thither to do harm. Hostile at all times, these spirits threaten a man most when he is passing through a crisis, and may then harm not only him, but those who are connected with him. Birth and death are the chief crises; they endanger the community, as well as the child or the corpse. But marriage is a crisis, too, and an-thropology explains the Moorish wedding ceremony as a *rite de passage,* as a device or collection of devices by which the bride and bridegroom are protected from evil spirits as they pass from virginity into the nuptial state. Their assistants need protec-tion, too; relatives, best men, bridesmaids, even the food must be defended, and an origin for our exclamation, "How glad I am it has gone off well!" has now been suggested. At every marriage there is danger of demoniacal possession. One slip in the ritual, and the newly-wed, particularly the bride, may bring disaster instead of increase into the tribe. Her veiling or boxing up, the disguising of her as a man with painted moustache, the disguising of the bridegroom as a female—these are devices to mislead the hostile powers. The guns fired by the men (wedding bells?), the quivering noise made by the women, the anointing with henna—these are to scare them away. The tap given by bridegroom to bride, or *vice versa,* the stone-throwing, the ceremonial frights are to expel them. The young wife in Andjra must go down to the beach and while seven waves break over her body say, "O my uncle, the Sea, I am troubled with spirits, give me children and peace."

Woman is unclean, and most unclean when she becomes the object of desire. That is the central danger. She is also holy, for the savage mind, seldom acting in what we deem a "natural" manner, connects susceptibilities to evil with power over it, and the wife who may pollute the flocks can under other circumstances spread blessings or serve as an asylum to the persecuted.

While not neglecting other influences in the Moorish rituals, Professor Westermarck lays most stress on fear. He attributes to fear many customs to which have subsequently been attached some other emotion—the emotion of joy, for instance, or the desire for offspring—and he shows that if either of the couple has been married before, the ritual in his or her case is greatly reduced, because the transition from virginity has already been made and consequently the devils have less power. Dealing in turn with the betrothal, the dowry, the preliminary

ceremonies in the houses of either, the fetching and reception of
the bride, and the subsequent ceremonies, he calls up a picture
of a primitive and anxious society, shadows of whose fear may
be traced in the hilarious agitations of England. Even our old
friend the old shoe is to be found in Morocco, but how devoid
of jollity; bride and bridegroom strike one another with it in the
hope of expelling the *bas*. And not for days and days—in some
tribes not for months—is it possible to say, "How well it has
all gone off! Oh, how thankful I am!" for evil retires reluctantly
from its great chance.

In the prevailing terror there are gleams of beauty. The
woman of Andjra has been already quoted. A bride among the
Tsul, if she loves her husband, can, while his head rests on her
arm, whisper inaudibly, "May you be fond of me as the dead
is fond of his grave; the speech of God, and the speech of the
Prophet, and the speech of Lady Fatima, the daughter of the
holy places, who took charms from seven seas." The little village
church, managing most things better, hears nothing like this,
nor has the wedding breakfast found an equivalent for the
feasting and the dancing and the drums of Fez, or entertained
guests of such physical splendor.

1914

The Rose Show

The Press and Poetry of Modern Persia BY E. G. BROWNE

In an essay that Professor Browne quotes, a modern Persian poet discusses the aims of poetry. "Trees must be known by their fruits," he asserts, and goes on to consider what fruit has been plucked from the trees of the past. Root and branch, he condemns his own literature. Its mysticism has produced idlers, its roses and nightingales libertines, its flattery tyrants, and its hyperboles untruthfulness. Away with it! What should the poet do instead? He should "imitate the poets of Europe." He should realize that "such poetry as does not convey some moral or lead to some philosophical conclusion is merely of the nature of empty phrases and idle tales and vapourings."

Here speaks the patriot, and between patriotism and poetry there is a profound, if unfortunate, antipathy. The poems that have helped men to be brave and honest and fierce are by an unlucky fate seldom beautiful. "God Save the King" is not beautiful. "We Want Eight and We Won't Wait" is little better.

Yet both of them have made history. It is unfortunate, but the truth is that Beauty is an unreliable houri, who never turns up when she would be really useful. Though warned against them for a thousand years, she lingers still among those nightingales and roses. Military operations do not attract her; no, nor constitutional experiments either; and, if we may judge from translations, she has averted her eyes not uncertainly from the patriots of Persia.

> *Henceforth all the girls shall be educated;*
> *All shall have their share in the colleges of science;*
> *They shall be equal with the boys in their rights of learning.*
> *Blessed is this participation of the World of Women!*

But it would, of course, be wrong to judge the verses collected by Professor Browne as literature. They are rather material for the historian, and should be considered in connection with the list of newspapers—371 in number—that precedes them, and with the account of the Persian revolution that follows them. Journalism in Persia waxes and wanes with the constitutional movement. It rises into prominence with the First National Assembly (1906–1908), flags during the autocracy of Mohammed Ali, revives after his expulsion, and increases in vigor up to the crisis of Christmas, 1911, when the Second National Assembly is closed. Mr. Shuster is dismissed, and Persia is left to the mercies of the Russian Bear and the British Lion. The history of this tragedy has yet to be written, but it is improbable that any Englishman will look back to the Anglo-Russian agreement with pride. We have betrayed Persia and endangered India. We have alienated the Indian Mohammedans, and led them to suspect a crusade against Islam. We have lost our honor, and gained nothing in exchange. It is natural that we, after the Russians, should be the Persian journalist's chief butt, that the caricaturist should show us throttling Mr. Shuster, and that the poet, forgetting his nightingales, should cry:

> *To London speed, O breeze of dawning day,*
> *Bear this my message to Sir Edward Grey.*

One cannot expect beauty from the shambles of Tabriz. Rage, indignation, hopes that die before they can be uttered— these are the muses of modern Persia, and though the products that Professor Browne edits with such learning and such generous enthusiasm may not rank high as literature, they are at all events the reflection of a nation's soul. And occasionally distinction inspires them.

> *O son (cries Persia to the poet), consider thy state!*
> *Seek the care of tomorrow by the efforts of today!*
> *Loose the chains from me, and only then take in thy hand*
> *the chain-like tresses of thy sweetheart.*
> *I am fevered, thou art glad; such heedlessness is a*
> *shame in a youth like thee!*
> *Through the blood of my young men the ground is all*
> *rosy red; come back and gaze for a moment on my*
> *rose-walks and rose show!*

We shall probably see further operations in that garden in the course of the next few months. Professor Browne, if we may judge by his concluding words, is inclined to be hopeful.

1914

To Simply Feel

Poems of Problems BY ELLA WHEELER WILCOX
Love's Legend BY H. FIELDING HALL

Can one feel too much? Ah, no, pants the heart. To feel everything always—for what else were we born? And most especially were we born to feel love. Away with reason—it chills.
Away with art—it confines. Away with the world and the
devil. Fling wide the floodgates to the natural emotions, and let
them sweep us whithersoever they will. Let us rise, if it so happens, from a low emotion to a high one; but, oh! let us always
feel, and urge others to do the same, for feeling is life.

Thus counsels the heart. The puritan has his answer ready,
and may be left to give it. But there are other answers besides
his, and it is interesting to attempt one. What is this Nemesis
that waits on unqualified emotion? Why is the writer who
tries simply to feel apt to simply feel before he has tried for
long? Is it a coincidence that an emotion and an infinitive
should so often split at the same moment? May they not be suffering shipwreck upon one rock, and, if so, what is the name of

242

that rock? These questions, among others, are suggested by the two books under review.

Let us begin with Mrs. Wilcox, the most widely read poet of our day. She tells us herself that—

> *women's souls,*
> *Like violet powder dropped on coals,*
> *Give forth their best in anguish,*

and it may be that she will yield something to the gentler fire of criticism. In *Poems of Problems* she continues a series that has already brought comfort to thousands of English school-girls and adult Americans—a series of verse utterances on the great things of this life and the next. Passion, Pleasure, Power, Cheer, Sentiment, Progress, and Experience have alike received treatment from her pen, and now it is the turn of eugenics and heredity. Here are delicate subjects, but she approaches them with the confidence of a capacious heart. Thanks to her intense feeling, she has access to Heaven, which proves to be far more unconventional than Dante or any of the Churches have dreamed. Mrs. Wilcox knows what God really minds, as apart from what He is supposed to mind, and anticipates a semiscien-tific Judgment Day, in which the unwed mother shall be pre-ferred before the childless wife, and the unsound father be healed. Meanwhile, there is much to do on earth:

> *From rights of parentage the sick and sinful must be barred,*
> *'Till Matron Science keeps our house, and at the door stands guard.*

Science is God; God, Science. Both are Love. Consequently, mankind will never dismiss its concierge—she will perform her duties so feelingly. She is not the slow spectre of the laborato-ries, athirst for truth, but an American lady of elevated morals, who knows right from wrong, she does hope, and is only too glad to lend the world a helping hand. Healthy and warm-hearted, she would make short work of the science of Anatole France. Monsieur Bergeret, it may be remembered, once lifted his eyes from his dishonor to the stars, and speculated whether life may not be a transient blight in the universe—a local malady by which the earth has been attacked, and the earth alone. But then Monsieur Bergeret was dyspeptic and French. How can life be a malady when we all regard one another as cordially as we do? And, anyway, why speculate at all, when to simply feel is sufficient?

Poems of Problems is an interesting document for the future historian of our society. It evidences a new demand on the part of the semieducated public—a demand for frankness and unconventionality. No one can call Mrs. Wilcox conventional. She airs subjects that orthodoxy would stifle, and the wideness of her circulation proves the need. But, though unconventional, she is never original. However scientific her Heaven, it remains replete with angels and Biblical talk. In fact, she is offering new dogmas for old, as did the Reformation, and may exemplify to the historian the transition between subservience and independent judgment. The educated public completed that transition fifty years ago. The semieducated—those who have learnt to read, but not yet how to read—are here seen making it. As a document, her poems are notable. As poems, despite their sincerity and feeling, they are not. Why? Before attempting an answer to this, let us turn to Mr. Fielding Hall.

The receptacle for Mr. Hall's emotion is cast in the form of a novel. *Love's Legend* tells of the honeymoon, estrangement, and reconciliation of one Mr. Gallio and Lesbia, his wife, intermixed with amorous episodes between the same adown a Burmese river. But all is subsidiary to feeling. The characters are bathed in feeling. It sprinkles the slightest of their actions, permeates the landscapes, and is threatened in the last sentence of the book for ever, ever, evermore.

Now, while agreeing with Mrs. Wilcox that love is every-thing, Mr. Hall draws a very different moral—so different that the two writers must hate one another like poison, and only a cold outsider can hope to read them both. If the lady is semi-Christian, the gentleman is neo-Oriental. Science, a matron for her, becomes a pasha for him—Pasha Science, as full of feeling as ever, but different in other ways. Mrs. Wilcox says that—

> In the banquet hall of Progress
> God has bidden to a feast
> All the women of the East.

Mr. Hall denies that such an invitation has been issued; he knows that progress is fatal for females—it so increases their husband's difficulties, and in consequence their own. A man is public property, a woman the private property of a man. Let her be told this by her parents, and no more, lest conjugal bliss be marred.

He states the problem as follows:

> Suppose you engaged a peach or an apricot to come to you to be eaten, but when she came you found her fixed idea was that she was to be placed under a glass case on a sideboard. It wasn't fair to bring up girls like that, it wasn't fair to us. Society has no right to deliberately and intentionally pervert a girl in this way.

And he asserts that nature decrees a double standard of mo-rality for the sexes. Woman must be pure. Man may disport himself before marriage on the boulevards. (What about the women with whom he disports himself? On this point Pasha Science is duly silent.) Woman takes. Man gives. Woman is the audience. Man the poet. These are hard lessons for a peach, nor does poor little Lesbia learn them without falling into the Irrawaddy, and losing all her European clothes. She has also to learn that God, instead of being in the sky, as Mrs. Wilcox sup-poses, is really inside one—a discovery unwelcome to her, but her husband will have no shirking. Now by an apt anecdote, now by persiflage or horseplay, now by intimidating silences, he leads her up to be all she should be. The quiet stream of her life joins the impetuous torrent of his at last, and they flow on to-gether in one mighty river of broadening emotion towards the sea, whence—solemn thought—they will one day re-emerge in the form of dew, and it will all happen over again.

Mr. Hall is a more skilful writer than Mrs. Wilcox, but his lack of nobility makes him less pleasant reading. Like her, he assumes that the two sexes are fundamentally distinct (have either of these scientific emotionalists read a line of science?); but, unlike her, he preaches that men are never to blame, women always; and since he is personally male, his sermon be-comes suspect. Were he cynical, he might be void of offence, but he writes in the name of high feeling and theosophy, and marital love, which makes him very hard to bear. Those who imagine that Mrs. Wilcox is mere silliness, would do well to glance at *Poems of Problems*—they will find among its crudities a real desire to elevate humanity. But those who have enjoyed *The Soul of a People* are advised not to spoil their recollection of that charming book by conning *Love's Legend*.

And now let us try to answer our question.

Love is everything. So both these writers assert. They are absolutely right. It is. But Lord Bacon was also right when he wrote that the true atheist is he who has become cauterized by handling holy things, and it is from this point of view that they should be criticized. They fail not because their outlook is narrow or their facts wrong or their style weak—it is possible to have all these defects and yet win through—but because they misuse emotion. Professing to feel, they have merely handled, and have tossed sanctities about like parcels, without trying to apprehend the contents. Love is not a word of four letters, nor God a word of three. Both occur on many a page of either book, yet are further than ever from us at the close. They can only approach us when they are instinct in the writer, when they are so completely in his possession that he scarcely thinks of mentioning them by name. Such a writer does not set out to "feel," because feeling is his starting point. He does not eulogize the heart or decry reason. He does not treat of emotion, because it is bound to appear incidentally, whatever his theme. Emotion is not a theme. It is the central fire and the external glow, but it is not a theme, and those who persist in handling it as if it were are trying to enter the Kingdom of Heaven by calling, "Lord, Lord!" and must remain, despite their protests, in the outer darkness. The fate of the emotionalist is ironic, and he will never escape it until he is less obsessed with the importance of emotion. When he is interested in people and things for their own sake, the hour of his deliverance has approached, and while stretching out his hand for some other purpose, he will discover—quite simply!—that he can feel.

1914

A New Novelist

The *Voyage Out* BY VIRGINIA WOOLF

One of the men in Mrs. Woolf's book complains: "Of course, we're always writing about women—abusing them, or jeering at them or worshipping them; but it's never come from women themselves. I believe we still don't know in the least how they live, or what they feel, or what they do precisely. . . . They won't tell you. Either they're afraid, or they've got a way of treating men." And perhaps the first comment to make on *The Voyage Out* is that it is absolutely unafraid, and that its courage springs, not from naïveté, but from education. Few women writers are educated. A gentleman ought not to say such a thing, but it is, unfortunately, true. Our Queens of the Pen are learned, sensitive, thoughtful even, but they are uneducated, they have never admitted the brain to the heart, much less let it roam over the body. They live in pieces, and their work, when it does live, lives similarly, devoid of all unity save what is imposed by a plot. Here at last is a book which attains unity as surely as *Wuthering Heights*, though by a different path, a book which, while written by a woman and presumably from a woman's point of view, soars straight out of local questionings into the intellectual day. The curious male may pick up a few scraps, but if wise he will lift his eyes to where there is neither marrying nor giving in marriage, to the mountains and forests and sea that circumscribe the characters, and to the final darkness that blots them out. After all, he will not have learnt how women live, any more than he has learnt from Shakespeare how men perform that process; he will only have lived more intensely himself, that is to say, will have encountered literature.

Mrs. Woolf's success is more remarkable since there is one serious defect in her equipment; her chief characters are not vivid. There is nothing false in them, but when she ceases to touch them they cease, they do not stroll out of their sentences, and even develop a tendency to merge shadowlike. Rachel and her aunt Helen are one example of this. Hewet and his friend Hirst another. The story opens with Helen. Helen, though an accomplished Bohemian, is discovered in tears close to Cleopatra's Needle—she is off for a holiday to South America, but does not like leaving the children. Her husband, a Pindaric scholar, beats the air with a stick until she has finished and can gain the boat, where Rachel, a pale idle girl of twenty-four, awaits them. Helen is bored at first. But at Lisbon they are joined by a kindly politician—he, like most of the minor characters, is sketched with fine foolery and malice—and he, by kissing Rachel, wakes her up. When he has disembarked, she expounds to her aunt, they become friends, and when the Voyage Out, so far as it is by water, has ended, she goes to spend the winter with Helen at Santa Marina. Below their villa in the English hotel dwell two young Cambridge intellectuals, Hewet and Hirst. The pairs become acquainted, and for a time there is a curious darkness, while one of the men—we know not which—and one of the women—we know not which—are nearing each other. When the darkness clears, Helen is defi-nitely the confidante, Hirst the onlooker, and Hewet and Ra-chel have, in the recesses of a primeval forest, become engaged to be married. The Villa acquiesces, the Hotel smirks, and until the final note, we expect wedding bells.

If the above criticism is correct, if Mrs. Woolf does not "do" her four main characters very vividly, and is apt to let them all become clever together, and differ only by their opinions, then on what does her success depend? Some readers—those who de-mand the milk of human kindness, even in its tinned form—will say that she has not succeeded; but the bigness of her achieve-ment should impress anyone weaned from baby food. She be-lieves in adventure—here is the main point—believes in it pas-sionately, and knows that it can only be undertaken alone. Human relations are no substitute for adventure, because when real they are uncomfortable, and when comfortable they must be unreal. It is for a voyage into solitude that man was created, and Rachel, Helen, Hewet, Hirst, all learn this lesson, which is exquisitely reinforced by the setting of tropical scenery—the soul, like the body, voyages at her own risk. "There must be a reason," sighs nice old Mrs. Thornbury, after the catastrophe. "It can't only be an accident. For if it was an accident—it need never have happened." Primeval thunderstorms answer Mrs. Thornbury. There is no reason. Why should an adventure ter-minate that way rather than this, since its essence is fearless motion? "It's life that matters," writes a novelist of a very dif-ferent type; "the process of discovering, the everlasting and perpetual process, not the discovery itself at all." Mrs. Woolf's vision may be inferior to Dostoevsky's—but she sees as clearly as he where efficiency ends and creation begins, and even more clearly that our supreme choice lies not between body and soul, but between immobility and motion. In her pages, body v. soul —that dreary medieval tug-of-war—does not find any place. It is as if the rope has broken, leaving pagans sprawling on one side and clergymen on the other, while overhead "long-tailed birds chattered and screamed and crossed from wood to wood, with golden eyes in their plumage."

It is tempting to analyze the closing chapters, which have an atmosphere unknown in English literature—the atmosphere of Jules Romains' *Mort de Quelqu'un*. But a word must be said about the comedy; the book is extremely amusing. The writer has a nice taste in old gentlemen, for instance. They talk like this:

> "Jenkinson of Cats—do you still keep up with him?"
>
> "As much as one ever does," said Mr. Pepper. "We meet annually. This year he has had the misfortune to lose his wife, which made it painful, of course."
>
> "Very painful," Ridley agreed.
>
> "There's an unmarried daughter who keeps house for him, I believe, but it's never the same, not at his age."
>
> Both gentlemen nodded sagely as they carved their apples.
>
> "There was a book, wasn't there?" Ridley inquired.
>
> "There *was* a book, but there never *will* be a book," said Mr. Pepper, with such fierceness that both ladies looked up at him.
>
> "There never will be a book, because someone else has written it for him," said Mr. Pepper with considerable acidity. "That's what comes of putting things off, and collecting fossils, and sticking Norman arches on one's pigsties."

In the humor there is something of Peacock. When the ball at the Santa Marina Hotel turns into a bacchanal, and the

aforesaid Mr. Pepper executes a pointed step that he has de-
rived from figure skating, there is an effect of cumulative drol-
lery that recalls the catastrophe in *Nightmare Abbey*, when
Mr. Toobad fell into the moat. The writer can sweep together
masses of characters for our amusement, then sweep them
away; her comedy does not counteract her tragedy, and at the
close enhances it, for we see that the Hotel and the Villa will
soon be dancing and gossiping just as before, that existence will
continue the same, exactly the same, for everyone, for everyone
except the reader; he, more fortunate than the actors, is established in the possession of beauty.

1915

Short Stories from Russia

The Steppe and Other Stories BY ANTON TCHEKOV,
TRANSLATED BY ADELINE LISTER KAY
Stories of Russian Life BY ANTON TCHEKOFF,
TRANSLATED BY MARIAN FELL
The Old House and Other Tales BY FEODOR SOLOGUB,
TRANSLATED BY JOHN COURNOS

Russian literature will scarcely come to its own until we cease to seek in it for the Russian spirit. We still read it for informa- tion, just as we used to read French literature for information about that other local product, la femme. La femme we have explored. M. Bourget has bared the inmost pulse of that in- credible machine, and now we only read French novels when they happen not to be dull. But the Russian spirit is still un- explored. We do not know what animates our great ally, and, naturally curious, we turn to her literature for what literature seldom provides—a generalization. Even Tchekov, who cares only for individual men, women, flowers, and so on, is pressed into this service and advertised by one of his publishers as writ- ing "Stories of Russian Life," and by the other as portraying "the resignation and patient idealism which is so characteristic of the Russian spirit." If he does so, it is accidentally. Tchekov is not an interpreter—at all events not in these stories. His only aim is to describe certain things and people in a way that shall be interesting and beautiful.

Tchekov possesses humor and tenderness, but perhaps his highest gift is negative: he gains his effect by neglecting what is usually regarded as effective. An English magazine editor once laid down that "the" short story, as he termed it, must go with a snap. If he was right, Tchekov is wrong. Consider "The Steppe." Noiseless throughout, it becomes inaudible at the close, rising out of hearing and sight, like rolling flax that a wind whirls into the sky. A little boy has to go to school. He starts in a carriage with his uncle and the village priest, then is transferred into a wool-wagon, where he travels a few days, bathing, laughing and crying, eating fish-gruel, getting soaked by a storm, and rejoining his uncle and the priest in a feverish condition, from which he soon recovers. That is all. There is no point, only a series of points. Most writers would have focussed on the fever, but Tchekov lets it flow by with the other facts, and does not give a single bad mark to the uncle for callousness, to the priest for superstition, or to the wagoners for incompetence. He is only concerned to make the little boy's journey interesting, and to fill every sentence—not just the show sentences—with beauty. We are left with a sense of completeness. We have travelled through the world of his creation, and enjoyed its imaginative fullness. Nothing has happened that might not happen in the world of daily life—that is to say, there has been no snap—but the particular sequence of the events is not to be experienced this side of poetry. Tchekov, if one cares to label him, is both realist and poet. With one hand he collects facts, with the other he arranges them and sets them flowing. The imagination he possesses is content with the earth and sun and stars that we know; it never attempts to gain beauty through distortion. It has nothing in common with fancy.

Or, again, consider "Agatha," a story in the second collection. The editor would prefer "Agatha" to "The Steppe," because it does contain a situation. But how tamely the situation is treated! It is not worked up, but merely flows by in the beautiful nocturnal river.

"In which country are the birds most at home, in ours or over there?" Savka asked.

"In ours, of course. They are hatched here, and here they raise their young. This is their native land, and they only fly away to escape being frozen to death."

"How strange!" he sighed, stretching. "One can't talk of anything but what is strange. Take that shouting bird over there, take people, take this little stone—there's a meaning in everything. Oh, if I had only known you were going to be here this evening, sir, I wouldn't have told that woman to come. She asked if she might."

"These affairs of yours with women will end badly some day," I said sadly.

"Never mind."

Then, after a moment's reflection, Savka added:

"So I have told the women, but they won't listen; the idiots don't care."

Silence fell. The shadows deepened, the outlines of all objects faded into the darkness. The streak of light behind the hill was altogether extinguished, and the stars shone ever brighter and brighter. The mournful, monotonous chirping of the crickets, the calling of the rail-bird, and the whistling of the quail seemed not to break the nocturnal silence, but rather to add to it a still greater depth. It was as if the stars, and not the birds and insects, were singing softly, and charming our ears as they looked down from heaven.

> Savka broke silence first. He slowly turned his regard to me, and
> said, "This is tedious for you, sir, I can see. Let's have supper."

Savka does not symbolize the Russian spirit, any more than
the quiet evening where they sat symbolizes life or death or
love. It is true that "there's a meaning in everything," but also
true that each thing means itself and not something else. Savka
is Savka, the evening an evening—a particular man and a particular scene that Tchekov wishes to describe. Such appears to
be his method. He avoids generalization, he even avoids climax,
because either would seduce him from the subject—and consequently from the poetry—in hand.

With Sologub it is otherwise. To his ingenious mind nothing
seems to mean much unless it means something else, and most
of the stories in *The Old House* entail a psychic to-do. They are
the work of a skilful writer, who has realized the literary value
of hallucination and metempsychosis, and knows that it is more
effective to say "This is—what?" than to say "This is a ghost."
Up to date in his methods, he combines the supernatural with
realism, occasionally with some success. "The Old House" tells
of the grandmother, mother, and sister of a young man who has
been hanged, of their daily wakenings, their toilets and prayers,
and breakfasts, and, mixed with these, their passionate desire
that he shall return, which leaves them nightly wailing to the
moon; the inference being that they are indeed approaching
him, but not by any human path, that the house and the woods
and fields surrounding it are soaked with the dead youth's personality, and causing them to join him through madness; with
the further inference that madness is more real a state than
sanity. The theme—from a literary point of view—is good, and
masterpieces have been written upon it; Villiers de L'Isle-
Adam's *Vera* is an example. But if we are to believe, the writer

must himself believe in it while he is writing. He need not believe in it during daily life—while lunching with the editor, for
instance—but he must while actually composing get into a
state where ghosts *do* exist, where madness *is* preferable; to use
the old term, he must be inspired, and Sologub has only theories
and fancies, that remain unfused by any central heat. He can
charm—as in the sister's invocation to Aphrodite—and he can
thrill, as in the final scene. But thrill and charm do not link up;
the theme remains psychic, not poetic, to the end.

His work recalls that of Algernon Blackwood in England.
There is the same cleverness of ideas, the same conversance
with modern research, the same attempt to guarantee the super-
natural by the natural, the same imaginative and emotional poverty. Excitement has to do all the writing, and when it flags—
oh my!

> In a barely audible voice the old woman mumbled: "Yes,
> I am a crow. And when I see a doomed person I have such a
> strong desire to caw."
> The old woman suddenly made a sweeping movement with
> her arms, and in a shrill voice cried out twice: "Kar-r, kar-r!"
> Alexandra Ivanovna shuddered and asked: "*Babushka,* at
> whom are you cawing?"
> The old woman answered: "At you, my dear, at you."
> It had become too painful to sit with the old woman any
> longer.

It has indeed, nor would one have sat so long but for Sologub's great success in Petrograd, where he has been hailed as
the spiritual kinsman of Tchekov. Judged by this volume (one
must remember he has written nineteen others), the success is
undeserved. And in any case, what kinship has he with the
author of "The Steppe," where life flows on, noble, imagina-

tive, profound, yet differing only in arrangement from the life that we know? Think of one of the rare occasions when Tche-kov does employ the supernatural—the sound of a breaking string in *The Cherry Orchard*. We do not ask whether a string really breaks in the dying heaven of old Russia, or whether, as Madame Ranevsky suggests, it is only a tub that has fallen into a mine. The sound flows past in the beautiful melancholy stream; it recurs when the stream, quiet to the end, slides over the precipice, and Firs lies down to die. Compare its music with the gabble of Sologub's golliwog-devil in "The Uniter of Souls," or with the creak of his movable walls in "The Invoker of the Beast"—walls which are said by the translator to be "a symbol of our own subtle insecurity," but do not become the less tedious on that account; compare it with the old woman who was really a crow, or with Alexandra Ivanovna, who is a white dog really, and killed by a man who is really a pig. Super-natural topsy-turvyings such as these may shock and thrill for the moment, but must die when the page is turned; while we go back with increasing pleasure to Savka, who is Savka, and to his supper, which is supper.

1915

Tate versus Chantrey

REPORT OF THE NATIONAL GALLERY COMMITTEE ON

MATTERS CONNECTED WITH THE

NATIONAL ARTS COLLECTIONS

Since the war began few of us have taken much interest in art. Literature is different; literature lies closer to our daily life, and can, like music, open doors that lead out of it, and be a positive support against anxiety and pain. But pictures and statues seem curiously remote at such a time as this. Rightly or wrongly, most of us regard them as luxuries, only to be enjoyed in holi- day mood, and their very mention provokes a sneer. For this reason the Report of the National Gallery Commmittee—a most important and entertaining document, which would at other times have kept the press busy for weeks—is likely to fall to the ground unnoticed. It is a pity that this should be so. There will be a world after the war, a world in which pictures and even statues must figure; and if the Committee's recom- mendations are adopted they are likely to figure less discredit- ably than they have in the past.

This Report deals in part with the leakage of masterpieces

out of this country during past years into America and Germany, but the most interesting section is concerned with the Chantrey Bequest. This Bequest (£2,100 per annum) was made by Sir Francis Chantrey to secure for the nation whatever was best in contemporary British art. His intentions are beyond dispute—the best, wherever obtainable; but unfortunately he appointed as administrators the President and Council of the Royal Academy, with results that are common knowledge. The Royal Academy—an institution neither officially nor actually representative of British art—has regarded the bequest as its own perquisite, and has spent it almost exclusively on the works of Academicians. These works it flings annually at the nation, to be housed at the national expense. There was a Committee of Inquiry some ten years ago, but nothing resulted. The Academy has the money and sticks to it, and the unlucky Tate Gallery is—at first sight—in its power, being legally compelled to nourish the Chantrey brood.

What a brood it is! What a spectacle are the rooms at Millbank that shelter it! There are a few works of merit, of genius even, but the rest are costume pieces, or examples of the kiss-mammy and wave-to-daddy schools. It is right that such pictures should be painted, for they give many people genuine pleasure, but it is not right they should cost so much, it is not right that they should be bought for the nation. Chantrey art, say its defenders, is popular, to which the reply is that popular art is never permanent; its place is consequently in a Christmas number, not in a national collection. The kiss-mammy of one generation is invariably nauseous to the next; daddy, who once wore corduroys and whiskers, wears khaki and a blob-moustache now; and ten years hence will have to wear something else if he is to maintain his emotional appeal. He is obviously a bad investment, even as a popular investment, but what is the Tate to do? The Chantrey dumps him, year after year. He is not only bad in himself, but—as the Report points out—he harms the Gallery by making it ridiculous. The funds of the Tate are so small that each year the Chantrey pictures must bulk larger in proportion to the rest. The standard they set is so low that artists or owners of modern masterpieces fight shy of a collection that includes them, and cannot be induced to present their pictures or "to sell at modest prices for the honor of being represented in the Collection as is frequently done in France." British painters "whose works are eagerly bought for Continental galleries," are unrepresented in their own country, while a "double standard of admission is set up," and the Tate sometimes refuses "pictures superior in artistic merit to those which are simultaneously purchased under the Chantrey Bequest."

What can free the poor Tate? In the first place, legislation. Parliament can put the Chantrey on a proper basis, and the Committee recommends that it should be asked to do this; the wishes of the testator will then be carried into effect, and his money purchase whatever is best in contemporary art. But, failing legislation, the Tate still has a powerful weapon. It is compelled to receive the Chantrey brood, but by a happy and Gilbertian chance is not compelled to exhibit it. It has the right to send it straight into the cellars, and the Committee recommends it should exercise this right—a right which was even admitted by the President of the Royal Academy, one of the witnesses called. The arrangement would not be ideal. The nation would be no nearer getting pictorial value for its £2,100, and the daddies and costume pieces would be debarred from their very real sphere of usefulness elsewhere. But it would be better than nothing. The Gallery would cease to be grotesque.

It could begin, however feebly, to represent contemporary art. And the Royal Academicians would have to retreat from an untenable position, and admit the right of a national collection to decide how a nation's bequest shall be spent. That they will retreat without such pressure is improbable, because they do honestly think that the Burlington brand is the best, and that they would not be doing their duty if they recommended any other. One cannot blame them. It is right they should believe in the tradition that has formed them, it is natural they should believe that old tired men are the best judges of beauty, it is inevitable that, thus believing, they should select for this year's Chantrey a nude statue—not a naked statue like M. Rombaux's, which would be not quite nice, but a dead decent studio nude; a small kiss-mammy, and a View. These are the nation's latest acquisitions. It remains to be seen what the Tate will do when they arrive.

1915

Reconstruction in the Marne
and the Meuse

Anyone who attended a picture-palace in the early months of
the war may remember an ingenious device that illustrated the
battle of the Marne and the subsequent German retreat to the
Aisne. The Germans, represented by little black blocks and an
occasional eagle, were seen leaping and sliding across the map
of France towards Paris, their prey. Outside Paris the Allies,
shown as shaded blocks, checked them, the turning movements
were executed, and then the eagles slipped back eastward, pursued by the strains of "Rule, Britannia" and the "Marseillaise."
It was an interesting film, and brought home to the ordinary
man the strategical side of the September invasions. But there
is one side of invasion it could not bring home: the destructive.
France is not a map, but France, and the German armies do not
advance over white paper and retreat leaving it white, but into
civilization that they leave a desert. Each of those little black
blocks leaves a stain behind—more than a stain, a festering sore

that eats inwards and spreads. Invasion is more than the destruction of property, it is more even than murder and pain. It is the herald of spiritual death. The survivors, when the tide of horror retreats, feel that it is sure to return, and that even if it does not, life is not worth living again. Before it came they could not imagine it would come, now they cannot imagine anything else. They have had an experience of which we, in our isled security, can have no conception; their mental state is now as far removed from ours as if it was on the other side of the grave.

What is being done for those survivors, for those who lay in the line of that German retreat between the Aisne and the Marne? France is a first-class power, with a past as splendid as our own and a reputation for humanity as great, and at first sight it seems impertinent for English people to offer her any assistance in connection with her war victims. But it must be remembered that on France falls the brunt of the war in the west—a war in which England has hitherto played a minor part. France is not negligent, nor is she poor, but she is busy, desperately busy. Though she can provide much of the stuff, e.g., materials to build huts, horses and petrol for transport, hotels and houses for hospitals, she cannot provide time and she cannot provide labor, because all her energies are employed in expelling the Germans. Consequently, she has been willing to accept the offer of the Society of Friends to work in the evacuated departments of the Marne and the Meuse, and the reports that they have issued—now about a dozen in number— give a vivid account of the destruction and of the attempts at reconstruction.

"Imagine," writes one of the workers, "a village in England— one that you are acquainted with: it may even be your home—

with some 700 houses, of which 650 have been burned to the ground, and then you will be able to form some idea of what is S—— now. The inhabitants left in astounding bewilderment, hardly able to believe that the German army was so close, and so in the hurry and scramble to get away they left everything behind them, innocently expecting to find their belongings again when they returned, scarcely crediting the Germans with such viciousness as led them to burn S—— to the ground. And so when they returned a few days after the German retreat, conceive their sorrow and chagrin on finding their houses razed to the ground and all trace of their possessions gone. All their hay and crops—no sight sadder than the grey heaps of powdered ashes—cattle, rabbits, and everything, burnt or destroyed. How I admire their courage as I see them grubbing about amongst their ruins, searching for some lost thing, or beginning—where would you begin?—to clear away the débris?"

The Society of Friends begins by sending out investigators, who are usually women who have been trained in social work. In accordance with their reports the other workers follow. Nurses visit patients in their own homes, builders erect huts for the peasants (who *must* get back to their ground and have nowhere to live in), and there is a growing department of agricultural relief. These are the four main divisions of activity, and about 125 volunteers from England are at present engaged in them. "It is not only the material help given," writes the secretary of the Relief Committee (Miss Ruth Fry): "the most important aspect of it all is the courage raised anew in these much-tried sufferers, to whom the coming of these helpers is a very impressive sign of the reality of our friendship." And she tells how the children in a ruined village will, at the investigating visit, stand about, bored and apathetic, as if life contains nothing but stagnation and despair, and how, when the Friends return, girt with a pleasing bustle of medicine bottles, or agricultural implements, or planks, the children will gradually recover interest and end by screaming at the motorcars, as all wellconducted children should. "Were the Germans to reoccupy the districts tomorrow, our work would not be wasted, because we have kept the people from idleness for a little and helped them to regain hope."

The work began in November, and at first the medical side predominated: for instance, a Maternity Hospital for the Marne refugees was organized at Châlons. Miss Pye, one of the organizers, thus describes a patient whom she went to fetch by car:

> In spite of the fact that we were unknown to Madame L., of a foreign country, arriving late in the dusk of a winter evening, she rose up, laid down her sewing, put on her hat and cloak, and came away with us into the dark. It was her first baby. Her husband, a compositor in Reims before he was called up, had been seriously wounded four months before, and since then she had had no news at all. She spoke during the long ride back of their happy life together, then of his being called out, of the horrors of the bombardment, and her six weeks' nightly sojourn in the cellars. She spoke of the Germans in Reims, but said they were "très gentils," and that many of her friends had found the same. One she met had been so sad, and had wept over having to fight and leave his wife and children. She showed him the picture of her husband, and he wished her good fortune and his safe return. Her courage was splendid. She said, "If he never comes back to me I must bring up my child and work for him; one must have courage these days; one has moments, but it is no good to weep, it only brings weakness." Just before a little daughter was born to her the news came that her husband was dead. Her courage never failed. "For my dear little girl I want to be strong," she said.

In the later reports it is agriculture that figures. The two departments are almost entirely rural, and a great effort is being made to continue their life. Most of the farm machines have been destroyed by fire—that is to say, they survive, but the iron is so soft that it bends at a touch—and to replace them about eighty mowing machines have been distributed among the villages on the co-operative system (an innovation among the French peasantry, this; in some districts there was opposition); while the Agricultural Relief of Allies Fund is helping the Friends to provide reapers and binders for the forthcoming harvest. This harvest was sown by Frenchwomen last autumn, who went out into the fields immediately after the German retreat and, as though they were themselves some process of nature, carried on the labor of countless generations, and prolonged the fertility of France into another spring. In comparison with their courage, their patriotism, what are the instruments of destruction? Like Madame L., they nurse the inviolable hope, they are tending the life of the earth, and it is to help them in this faith, beside which war is a phantom, that the Society of Friends is working.

To an outsider, this insistence on hope, this attempt at *spiritual* reconstruction, whatever the fortunes of battle, seems particularly characteristic of the Quaker mind. The supreme evil of war is surely not death, but despair—the feeling that the incursion of the soul into matter has been a mistake, that we may just as well sit brooding among the ashes of happiness and beauty, that it is useless to work, useless to give help and even to receive it. We know this feeling even in England, where the war has touched us comparatively little. As casualty list succeeds casualty list, the whole of civilization seems sliding; and what must it be for the French, who have known war's full physical horror? Against such despair the Quaker fights. He believes that though civilization may slide, the power of which civilization is only a partial expression stands firm, being rooted in humanity. Or—to adapt that image of the cinematograph and its shifting blocks—he believes that no space that the armies of love have once traversed is ever the same again. There is always a radiant trace, always a lingering glory, always a glow that strengthens inwardly and is ready to shine outwardly as soon as clouds lift and the battle smoke thins under the winds of time.

1915

Forster's Publications
1900-1915

A CHRONOLOGY

Selections included in this volume are marked with an asterisk (*). Selections previously collected are identified as follows: *The Celestial Omnibus* (CO), *The Eternal Moment* (EM), *Abinger Harvest* (AH). Books are in capitals, short stories in italics. Details of publication may be found in *A Bibliography of E. M. Forster* by B. J. Kirkpatrick (1968).

1900

*On Grinds. *1 February 1900.*
*On Bicycling. *10 May 1900.*
*The Cambridge Theophrastus: The Stall-Holder. *1 June 1900.*
*A Long Day. *1 June 1900.*
*A Tragic Interior. *21 November 1900.*

*The Pack of Anchises. *21 November 1900.*
*The Cambridge Theophrastus: The Early Father. *21 November 1900.*

1901
*A Brisk Walk. *21 February 1901.*
*A Tragic Interior, 2. *21 February 1901.*
*Strivings after Historical Style. *June 1901.*

1903
Macolnia Shops. *November 1903.* (AH)
Albergo Empedocle. December 1903.

1904
Cnidus. *March 1904.* (AH)
*A Day Off. *14 May 1904.*
The Road from Colonus. June 1904. (CO)
The Story of a Panic. August 1904. (CO)
The Other Side of the Hedge. November 1904. (CO)

1905
Cardan. *April 1905.* (AH)
The Eternal Moment. June 1905. (EM)
Gemistus Pletho. *October 1905.* (AH)
WHERE ANGELS FEAR TO TREAD. c. *4 October 1905.*

1906
*Rostock and Wismar. *June 1906.*

Introduction to THE AENEID (trans. E. F. Taylor). *July 1906.*
*Literary Eccentrics: A Review. *October 1906.*

1907

*Pessimism in Literature. *January-February 1907.*
THE LONGEST JOURNEY. *8 April 1907.*
The Curate's Friend. October 1907. (CO)

1908

The Celestial Omnibus. January 1908. (CO)
*Dante. *February-April 1908.*
A ROOM WITH A VIEW. *14 October 1908.*

1909

Other Kingdom. July 1909. (CO)
The Machine Stops. Michaelmas Term, 1909. (EM)

1910

HOWARDS END. *18 October 1910.*

1911

Mr. Andrews. April 1911. (EM)
THE CELESTIAL OMNIBUS AND OTHER STORIES.
11 May 1911.
* Mr. Walsh's Secret History of the Victorian Movement.
June 1911.

*The Beauty of Life. *October 1911.*
The Point of It. November 1911. (EM)

1912

*An Allegory(?). *June 1912.*
Co-operation. June 1912. (EM)
*Inspiration. *July 1912.*

1913

*Iron Horses in India. *December 1913.*

1914

Adrift in India: The Nine Gems of Ujjain. *21 March 1914.*
  (AH)
*The Indian Mind. *28 March 1914.*
Adrift in India, 2: Advance, India! *11 April 1914.* (AH)
*The Wedding. *2 May 1914.*
Adrift in India, 3: In Rajasthan. *16 May 1914.* (AH)
*The Gods of India. *30 May 1914.*
Chitra. *13 June 1914.* (AH)
*The Age of Misery. *27 June 1914.*
*The Rose Show. *11 July 1914.*
Adrift in India, 4: The Suppliant. *25 July 1914.* (AH)
*To Simply Feel. *8 August 1914.*
*The Elder Tagore. *11 November 1914.*

1915

*The Indian Boom. *2 February 1915.*

*The Functions of Literature in War-time. *March 1915.*
*A Great Anglo-Indian. *29 March 1915.*
*A New Novelist. *8 April 1915.*
*The Mission of Hinduism. *30 April 1915.*
*Tate versus Chantrey. *26 May 1915.*
*Short Stories from Russia. *24 July 1915.*
*Reconstruction in the Marne and the Meuse. *30 August 1915.*